Home by Another Way

Other Books by Nancy N. Rue

Row This Boat Ashore

The Janis Project

Home by Another Way

Nancy N. Rue

CROSSWAY BOOKS • WHEATON, ILLINOIS
A DIVISION OF GOOD NEWS PUBLISHERS

Home by Another Way.

Copyright © 1991 by Nancy N. Rue.

Published by Crossway Books, a division of
Good News Publishers, 1300 Crescent Street, Wheaton, Illinois 60187.

Cover illustration: David Yorke

First printing, 1991

Printed in the United States of America

ISBN 0-89107-633-6

99		98		97		96		95		94		93		92		91
15	14	13	12	11	10	9	8	7	6	5	4	3	2	1

For all the people
who have helped
me find my way home—
but especially
for Jim

1

MONDAY was the party. Tuesday I saw Mouse for the last time.

Now it was Wednesday, after school, and for the first time in months I didn't have anyplace to go.

So there I was, lying on my back on my queen-sized water bed with my feet up on the dirty spot on the wallpaper—

Hey, give me a break. My room is the only really sloppy thing in my life—okay, except maybe my grades—and it doesn't even start to measure up to some of my friends' rooms. Nathan's got mold growing under his bed. Jon Ricco's got clothes on the floor that he wore once when he was in junior high, threw there, and never saw again. So my measly jumble of tapes and diving books and my one—count it!—one dirty bowl from last night's snack of Top Ramen doesn't qualify me as a typical sixteen-year-old male slob.

Neither does one dirty spot on the wallpaper. I even had my shoes off that Wednesday afternoon when I was lying there, arms behind my head like usual, with Lou curled up in one of my armpits.

Lou's my cat, okay? He's a little strange. He likes my armpits, and he likes to eat dental floss—used or unused. But he sits in the window and looks out over Oakland and waits for me to come home, and when I do he's there for me. He's named after Greg Louganis—come on, would you call a cat "Greg"?—

7

and since I can't have the Winner himself here keeping me straight on my dives, I can at least have a namesake who keeps his mouth shut—except when he sees the birds out on the deck and sits in the window and talks to them in a voice he thinks is going to fool them into taking him for a sparrow. Hey, we all have our dreams.

I had mine too, until that Wednesday when I found myself lying there ready to dream—and there was nothing to plug in.

Any other Wednesday—or Friday, or Monday, or Saturday at 3 A.M. for Pete's sake—what I was plugging in would've been pretty predictable. I'd be imagining a dive. I never would have gotten off the platform if I didn't walk through my diving moves in my mind a hundred times.

Or I was praying. The only place I could ever get in touch with God was in my room, feet up on the wall. And I never would've gotten *on* the platform if it hadn't been for Christ. I'd have just as soon had a root canal as tell anybody this, but I could close my eyes and get a real clear image of Him, dusting off his sandals and saying, "Man, what a day. How was yours, guy?" And then I'd go for it, dump it all on Him. It was during one of those conversations that I thought He said to me, "Diving's where it's at for you, Josh. Reach a pinnacle of excellence there and you've got it."

I guess I had it all messed up. I always thought if I perfected the dives and reached for the top I'd have it made.

Right.

That Wednesday I didn't imagine dives. I didn't even pray. No, man, I *thought*. And then I thought about what I was thinking. It was like something some Monterey-Jack and artichoke-eating yuppie would do.

I was asking myself weird things. Like, "Who are you *now*, Josh Daniels?" And like, "What is it you want? I mean, *for real*." And like, "That plan you thought you had all worked out with God. Something was missing, wasn't it?"

Then, of course, that led to the rewinding and replaying of the tape. No, not of the tapes I and everybody else in the junior class at California Christian Academy listened to. No, this was the Mental-Memorex recording of what had happened. And I'd rewound and replayed the memories so many times in the last four days, they were wearing out my heads. But it was like I had to keep seeing it all in my mind, because it was what *happened* that made me start asking myself all those questions that were driving me off the end of my psychological diving board.

It was what *happened* that turned my nice, comfortable Used-to-be into the upside-down Now.

I guess that's why I kept rewinding what happened in my brain and playing it over and over. Maybe *this* time whatever was missing all this time would fall into place. Maybe if I replayed it just one more time—

O KAY, I said to myself that first Monday. *It doesn't matter that everybody on this bus is either shorter than you, darker than you, or has slantier eyes than you. You have a right to be on it. Just look straight ahead, act cool, and for Pete's sake don't miss the stop—*

I grabbed at the signal cord with a jerk that almost knocked the Chinese lady next to me headlong into her shopping bag. Or was she Korean? Who could tell—they all looked alike to—well, you've heard that before.

I muttered something about being sorry, but she just stared at the floor.

Not so the black kid across the aisle. He hissed at me until I was practically out the door.

"How about giving me a little more warning next time, huh?" the bus driver said.

He was white, so I looked over my shoulder at him and hoisted my L.A. Gear bag between us. "Hey, give me a break," I said. "I don't get out much, okay?"

There was a general jeering from the bus, and as the doors closed flatulently in back of me, I think the driver called me the intelligent behind of some animal.

I hadn't actually been lying to the bus driver. I *didn't* get out much—at least not out of the neighborhood where my mom and I lived in a suburban condo with mini-blinds and orange trees and a hot tub that sat ten. I couldn't tell you the last time I'd been in downtown Oakland—and I'd sure never been there alone.

I'd taken a sudden interest in reading the paper since my dad had first told me he'd set this up for me. And every time I read about another stabbing, mugging, or disassembling of a sleeping bum by a street gang of twelve-year-olds, I pictured myself getting off the bus and being immediately and simultaneously stabbed, mugged *and* disassembled by anybody who happened to be standing around.

So here I was, doing everything I could not to reach into my sweats pocket and pull out the directions to the Municipal Pool one more time and consult it here on the corner where the nearest waiting criminal could scope me out—

Josh, man, get real, I thought. *Just walk down the street like you belong here.*

Right. One glance into the next plate-glass window with the long, suspicious-looking crack slashed across it and I almost laughed out loud.

The kid I saw in the window was middle-class, clean-cut, dark-haired, skinny, six foot one, with blue eyes that had never seen violence he wasn't separated from by a TV screen, and a stupid turned-up nose he'd inherited from his mother that made him look about as tough as those models that advertise running shorts in magazines.

Yeah, I fit right in.

The people I was hurrying past were all either looking furtively at me over the top of a burrito wrapped in waxed paper, sidling by me with chow mein on their breath, or staring at me out of chocolate-brown faces that read, "What are you *doin'* in this neighborhood, honkie?"

I realized with a jolt that that comment was actually being lashed at me from a mouth that had parted company with most of its teeth.

The only thing I had going for me was that he—and the two guys with him—were on the other side of a chain-link fence around a vacant lot.

"I'm talkin' to you, honkie. What are you doin' here?"

"You are lost, man," said another one. I think he was Mexican. It was hard to tell when you were staring straight ahead and walking as fast as you could without looking like you were walking as fast as you could.

The second black kid flipped himself up to the top of the fence, dangling the biggest tennis shoe I ever saw inches from my face. "Maybe we can show this boy the way. Where to, son?"

I kept walking.

"You rude, boy."

"Maybe he don't speak English!" the Mexican said, and then hurled a hunk of spit that landed right in front of me.

I sidestepped it and walked faster. My throat was burning so bad I could hardly swallow. It was just like a segment off the "After School Special." When was somebody going to turn off the cameras and holler, "Cut!"?

"Hey, honkie, can't you answer when somebody talking to you?"

They're just bluffing, Josh, keep walking.

"Whatsa matter, you deaf?"

Ignore them. You're almost to the end of the fence. They're not going to climb over it just to harass you if you don't give them any—

"Speak, boy, speak! Arf, arf!"

—fuel for the fire. Just a couple more steps.

"Heel, boy. Heel!"

The banter stopped, and so did I. That last command had come from a very small mouth that was poking through a lower diamond on the chain-link fence. Dark almond-shaped eyes sparkled out at me. "Sit," said a pint-sized Ho Chi Minh.

Laughter erupted from the dark-skinned pack like so many zits.

"Tell him, Chinky-San!" said the Mexican to the kid of about nine whose eyes had by now crinkled shut in total crack-up over his own demented little wit.

Uh, don't keep walking, Josh, I said to me, *or you'll never look at yourself in another mirror.*

I turned slowly and surveyed them all with the icy stare I usually reserve for my mother. I was sure it was pretty luke-warm at that point, but the Oriental kid was practically drum-ming his fingernails in expectation.

"Excuse me," I said. "If you guys are looking for the City Pound, it's ten blocks that way. You hang a left and you're there. They'll check you right in."

The biggest black kid blinked.

"Oh—oh," said Big Foot. "He got a smart mouf."

"The speech therapist is right next door to it," I said, back-ing up a few steps before I turned and took off at an almost-trot. "You can catch him too."

I got around the corner without hearing the pounding of rubber soles behind me. The spewing of cuss words—some of which I was going to have to run by the Assorted Buddies because I'd never even heard them before—faded once I jay-walked toward a crowded market and cut a corner through a newsstand. The dude selling newspapers cussed at me too, but at least they weren't following me. I didn't kid myself. I hadn't even begun to match them. They were just surprised for a second.

That morning I'd thought it was going to be unpredictable enough for one afternoon just to meet my dad's choice of a pro-fessional coach. I hadn't really, I mean not *really*, expected to meet a streeet gang, complete with a trainee, the very first *day*.

The actual neighborhood where the pool was wasn't as bad as the bus stop area, where all you saw were temporary fences and boarded-up barricades blocking the sidewalks. At least here you could pick out an unemployment office and a health clinic, and it looked like the people going in were too busy just trying to survive to worry about whether I had the wrong color skin. It seemed okay to stop and take out the directions, written in my mother's unmistakable chubby-round handwriting.

"Now, use the Tribune Tower as a point of reference," she'd said.

I looked up. Yep. There it was, looking over the reconstruction like a critical old grandfather. And there was the pool, and with it the next step in getting me closer to my dream.

Ever since I'd joined the swim team freshman year and Coach Morrell had said, "You're a natural born diver, Daniels. Get on that board"—and ever since I'd started taking every medal at every local, state, and regional high school meet—and ever since I'd been mesmerized by Greg Louganis taking it all at the '88 Olympics—ever since then, I'd known I had to do it too. It was like being under a spell. Nobody else knew it yet, not even my dad, but I had to dive in the Olympics, no matter what it took.

And because, cushy as it is, California Christian doesn't have a diving platform—and because I'd long since mastered everything my high school coach could teach me—and because my father was, let's face it, loaded—because of all that I'd asked for a coach for my birthday. I was already slated for the Regionals in a couple of months. If I did well, I'd get into the Nationals. And if I made a good showing in the Nationals, I'd get into the trials. If I made it through the trials, I was on my way to—who knows where? The Olympics? If this guy was everything he was supposed to be, his one-on-one coaching was going to help get me there.

But there was going to be no *if* about it. I pushed open the glass doors of the Municipal Pool and felt the blast of heat and chlorine on my face. I was home.

The place was empty, which meant it wouldn't be hard to pick out Mouse Tulley. That was the coach's name—Mouse. My dad had said over the phone that was probably because he was a "short little . . ." Well, I won't give you the rest of his description. "Dad swears around you because he wants you to feel like you're one of his buddies," my sister Meg had told me. "It's supposed to make you feel like an equal."

I swung my bag over my shoulder and rang the bell on the vacant counter, smirking to myself. What was I going to say to whoever showed up—"Have you seen a short little so-and-so named Mouse?"

"Josh?"

I turned around to face a guy who looked about as much like a mouse as the black kid with the size 13 feet.

He wasn't tall. In fact he was probably only about five foot seven. But I wouldn't have called him short, little, or a so-and-so.

Dripping wet and dressed only in a red Speedo, he had a classic diver's body—big worked-out shoulders, skinny waist, legs like well-oiled machines. He ran his hand over the dark hair that was slicked back from swimming and scoped me out with small, dark, close-together eyes.

"Mr. Tulley?" I said.

"Mouse," he said. A pleasant ripple—you couldn't call it a smile really—passed over his face.

I nodded.

"So get your suit on," he said. "Let's go to work."

"That's why I'm here," I said.

A girl with an overbite and a body like a fast-moving bowling ball gave me a locker and ran through the locker room rules. It came out something like no-smoking-no-drinking-no-glass-containers-no-singing-in-the-showers.

That's okay, sweetheart, I thought as I pulled on my trunks. *I don't have time for any of that stuff. I'm here to dive.*

Mouse was testing the springboard when I got out to the pool, and I sat down on the edge to watch.

My eyes immediately went to the square cement monster that loomed over the whole picture.

The diving platform.

That was part of the reason I was here. They don't do platform diving in high school. It's too expensive because it takes a really deep pool. Even an intermediate platform is over sixteen feet above the water. You do a dive from one of those and you've got to have some room after you rip through the surface.

Even as I thought about it, butterflies were doing two and a halfs in my stomach. I knew this platfoorm was a seven and a half meter job, twenty-four feet above the surface. Which of course was nothing compared to the 10-meter platform I'd be using in competition. Thirty-three feet in the air.

I'd never dived off of any of them—nothing that didn't

spring with me and lightly move away as I left it for the water. I'd never dove off of anything that had the power to crack my skull open if I made a mistake and hit it.

I gave Mouse my full attention. My dad had said he was the best, but I was going to the Olympics. I wasn't going to waste my time trying to get there if this guy wasn't everything he was supposed to be.

Mouse went to the start of the board and stood, almost as if at attention, for a few seconds. If he was like me, the upcoming dive was flipping by in his mind like cards in a deck.

Then he strolled easily to the end of the board and his knees lifted, pulled by the same magic string that lifted his arms and brought his body straight back to the board.

He pulled up again into a perfect cane-like curve. A forward dive. A one-half twist. An entry that ripped the water with barely a splash.

Okay. Okay. He knows some stuff.

"All right," he said again when he got to the edge of the pool, "let's go to work."

I started to get up. "What do you want to see?"

"I've seen your fancy stuff," he said.

I stopped in mid-stance. "You have?"

"Saw your last meet."

"Oh. I didn't know my dad gave you the schedule."

"He didn't," Mouse said. "Just warm up a little. Then we'll look at some dives."

This guy, I decided later, had understatement down to an art. The unexplained remarks. The one-word answers. The term "warm-up." Ha. Try "work up a sweat that would make Mike Tyson look like a piece of dried fruit." By the time I got on the board, my mouth had turned to fiberglass.

There was something about diving for me. Total concentration was the name of the game. When I was out there doing it, I was aware every move had to be perfectly timed. That my form had to be flawless. That every tiny detail from the tilt of my chin to the point of my toes had to be absolutely precise. But even though it took everything, that's what I liked about it. It was all black and white. No mud. No confusion. I was in control.

I did a whole series for Mouse, although after the first dive he wasn't there anymore. I was in my own world. Backward dive, layout position—reverse dive, pike position—inward dive, pike position—forward dive, half twist. Stretching myself. Driving myself. Because that's what it took.

"Josh!"

I jolted back in from an approach.

Mouse was looking at me steadily from those close-together eyes. "Good enough," he said. "Let's take a break and talk."

I did a forward and swam to the side. He tossed me a towel, and I went after my hair with it.

"You're good," he said.

I know that, fella. Why else would I be here? "Thanks."

"It's easy to see why you're taking the high school titles."

Right again. "Thanks."

"If you go to the Regionals diving just the way you did today . . ."

"Th—"

". . . you won't get past the second round."

"—anks" faded from my lips.

Mouse looked at me narrowly. "What is it exactly that you want out of diving?"

Nobody had ever asked me that before. Of course I knew the answer. But I wasn't sure I wanted anybody else to know yet. Still . . . this guy was making me itch.

I looked back at him. "I want to be world class," I said. "I want the Olympics."

There. You've said it. It's out there.

"Newcomers don't just go to the Olympics," he said.

"I know that."

"Either you're a National medal winner or you've been near the top for a long time."

"Okay, but—"

"The pressure's powerful. You have to be well-seasoned."

I looked up from the towel I was now wringing so hard the terry cloth stubbles were digging into my flesh.

Great. My own father has set me up with one of those sneering coaches you love to hate.

Actually, Mouse wasn't sneering. His eyes were calm and even. I hated that more—and I didn't love doing it.

"You can't just be a 'good diver,'" he said. "You have to have something special. And you have several counts against you. You don't have the ideal diver's body for openers. You're fairly supple and coordinated, but you're tall. If you're short you have easier rotation. The taller you are the closer you spin."

I almost ripped the towel. "Yeah, but—"

"Your legs are pipe cleaners. It's going to take a commitment to some work with weights. You as a diver are your own most important equipment."

"Okay, yeah, but—"

"Your saves are bad. You've got—"

"Are you trying to tell me to forget about the Olympics?" I said. By now I had the towel around my neck, and I was hanging onto both ends with my fists. "Because if you are, man—"

"Hey—"

"I mean, I'm *going*—"

"Put a lid on it, okay? Just for a second."

I did, but I could feel my eyes going to slits.

He watched me—I guess to be sure my mouth wasn't going to open when his did. "If you're willing to unlearn some bad habits . . . If you're willing to let me be the boss and let me have the answers . . . If—"

His voice dropped, and he shrugged. "I think you can do it."

"I *know* I can do it."

"Okay then—those are my terms."

My dad was right. He was a short little so-and-so. But nobody—nobody!—was going to keep me from having what I knew was mine.

"Okay," I said.

Although he left then and I stomped into the locker room

and stomped all the way to the bus stop, my side of the conversation with him continued in my brain.

Why did you take it on yourself to go to my meets? Why are you even here, Bucko, if you have all those ifs in your contract? The contract. Of course. You're in it for the money.

I didn't meet No Teeth or Big Black Foot or Acapulco Al or even Karate Kid Junior on my way back to the bus stop.

The mood I was in, if I had, I think I'd have punched them all right out.

3

"GIVE it up, Daniels. Admit defeat. Either you come quietly or we take you by force. Young Jon—"

Young Jon Ricco held up a piece of rope and smiled the Latin smile he usually reserves for slimy situations.

"What's it going to be?" Nathan said.

I looked up from my water bed at the three of them, the "Assorted Buddies" as my mother called them, standing there grinning down at me.

"Neither," I said.

"Those are your only two choices, right, Brain?" Nathan said.

Brain nodded. Young Jon Ricco snapped the piece of rope, and I snorted.

"Snort no more," Nathan said. "You're coming with us."

"I can't."

Nathan wandered over to where Lou was sitting on the windowsill picking a piece of dental floss out of his paw. "Come party with us, my man, or the cat buys the big one."

He picked up Lou and buried the feline's face in his palm. A low growl came from between Nathan's fingers.

"Josh is not taking us seriously," Nathan said.

Young Jon sighed and came at me with the rope. I shoved him off, still snickering.

"I can't go with you guys," I said.

Nathan let out a derisive hiss. "Come on, Daniels. What's your problem? You have to go dive *tonight*? Saturday night? In beautiful suburban Oakland?"

"No—"

"Then get off your tail and come with us. Kim Barnes is having a party."

"And after that Jill Pronk." Young Jon wiggled his eyebrows. The kid doesn't have brain one, but women zap to him like sandspurs to shoelaces. To me that would be just about as annoying.

"Look, I'm serious, man." Nathan dumped Lou on the carpet and stabbed his hands onto his belt buckle. "You are getting totally boring with this diving stuff. You can't even hang with us anymore, and it's ticking me off."

"So be ticked. I have to go visit my dad in San Francisco tonight."

"Your dad?" Nathan looked at me like I'd just admitted to wearing pink boxers. "You never see your old man."

I got up and pulled off my T-shirt and tossed it onto the pile of dirty clothes by the door which by tomorrow morning would be miraculously turned into a stack of clean, neatly folded laundry.

"He wants to know how it's going."

"How what's going?" Jon said.

"The diving." Nathan curled his lip. "It's all he thinks about. He's getting boring."

Young Jon yawned until I could see his tonsils and then grinned at Brain, who answered with a twitch on one side of his mouth.

"Hey, what can I say to my dad?"

"You can say no," Nathan said.

I poked my head through the hole of a clean T-shirt and stared at him. "Come *on*—"

"Okay," Brain said. "Let's blow and let the man do his sonly duty."

We all looked at Brain. Usually we did when he said something because half the time he didn't say anything at all. People thought we called him Brain because he wasn't bright enough to talk. Actually it was because his name was really Brian and he'd made the mistake of revealing to us one night that until he was in about seventh grade he always got the letters switched around when he wrote his name.

"Okay, do it," Nathan said in disgust and feigned a punch at my Greg Louganis poster. "But you're going out with us next weekend."

"Maybe," I said.

"No maybes. Friday night you're going out with us."

"Yeah," Young Jon echoed. He twirled the rope and stuck it in the pocket of his jeans. How I'm not sure. He wore them so tight I don't know how he could even get a dime into them. As they left, Brain just twitched his mouth at me.

Those were my friends. The ones I met in the courtyard at California Christian every Monday through Friday. The ones I "got by" in class with. The ones I'd been on a path with since junior high.

"What an assortment," my mother always said. That's why she gave them the title "The Assorted Buddies." I never called them that, of course. You just don't pick up your mother's pet phrases. But I had to admit it fit.

Nathan was skinny and wiry and straw-haired and had eyes like a pot smoker. But he didn't smoke dope. That dead look came from apathy, not grass, and about the only thing that could bring it to life was a party on the horizon. We'd been best friends since sixth grade when I'd first moved to Oakland after the divorce. He was the one who had tried to convince me it was no big deal. Take it from him, you could live without your "old man."

We'd invited Young Jon Ricco to start meeting us in the courtyard freshman year, largely because he in turn could pick up any chick and deliver her to our door. That didn't appeal to me the way it did Nathan. Especially since I'd started to dive. I didn't have time for girls—an amazing phenomenon that baffled both of them. Young Jon—so called because he had a father with the same name (Old Jon) and because he had big brown little-boy eyes that turned girls into stuttering idiots, as if they weren't already—anyway, he kept us in possession of his mother's homemade pizza and went along with just about anything Nathan and I came up with. He'd have eaten a jar of unpopped popcorn if Nathan had told him it would be fun—and would have sworn afterward that it was.

Brain—Brian—had joined us in the yard sophomore year. I think Nathan had included him because when he'd first started going to California Christian he'd given the impression he could be talked into stuff the way Young Jon was. When Nathan found out that wasn't the case, he figured that was cool too. The dude tipped the scales at 180 plus and towered over most of the basketball team with total lack of interest. One weird thing about Brain was that everything on him was the same kind of beige color—his eyes, his hair, his skin. He reminded me of porridge, but at least he wasn't getting in my face.

The hassles, I realized as I stuffed a toothbrush and some clean socks into my Gear bag, had been going on for a couple of months now, and it was all because I wasn't available for the weekend party tours.

I couldn't blame the A.B.'s. They didn't get it, and I wasn't doing a whole lot to help them get it.

They'd figured out diving was taking up all my spare time, and some of my not-so-spare too. It was no secret that my grades were less than sterling and that Mrs. Sanderson, our English teacher, was constantly on my case about overdue book reports. But they didn't know about the coach or my plans for going to the Olympics—and I wasn't about to tell them. They'd think I'd landed wrong on my head in a recent one and a half gainer, and I'd be social history.

So, yeah, they were my friends, but I was starting to make up excuses not to meet them before school—that kind of stuff.

I hadn't really lied to them that night, though. I really was going to see my dad in the City. The part I had sort of stepped around was that I wanted to go.

I hardly ever saw my dad because he traveled and was busy running Daniels Properties. When he'd suggested I swing by sometime to give him the scoop on the new coach I'd scrambled at the chance. His interest in my diving was the first thing he'd had time for in my life for a long time, and I wanted to share it with him. But my friends, who thought the word "parent" was synonymous with "algebra homework," wouldn't have understood that. They all had parents who bought them top of the line everything and had fifty-thousand-dollar college funds set aside for them—just like I did. But they didn't seem to care if there was anything more, and I did.

I swung my bag over my shoulder, chucked Lou under the chin, and snapped out the light. Downstairs in the kitchen my mother was at the counter, smothered in the ferns she was misting.

"Honey, are you sure you don't want me to drive you?"

Am I sure I don't want to have my nose pierced?

"Yeah," I said, omitting the tempting *Just as sure as I was the first three times you asked me that.* "I told you, I'm taking BART," I said. "We got anything to eat?"

"I thought you were going to dinner with your father," she said, but she put down the spray bottle and started opening cabinets anyway.

"I can get it," I said, and went for the refrigerator before she had a chance to whip up a gourmet burger or start sautéing mushrooms. Of course, I *liked* sautéed 'shrooms. "We *are* going out," I said. "I'm just hungry now."

She smiled at me. "Of course. You're sixteen. If you weren't hungry at any given moment I'd take you to the doctor."

I stuck the industrial size jar of jelly under one arm, a loaf of oatmeal bread under the other, and grabbed a gallon jug of milk. And grimaced. My mother is head of Christian education at a big suburban Oakland church. I guess because of that she thinks she knows a lot about kids. Okay—yeah—maybe she does. But for some reason I hated it when she understood me all the time. I got sick of being understood.

"I'm not going to tell you to be careful getting to the station and all that," she said.

You're telling me now while you're not telling me.
"I know you hate that."
Yeah, I hate it. And I hate it when you know I hate it.
She dimpled at me. My mother doesn't smile—she dimples. People—OK, girls—say I do that too. Now *that* I really hate.
"So just—be cool," she said.
Aw, man!
I stuffed the sandwich in my Gear bag. "See ya tomorrow," I said.
"Have fun, honey. Give that old Meggie a kiss for me."
"Yup."
"I'll be fine. Denise is coming over for me to give her a perm."
"Great."
"And tell your dad hi."
Hi, Dad. Your ex-wife sends her regards. Lady—would you let me get out of here?
I guess if I'd said everything to my mother that I felt like saying, I'd have had to be fitted for dentures. I thought about that later when I was on the train, sliding toward the City. But I decided, no . . . I think she'd have *understood* the deep, hidden causes for my wise-guy attitude.
It was an unusually clear night in San Francisco. If I'd had more cash on me I'd have told the cab driver to drive past Fisherman's Wharf, a couple miles out of the way, just so I could lean out the window and catch the sea lions who had moved in down by the Pier. Now those suckers could *dive*.
But I'd used most of the last hunk of dough my dad had sent me to buy Greg Louganis's book, a silver Speedo I planned to wear in the Regionals, and, just that week, a membership at the health club. Pipe cleaners for legs. Bet me, buddy.
And besides—I wanted to see my dad.
I took the steps two at a time in a leap up to the condo he and my sister Meg lived in and pushed the buzzer on the wrought-iron gate. His place had better security than Folsom Prison. Couldn't say I blamed him. He claimed—and Meg said,

oh yeah, he knew, down to the penny—that the paintings on his walls alone were worth a couple of hundred thousand. "I'm in the wrong business," Meg had said to me the last time my father had bought a painting at an auction. "I'm part of research that could someday save people's lives, and I can't even make enough to qualify for an American Express Gold. These jokers stand across the room and throw a wet paintbrush at a canvas and people like Dad pay them fifty thousand dollars." Not that my sister Meg wanted an American Express Gold Card. She'd rather call me from a phone booth and keep putting in quarters than run up a phone bill.

When I rang the bell the second time, Meg herself appeared at the front door and crossed the court in a bathrobe with her hair wrapped in a towel. I mashed the button again, just for grins.

"Relax, little brother," she said. "I was in the shower."

"Good. I could smell you all the way across the Bay before."

"Nah. That was your upper lip."

She grinned. Meg has dimples too. It's the curse of Sara Daniels. But Meg doesn't dimple. She gives you an honest smile out of a face with too many freckles.

"Get in here," she said. "What's happening?"

I followed her into the house. After college Meg had moved in with Dad so she could keep costs down while she got settled in her first job. She had, shall we say, all the comforts of home and then some.

"Take off your shoes," she said.

"New carpeting?"

Meg wiggled her bare feet in the shrimp-colored rug whose fibers came up over her toes and buried them. "For what he paid for a square foot of this stuff, you could feed a family of five for a week."

"You lie."

"Yeah, but not by much."

I set my bag on the tile in the foyer and scanned the room whose glass tables and eyes-on-San-Francisco windows sparkled with the maid's touch. The picture was jarred by Meg's spatter of books, maps, and granola bar wrappers. I had a sinking feeling.

"Where's Dad?"

She folded her arms and walked to the couch. "He didn't call you?"

"Where is he?"

"Denver."

"Oh." I sank.

"He told me he was going to call you—Thursday, when he knew he had to go check on—well, what difference does it make? He left and he didn't tell you."

"It's okay." I picked up the TV remote, and she snatched it from me.

"The heck it is. That was downright rude of him to do, Josh."

"It's no big deal. He runs a big business. He's busy."

"Too busy to pick up the phone and be considerate?"

"Look, just drop it."

Meg looked up at me from the couch, her freckles working overtime. "Okay—but only temporarily."

"You're a nag."

"Yep. Sit down."

She whipped the towel off her head and shook her massive head of black unruly hair like a dog. Drops splattered all over the glass-topped coffee table.

"You're also a pig," I said. "Doesn't Dad get mad at you for trashing the place?"

"You know I only do it because I have to be so neat at the lab. Besides, I only do it when he isn't here, and I don't call it trashing the place . . . I call it relaxing and *living* for Pete's sake. Do you remember him being that fastidious when he and Mom were still married?"

I blinked at her.

"Of course you don't because he didn't have to be. Does she still wash your socks before they even get cold?"

I grinned. "Yeah."

"You're a brat."

She went after her mane with a brush. She goes at every-thing like I go at diving—like there's no tomorrow.

"So are you going out or something?" I said, reaching for the remote again.

"Would you put that darn thing down? No, I'm not going out. I'm taking tonight to get some space."

"Oh—ex-cuse me!"

"You're invited to get it with me. I haven't seen you in months, Baby B. Since New Year's Day?"

"Yeah, but if you've got stuff to do—"

"Shut up. No, don't shut up. Call Papa Luigi's and order us a pizza."

"Yes, ma'am."

"No—order two," she called as I headed for the phone. "I've got a two-for-one coupon."

Meg was the only twenty-one-year-old person I knew who actually used coupons. She'd always been like that. She made more trips to Europe and Asia when she was in college than the average President did his whole term in office—and always came back with pocket change.

"Vegetarian, okay?" I said.

"What?" She gave a mock shriek. "No sausage? No pep-peroni? No cholesterol on a thin and crispy crust? You're *meshugena*!"

That meant crazy. Meg was always picking up stuff to say from people she met riding on airplanes or standing in line at the deli. That particular one was Yiddish.

"I'm supposed to eat a lot of veggies."

"Oh—the new coach."

When I came back from ordering the pizza, Meg had her hair up in the usual ponytail and had changed into jeans and a T-shirt that said, "Where the heck is Medford, Oregon?" Meg was like a walking travelogue. She'd have had to go naked half the time if it weren't for her geographical T-shirt collection.

"So how did it go with the Big Bucks Coach this week?" she said.

I nodded.

One of her eyebrows shot up. "What does that mean?"

"He's okay."

"Liar."

"He's working out. What do you want me to tell you?"

"Oh—why not start with the truth?" She looked at me closely. "Is he a real jerk? Is he mean to you?"

I chopped out a sigh. "Would you get out of my face?"

"No, not at all."

She tapped her nose several times with her finger until her freckles danced. She was waiting.

"He's a good diver," I said finally.

"How good?"

"Real good."

"Better than you?"

I stared at her. "Of course he's better than me!"

"That's a start anyway."

I shoved at her with my foot. "What's that supposed to mean?"

"I know how you are about your own . . . expertise," she said. "If you say somebody's better than you think you are, they must be good."

"What—I'm not supposed to have confidence?" My grin was fading.

"I didn't say that. Go on. What's this guy like? What's his name anyway?"

"Mouse."

"Great."

"Yeah. He's kind of a little guy."

"Dad told me. A short little so-and-so."

"He knows his stuff."

"But . . ."

"No buts."

"Jo-osh!"

The doorbell rang, and she got up. "I want to know," she said.

The chick had laser beams for intuition.

"All right," she said when she came back. She dropped both vegetarian pizzas on the coffee table. "We don't get up until we finish both of these off—and until I finish you off. What's going on?"

"It's no big deal," I said, reaching for a piece with extra-thick crust. "This coach gets me out there and makes me show him my dives, and then he picks me apart. And it's been like that all week. I can do it if I really want to work at it, he tells me, but I'm working against pipe cleaner legs—"

"I love it!"

"—I'm too tall. I don't 'save.'"

"What's 'save'?"

"It's where you go after you hit the water. You can either go for the bottom or you can keep spinning as you go under water. He calls that going with the flow."

"So what difference does it make what you do once you're in the water?"

"That's what I want to know!" Actually Mouse had told me. He'd said I could use a good save to correct mistakes, like too much spin, and make it look like I was making a perfect vertical entry into the water. But I figured if he was going to teach me so much, I wasn't going to make mistakes.

"He's okay," I went on. "It's just . . . I don't think he really believes I'm going to do this."

"What?"

"Go to . . ." I stopped. "If I'm going to have a coach, I want somebody that believes in me. I'm *good*."

"That's what they say."

"And I'm going to show the—"

"Short little shrimp," Meg finished for me. "So do it."

I picked up the last piece from the first box. "I'm going to."

"So what's with your life?" I said. "How's the doctor?"

A big smile crinkled all the freckles on her cheeks into two crescent moons.

"Does that answer your question?" she said.

"Yeah, but I know you're going to give me another twenty minutes of conversation on the guy, so go ahead."

"Actually, Josh—" She folded her legs under her and squeezed her shoulders together.

"What? Trouble in the Garden of Eden? Oh no!"

I had never known Meg to date a whole lot. Not that I'd paid that much attention when she was in high school, and she hadn't even been around when she was in college. But there had never been letters and phone calls about this guy or that guy, the way girls usually acted. At least until she'd gone to work at the cancer research lab and met—*him*. Carl Avery. A doctor. A Christian doctor, no less. My mother was about to bust a dimple over the situation. Meg in love. It wasn't my bag, but she was happy.

"So what's the story? You found out he's an alcoholic?" I said.

"No—"

"Transvestite?"

"Josh!"

"So what's going on?"

"I found out he's really in love with me."

I looked blankly around the room. "So what's the problem? I thought that was what you women wanted."

"Would you please not refer to us females as 'you women'?"

"All right, all right. Lighten up."

"It *is* what *I* wanted. Me. Individual. Meg Daniels—"

"Okay, okay!"

"But now that means—decisions."

"Decisions."

"Get a clue, Josh. I think he's going to ask me to marry him, and I don't know what to say!"

"Looks like you got two choices."

"Joshua, everything is not black and white. I'm serious now." She leaned her forehead into her palm, proof to me that she was indeed serious. I'd only seen her do that twice—once when my parents told us they were getting a divorce, and once when my grandmother died. This was heavy. I put my crust back in the box.

"You don't want to get married," I said.

"I don't know. I mean, I love Carl. I do."

That didn't mean a whole lot to me, but I nodded.

"But I'm so independent. I do what I please when I please. I mean, you can't do that when you have a husband."

"I guess not."

"And look at the role models we have. I'm not sure I know how to be a married person. The only example I have is Mom and Dad—and they didn't exactly succeed."

We were both quiet for a second. The subject of our parents' breaking up, even though it had been five years, tended to do that to us. Another thing I never told the Assorted Buddies.

"So what are you going to do?" I said finally.

"Stall him," she said.

"Coward."

"You bet! Why do you think I'm not out with him tonight?"

"You're taking some space."

"You got it." She sloshed some apple juice into my glass. "You know, Dad really could have called you back this week and told you he wasn't going to be here."

I looked around vaguely. "I'm having a little trouble keeping up with these channel changes."

"Josh, when are you going to get a clue? Yes, Dad provides the college fund and the big-time coach and the—"

"What clue? Man, Meg—"

"Okay, okay, forget it." She leaned toward me on the couch and looked at me like optometrists do when they're searching your eyes. "But if you run into trouble with Dad, please come to me."

◆   ◆   ◆

Man, I thought later as I lay in Dad's guest room with my

feet barely touching the wall, *when I know something I know it. When's the rest of the world going to leave me alone about it?*

When I put on my silver Speedo and kick tail at the Regionals and Dad leads the ovation in the stands—then maybe. Then for sure.

4

"HON-KEE! Whatchoo doin' today? Goin' to the beau-ty parlor?"

"No, man. He got a violin lesson today."

No, man, I got an appointment with my shrink, because to be going through all this I gotta be crazy.

"Whatcha got in the bag, *gringo*?" the Mexican kid said as he swung himself over the fence and into my path.

"My black belt, a thirty-eight, and a set of brass knuckles. Hey, do you mind? I have places to go."

It was the third day that week—and the fifth day out of the eight I'd been taking the bus to the pool—that the three of them had harassed me, so I'd had some time to get my "smart-mouf" replies ready. Matter of fact, I'd been lying awake nights coming up with them. My best one for Tuesday had been the one I'd thrown out for No Teeth: "Hey, pal, there's a great orthodontist over on Eighth Street. Tell him I sent you." Then I'd flipped him a quarter.

I won't mention what he flipped me back.

It seemed like as long as I kept walking and spitting out the comebacks—fast and cool and sarcastic—they didn't show any signs of whipping out switchblades and ripping up my body for spare parts.

But that didn't keep my veins from turning to barbed wire every time they appeared at the fence.

"You need to find yourself a serious other route, boy," Big Black Foot said that particular day.

"You guys oughta find yourselves a serious other playground," I said. "Aren't you a little big to be playing with these children?" I nodded sharply toward the Oriental kid who was striding, Ho Chi Minh eyes aglow, steadily toward us. I bet that kid could've strolled through the Demilitarized Zone if he'd wanted to. He hadn't missed a day of hassling me yet. The kid had guts. He scared me more than they did.

"Is that white boy back again?" he said. There always seemed to be a chortle lurking in the back of his throat when he talked.

"Yeah, he— " No Teeth started to say. But I swung my bag over my back and picked up my pace. I'd never stopped walking, like usual, and, like usual, the two black guys had followed me from inside the fence while the Mexican did the hat dance around me on the outside. Like usual, when the kid turned up for some reason I wanted to get out of there more than ever. It was always a matter of coming up with a statement they had to think about for a minute while I threw it into fourth and screeched around the corner. So far one of them had always thrown me the straight line I needed.

"Yeah, Baby San," Big Black Foot said, "the pretty white boy gonna go to the op-era."

Great. What the heck was I supposed to do with that?

"No," said No Teeth, "he goin' to the symphony."

Okay. Now you're throwing me some possibilities—

"No, man!" Acapulco Al was getting into it. "He goin' to the ballet!"

All right. "You guys are close," I said, "but sorry, no prize. I'm going to the movies—and you ought to come along." *Hang in there, Josh, you're almost to the end of the fence.* "You could definitely relate." *Please—let this work.* "They're showing 'The Three Stooges.'" I looked down at the kid, who was practically trying to crawl through a chain-link diamond. "Explain that to them while I'm gone, will you, kid?" I said.

And then I took off—heart slamming, pits dripping like a

lawn sprinkler. Like usual, they just hung at the end of the fence and swore at me. It was totally weird how they didn't follow me—but I sure wasn't going to go back and ask them why.

By the time I got to the pool, my pulse had slowed to a mere race and I could go and check in with Mouse's secretary—Overbite Betty—without looking like I'd just had a serious run-in with Arnold Schwarzenegger.

While I changed into my trunks I could also shift gears, from "scared half out of my Nikes" to a simple "on guard"—for what was going to come out of the mouth of the Mouse today.

To understate it just a scosch, as my mother would say, it didn't go well.

He was executing a dive, as always, when I got out to the pool. It was just a simple back dive, but—much as I hated to admit it—he looked like a switchblade closing cleanly into the water. He made it look like an art form.

"Diving isn't like other sports," he'd said the day before. "It's pure art. Any dive you do should be a smooth blend of all those fast actions you're doing. It has to look effortless. It's got to be elegant, or you're just a jock. Ever watch Louganis dive?"

Do I ever breathe, swallow, or blink?

I'd nodded sullenly.

"He doesn't just dive. He performs. He's the closest to perfect the art has ever known."

Josh Daniels will be too, buddy. Just hold on to your Speedo because here he comes.

When he got to the edge of the pool now, he just looked at me through his narrow eyes and said, "Why don't you get warmed up?"

Two days ago we'd started skipping the "hi's" and the "how are ya'?s."

I spent twenty minutes warming up. Man, I hated to say it, even to myself, but his killer workout was helping. And so was the weight training I did every night after dinner at the health club—compliments of my father's MasterCard. His secretary had given me the number over the phone per my dad's instructions. "Anything my man wants," she'd quoted to me. I'd told her to tell him he could stop by practice anytime.

I was headed for the board after my warm-up when Mouse stopped me.

"Hey—let's talk a minute first."

Another lecture.

I shrugged and squatted on the cement with him.

"We're going to concentrate on your entries today," he said.

Nobody ever complained about my entries before.

"Yours aren't bad."

Gee, thanks.

"But you have a tendency to go at the water like it's a target."

Do you have a problem with that?

"That isn't the best approach."

Guess you do.

"I want you to start thinking of the surface of the water as a curtain that you have to go *through*—instead of *at*—so that you're reaching for the bottom, not the top. It'll help you stretch the dive down. If you concentrate on the follow-through it's funny how that improves your entry."

He stopped and looked at me for a long minute. I can only imagine what was registering on my face—but, man, I was trying to keep it totally blank.

"Are you with me at all?" he said.

I nodded.

"Then let's get up there and dive."

He didn't pat me on the butt the way most coaches do. He just put his hands on his hips and waited for me to move. And I could forget getting any of the "positive reinforcement" my mother was always saying young people needed as much as they craved pizza.

Nah, what I was going to get, for the eighth day in a row, was his hook—catching the slightest flaw in my timing, my form, the way I held my mouth for Pete's sake.

"Okay," he called as I mounted the board, "think of a slit

opening in that curtain." He paused, then added, "You're going to drop your whole body cleanly through that slit."

I heard you the first time.

I opened my mouth, but his voice came out.

"Josh—"

I looked at him sharply.

"Losers form their excuses before they even get on the board."

I shut my mouth and dove.

And dove. And dove. Six more times before he called me over to the side.

"Not bad. Not bad at all. Now you don't want flat feet, but you do want flat hands. This time—"

This time.

"—grab one hand with the other so you form a flat surface. That'll give you a real good rip entry."

I read that in Louganis's book.

"I read that," I said.

He looked surprised.

"You're reading about diving?"

Yeah. Now are you going to tell me not to do that?

"Yeah," I said.

"Good. I'll bring you more stuff. If you really want to do this—"

Man, how many times do I have to tell you?

"—it means totally immersing yourself in it."

"I know that," I said testily.

Are you going to give me this kind of grief when my dad comes to watch me practice? How badly do you need this job, fella?

◆　　◆　　◆

It was almost dark by the time I got out of there that day, and I knew I was going to have to take a later bus. I was gathering up a pretty good flock of butterflies in my stomach when I got to the fenced-in vacant lot. Big Black and his pals had never been there when I took the return trip to the bus stop, but it was later than usual, and they weren't three people I wanted to run into at dusk.

They weren't there, so I slowed down a little to avoid getting to the bus stop too early and having to hang out with the group that was going off to the graveyard shift with their thermoses of egg foo yung. Big mistake. Something grabbed my leg almost the minute I got parallel to the fence.

"Hey!" I yelled. It was too late to try to be cool.

There was a throaty chortle down by my ankle. My body turned to relieved jello.

"You!" I said.

"Yeah." The Oriental kid grinned shamelessly from behind the fenced diamonds.

"Come on, kid, give me a break."

"Don't have any breaks," he said.

"Very funny."

"But I got a pear."

"What?"

I'd started walking again, but I stopped as he painstakingly pushed a large, ripe pear through a bent-out place in the fence.

"Take it," he said.

There was something so cut and dried in the way he said it, I found myself sticking out my hand and taking the thing. But then I shoved it back through.

"I don't take handouts, kid," I said.

"It's not a handout. I stole it."

"Aw, man!"

"From the old man at the Market. It was easy. He's a 'tard."

"'Tard?"

"Like a re-tard."

"Look, if you were that hungry, why didn't you eat it yourself?"

"I didn't take it for me," he said. "I took it for you." He looked at his watchless wrist. "You late today."

"I got held up by—Hey, what are you, my bodyguard? Get out!"

I took off down the outside of the fence. Good grief—I'd almost started explaining myself to this little slant-eyed reject from Sesame Street. How the blazes did he know what my schedule was, anyway? The kid was giving me the creeps.

"You gonna get pretty hungry on that bus, man," he said.

The pear came out through another hole.

"I'll deal with it," I said. I kept walking.

"Everybody else be eating egg rolls or potato chips. You won't have nothing."

"Anything."

There was a chortle. "That's what my sister says."

I stopped. "Well, tell your sister she ought to keep you on a leash."

The pear came out through a third hole. Behind it, black eyes sparkled in the gathering darkness.

"All right," I said, grabbing it. "Now go home, will you?"

"You too, white boy."

"My name is not 'white boy,'" I said.

"What is it?"

I caught myself with a *J* about to spill over my lips. "None of your business."

"Mine Phong," he said.

"Oh, yeah? Well, thanks for the pear . . . Phong. Now beat it!"

But of course he didn't. I did.

And as soon as I got around the corner, I pitched the pear into a dumpster.

◆　　◆　　◆

It was completely dark when I got home. From the sidewalk I could only see the outline of Lou sitting in my bedroom window. The dude was practically tapping his fingernails on the windowsill and saying, "Where have *you* been?"

"Be right up, pal," I said.

Lou in the armpit—a bowl of Top Ramen—feet up on the wallpaper—that's what I needed to grind this day to a halt before I went down to the health club. My version of Miller Time.

But a shriek from the kitchen greeted me the minute I got the front door open. If you didn't know Denise Stahl, you'd think somebody was being slain with a butcher knife over the bread board. Personally I knew it was Denise—laughing. Great. Perfect end to a perfect day. So much for Miller Time, in any version.

I tried to get upstairs without checking in, but my mother could smell me the second I stepped into the house.

"Is that you, Joshua?"

No, it's Jack the Ripper, but—

"Honey, come on in. Denise is making—"

Shriek. "*Trying* to make—!"

"—potato skins. Now, they're going to be good. They just look a scosch like they've already been chewed up is all. It'll save us the trouble."

There was no point in trying to get out of it. My mother would've brought the blasted things up to my room on a silver tray with a glass of Gatorade in a crystal goblet and a candle on the side.

I backed up and went into the kitchen. Denise was sprawled over the butcher-block table, crumbling bacon onto a tray of skins from a high altitude. My mother was right. They did look half-eaten. For that matter, so did Denise's hair.

I must have been staring at it, because one hand went up to her bangs, and she scattered bacon all over the floor in the process.

Denise shrieked—of course. Man, the chick always laughed like a turkey breathing its last the night before Thanksgiving.

"You're looking at my handiwork," Mom said. She had the broom out already and was scooping bacon into a dustpan. "Doesn't she look cute with a perm?"

She looks like a schnauzer.

Shriek. "I look like a poodle!"

Okay. I was close.

"You do not!" Mom took a gentle swipe at Denise's Pepsi-brown snarls on her way back to the broom closet. "It will settle into itself. It's just a little wild right now."

The question was, when was Denise going to settle into *her*self? Everything about her was wild as far as I was concerned. Long arms and legs flying all over. An aluminum-braces smile that was too big for her face. Eyes that were too, for that matter. They were the same color as her hair, which made it look like everything about her was constantly standing on end. She reminded me of Odie in the Garfield comic strip.

"A *little* wild!" she said. "I can't even get, like, a comb through it."

Obviously.

"You aren't supposed to," Mom said. "That's the beauty of it."

The beauty. Okay.

Mom poked me. "Joshua, try the skins. You're a great guinea pig."

"I don't think so!" Denise said, snatching the pan of potatoes away from Mom and, of course, narrowly missing sliding half of them off onto the floor. "He'll eat *anything*. We won't know if they're really any good."

Oh, believe me, I'll tell you.

"Joshua, you have to swear to be honest," Mom said, loading up a plate for me and going for the ranch dressing.

I swung my Gear bag over my shoulder for effect. "I'm not going to eat until I get back from the club. And I'm not supposed to eat that stuff anyway."

Denise's face fell. In fact, for somebody who thought I was a garbage disposal, it crashed right to the no-wax floor, bounced back up, and creamed in again. Why me? Why was it me a chick like Denise had to get a crush on? And then why did my mother have to take her on as a project and have her over to the house for cooking lessons and home permanents and nail re-dos practically three nights a week? Denise was a sophomore at California Christian. I could have avoided her about 80 percent of the time if my mother hadn't taken her under her wing and wasn't mother-henning her to death.

Shriek. "Okay! Fine! But when I bake brownies, don't come crying to me for a crumb!"

"No problem! I can't eat those either," I said, escaping up the stairs. That must be what it was like to have a younger sister. At least she didn't live with us. Yet.

◆　　◆　　◆

It was 11 o'clock before "Miller Time" actually came around. I went to the club and did double my usual work with weights, all to the silent rhythm of "I'll-show-you-Mouse-I'll-show-you-entries-I'll-show-you-art-form." Then I came home, showered for the third time that day, sneaked into the kitchen after Mom had gone to bed, and ate a whole head of lettuce drowned in a bottle of French dressing—and two potato skins. They weren't bad cold. Not enough bacon on them though. A tug-of-war with some peppermint-flavored dental floss followed, which, per usual, Lou won.

By then there was no time for homework. It was on the way to midnight when Lou snuggled into my armpit and I propped my feet up on the wallpaper and the dives started on the ceiling.

One-and-a-half gainer.

Forward with a double twist.

Jackknife. Clean entry.

Pretty.

But was it art?

By the time Christ came in and started dusting off His sandals, things were getting a little blurry. Like usual, I thanked Him for becoming part of my life and for making me a diver and leading me toward a goal that was going to seal who I was—for me and for everybody else. And I asked for His help dealing with Mouse.

I even asked Him to help out with Denise's hair. I guess that's where the edges started to blur, because from there I was off on a catalogue list of how many times I'd had to deal with people getting in my face in one day. Mouse. Denise. Mom. Those three losers behind the fence. Dong.

No—Wong.

No—Phong.

Lou purred.

Yeah, that was it.

Phong.

THERE was always a "but" in his voice.
That was the thing with Mouse Tulley.
"Okay, good save, nice save, *but—*"
"Those entries are looking good, *but—*"
"Now that was almost art, *but—*"
He never said what a but was. However, it was getting to the point where I wanted to come out with the "buts" that were in *my* head.

You're a good diver, okay, but you're a lousy coach.

You're teaching me technique, but you don't believe in me.

You plaster on a smile every time I walk out of the locker room, but you aren't getting a real big kick out of coaching me.

So the but attitude was the one I was wearing the next day when I got to the pool. I'd started it with feet on wallpaper the night before: *God, I'm working my tail off to get where You want me to go, but this guy is getting in my way. Have You noticed?*

My attitude wasn't watered down by No Teeth *et al.,* either, because only the kid, Phong, had been at the usual spot when I'd gotten off the bus, his eyes looking through diamond-shaped fence spectacles.

"Hey! None of your business!" he said.

In spite of myself I stopped. "What's none of my business?"

45

"You said your name was 'None of Your Business.'"

"I did not. You asked me my name, and I said —"

"'None of Your Business'!"

The kid was way too young to be as quick a wise guy as I was. The thought of this almond-eyed Jay Leno being a match for me kept me rooted to the sidewalk.

"My name sure isn't 'None of Your Business,'" I said.

"What is it then?"

I glanced around for No Teeth or Acapulco Al. All I needed was for them to get ahold of my name. I'd be dogmeat the next time I went by.

"J.D.," I said finally, although *why* I couldn't tell you. Next thing I knew I'd be feeding him my Social Security number.

"Where do you go every day?" he said.

"To the pool." *Oh, and by the way, 570-74—*

"What for?" he said.

"To . . . None of your business!"

"Oh. Same as your name."

He grinned, and when he did his eyes disappeared into about sixteen folds of pecan-colored flesh. I squinted mine back at him.

"Look, Chinky-San—"

"No." He shook his head, still grinning. "That shows how much you know. Chinky—Chinese. San—Japanese. Phong—Vietnamese."

Great. A refugee from Saigon dogging my trail.

"Okay, Vietnamese Phong, I gotta go."

"I'll go with you."

I stopped so fast my Gear bag hit me in the head.

"No way!"

"Why?" he said. He was already halfway up the fence.

"Because, man—" I was groping. "What about your mother or something?"

"What about her?"

Good comeback. Sounded like something I would say.

"You gotta have somebody's permission, man."

He climbed another couple of diamonds and grinned. "I'll get it."

"Right," I said. No problem. A kid this feisty probably didn't even have a mother.

"So long, J.D.," he said as I passed the end of the fence.

"So long, Phong," I said.

"Hey! So-Long Phong!" He said it in a singsong voice. But come to think of it, everything he said came out like he was about to burst into a tune.

He said "So-Long Phong" about three more times as I walked away. When he stopped, I sneaked a glance behind me. He was almost to the top of the fence, peering wistfully through the diamonds. Something went through me, but I shook it off. *You're a spunky little kid, Phong*, I thought instead, *but don't dog me.*

So by the time I got to the pool I'd been spewing out "buts" all day, and I was primed for Mouse and his unspoken ones.

But he didn't say much of anything. I went through the warm-up, did the usual routine, and displayed enough rip entries to make Louganis himself sit up and take note as far as I was concerned. The whole time I worked, Mouse didn't say anything—until I did my last dive, and then he motioned me over to the side.

"Two things," he said.

Here come the buts.

"Yeah?"

"One: Next week we start work on the platform."

Oh. The concrete Gargantua. Twenty-four feet in the air. "Okay," I said.

"Whole new ball game. Be prepared to start learning to dive all over again."

He was looking at me, so I raised my eyebrows, but my heart was slamming.

"Two: I brought some books for you. Beth has them at the desk."

Overbite Betty? Gee, it'll be a treat to touch bases with her. I've been meaning to stop by for a chat.

"Read them when you get a chance." He gave a throaty chuckle. "They might change your mind about this mess you're getting yourself into."

"Nothing's going to sway me," I said.

He didn't answer, but there was a "but" right in the middle of his silence.

After I showered I shoved the books off Overbite Betty's counter and into my bag without looking at the titles. I knew if I saw *Basic Fundamentals of Diving For Beginners*, Mouse was going into the Municipal Pool on the end of my foot.

Between the weight of the four books in my bag and the weight of his "ifs" and "buts" on my mind, I was lugging it getting to the bus stop. Nobody was at the fence.

At least not until a hand stuck a piece of paper through a bent-out place level with my belly button.

"Here!" Phong said.

"Here what?" I stared down at it.

"Permission."

I heard myself snort. "So you do have a mother."

"Did you think I was made in a factory?"

"Yeah, I thought you were made in a factory. Lucky for us they never made another one."

"Yeah. My sister says I'm unique." He crinkled his eyes.

"You could say that," I said. I took the note which he was by now rustling impatiently against my sweats and opened it. I had to look at it twice to see that it wasn't typed on one of those typewriters that types like cursive. If I ever produced handwriting like that, Mrs. Sanderson would have a massive coronary.

Dear Mr. J.D. (*it read*),

Phong says you have invited him to go to the pool after school with permission. Yes—if you will write back a note. Also, I hope there is no charge.

Tram Truong

I looked up at Phong with, I know, my mouth flopped open. He'd been staring intently at me as I read, and now his eyes lit up like birthday-candle flames.

"*I* invited *you*?" I said, tapping the note.

The flames didn't even flicker. "It sounded better that way."

I snorted. "Give me a break, man!"

"So?"

"So—*what*?"

"You write a note for tomorrow."

It was more a statement than a question—kind of like a teacher saying, "You do have your homework ready." Maybe that was why I started scrounging in my bag for a pen and turned the note over to write on the back.

Or maybe it was because, in spite of the crinkles of skin around his eyes, the candle flames in them were starting to fade.

Or maybe it was because deep down inside, Josh Daniels was a marshmallow-hearted, no-backbone sucker.

Dear Mrs. Truong (*I wrote, in shall we say, less than perfect cursive*),

Phong ~~can~~ may go with me to the municipal pool Monday if he wants.

I paused and considered adding, *but I didn't invite him!*
Phong's creamy beige fingers curled tighter around the chain link, so I went on.

He doesn't need money because we won't be swimming.

I looked up at him again. His eyes were going from the paper, up to my face, and back again.

"Go on," he said.

"Man, lighten *up*."

I will be busy, so I can't watch him or anything.

Should I write, *I can't be responsible if he falls headfirst into the deep end?* No, because I might be the one pushing him in.

I signed an illegible "J.D." and stuck the note back through the fence.

"Not tomorrow," I said. "Be waiting Monday. I'll be by at—"

"I know." The flames were back, at torch strength. "I'll be here—man."

I don't doubt it—man. I could already see the bus coming, and I took off down the sidewalk.

But I did look back once. Phong was at the top of the fence, arms folded on the bar, chin resting on them. When he saw me looking he pointed to the spot.

Yeah, kid, I'll be here, I thought.

But I just nodded and pointed too.

"JOSHUA, I know you're vying for the Oscar Madison Award, but I think the condition of Lou's litterbox qualifies as overkill."

Mom looked at me from over the top of her half-glasses and, of course, dimpled. Denise, of course, shrieked.

I growled into the refrigerator. "I came down here for a sandwich—"

"And you got a load of grief, I know. Poor baby. What kind of sandwich do you want?"

"I don't know." I slammed the door so hard the salad dressing bottles rattled.

"I'll make you a Santa Barbara. You go change the litterbox, and your sandwich will be all ready when you get back."

"I'll get it done, Mom," I said, though I doubt she understood me, my teeth were clenched so tight.

But of course she understood me. She always understood me. I hated that.

"Sometime in this decade," she said mildly.

"What's a Santa Barbara?" Denise said.

"Black rye. Tomatoes. Jack cheese. Sprouts."

Shriek. "You eat sprouts on your sandwich?"

"Not if I can help it," I said, looking at my mother.

More dimples. "Okay, one Santa Barbara sandwich minus the sprouts."

"Mom—"

"You want one, Denny-Penny?"

Denny-Pe—all right, get the net. "Mom . . . Hey, you—you with the tomato in your hand."

"What, Joshua?"

"Scratch the Santa Barbara. Just give me a grilled cheese or something, okay?"

"You got it. Denny, grilled cheese okay with you?"

"And I'll eat it up in my room," I said. "I gotta study."

"On a Friday night?" Denise said. "I'm impressed."

Don't be too impressed. I just thought of it myself.

One glance at Denise warming up to the idea of cozily sharing a grilled cheese with me in the breakfast nook and I felt like curling up with a good U.S. Constitution textbook.

I really am being more of a jerk than usual, I thought as I went up to my bathroom and picked up Lou's litterbox filled with a week's worth of what Meg called kitty hors d'oeuvres. *But so is everybody else.*

There'd been an accident at the freeway exit that afternoon, so the bus was late getting me to the stop, I remembered. Then I'd run as far as the fence. Big Black Foot and his henchmen had been there, and Acapulco Al had been having an off day so that when he gave his usual spit into my path he missed and hung a wad of saliva right in the middle of the toe of my left Reebok. So-Long Phong had laughed so hard his eyes had disappeared altogether, and then when I'd turned the corner I caught a glimpse of him out of the corner of my eye, hanging at the top of the fence, staring after me, eyes big as—well, as big as big almonds. It stuck in my mind like one of those paintings of big-eyed kids you see at garage sales. Man!

And then there was Mouse. I did everything he told me to. I mean everything. My ears were even pointed right, for Pete's sake. And still it was, "Nice. Now if you're willing to give this everything you've got—"

Man, get a clue. What do I have to do, open a vein?

"—find yourself a trampoline and do as many somersaults as you can. Do them until you want to puke."

I already do.

So coming home to my mother's mandates for the day—all frosted with "I know what it's like to be a sixteen-year-old boy, Joshua"—nudged my general overall wise-guyness up about three notches.

How does a forty-five-year-old woman know what it's like to be a sixteen-year-old boy? I'm not even sure I know.

"What *is* a 'normal' sixteen-year-old boy, Lou, my man?" I said as I tossed the empty litterbox into the bathtub and sprayed hot water into it. Lou jumped up on the edge of the tub to watch the process, but didn't answer. That's what I liked about him.

"Does he go out partying just because his friends do, and does he smart-mouth his mother just because she thinks she understands where his head is?" I smacked the box on the side of the tub and watched the drops fly. "Oh well. Does one out of two make me normal?"

Lou looked at me solemnly and blinked.

"Guess not."

That was, of course, no news to me. I was feeling less and less normal all the time. Here it was Friday night. I'd purposely shown up in the courtyard that morning to tell the Buddies I wasn't going with them to Zondra Shannon's beer bl—oh, excuse me—"get-together for students from California Christian Academy."

"You're going, man," Nathan had said. "You promised."

Nope. I was going to the health club to lift weights. And then I was going to put my feet up on the wallpaper. Because one of these Friday nights I was going to the Olympics.

My mother poked her head in the door. "Your sandwich is on your bed. Denise and I are off to Belinda Addison's wedding shower." She settled against the door frame.

We could be here for days.

"Can you believe our little Belinda is old enough to get married? You kids grow up too fast."

She straightened and went out. I thought she was through, so I took a breath, but her head came back in. "And you're the worst offender," she said. Her dimples deepened. These weren't her smile dimples. These were the heavy-concern variety. "Do something fun tonight. Don't let these years slip away."

Break out the violins.

"Okay, Mom."

"'Get out of my face, Mom,'" she half-said, half-sang down the stairs. She reminded me of So-Long Phong.

There was not only a grilled cheese sandwich, made with Monterey jack, cheddar, *and* mozzarella, on a plate on my bed. There was a dill pickle on the side, a basket of sour-cream-and-onion potato chips, and a banana protein shake. The only thing missing was the waitress with the annoying questions.

"Josh?"

Or not.

I pushed open the door for Denise, but not before I flipped open a book I could have my nose in when she came in.

"What?" I said at six on a testiness scale of one to ten.

"Your mom wants to know if you, like, need anything else before we go."

"Nah."

"Okay. We're out of here." She waved an arm as she turned to go and set the sea-gull mobile on my ceiling dancing.

"Oh, I'm sorry!" she said, half-shrieking, half-moaning. She grabbed at it to stop it.

"Just forget it," I said.

"No, I can—"

"It's okay—"

"Here, I've got it—"

"Denise!"

"What?"

She blinked her too-big eyes at me, and for a second she looked like Lou. Except Lou doesn't have poodle hair and braces.

"It'll stop by itself. Go to your—wedding shower."

She folded her arms across the front of her sweatshirt and made the shoulder pads bunch up against her neck. Why did women wear shoulder pads under their sweatshirts, for Pete's sake? They made Denise look like Olive Oil going out for middle linebacker.

"Do you know how much I hate wedding showers?" she said. She glanced over her shoulder and lowered her voice. "All those women making jokes about, like, honeymoons and stuff, y' know. It's embarrassing."

"So why are you going?"

I could have immediately slit my throat. You don't ask Denise Stahl a question unless you've got twenty or thirty minutes to spare.

"—because Belinda's been going to our church since, well, since, let's see, I was in, like, third—"

"Denny-Penny!" my mother called from downstairs. "Are you coming, girl?"

Denise rolled her eyes. "Gotta go, Josh."

Gee. Too bad.

She turned to go and then, of course, stopped. "I'm glad you're not going to that party at Zondra's. Those things are getting way out of hand."

"A little sour grapes, Denise?" I said.

She cocked her head. "What do you mean?"

Because you weren't invited, I thought. But I do have a few shards of niceness lying around. "Nothing," I said. "You better go. I can hear Sara tapping her foot."

Shriek. And then, ah, peace—she was gone.

I sighed and glanced down at the book I'd opened. *Tales of Gold*, it said. One of the books Mouse had given me, which of course I hadn't bothered to pick up and probably wouldn't have yet if I hadn't needed a ploy.

I fanned a couple of pages. *Tales of Gold* was about Olympic gold medalists. The diving section was clipped off. I slipped off the paper clip and proceeded to fold it out into a straight line while, in spite of myself, I read.

Pete Desjardins won the silver medal for diving in Paris in 1924. He was 17.

Aileen Riggin won the springboard diving title in 1920, the youngest Olympian at the Games. She was 14.

Dorothy Poynton Hill won the silver medal on the spring-board in 1928, the youngest American ever to win an Olympic medal. She turned 13 on the ship going to Amsterdam.

Although Victoria Draves didn't even start diving until she was 16, she was the first woman to win both diving events in the same Olympics.

Joshua Daniels will win both titles in the 1992 Games. If these kids can do it, so can he.

Okay, so I didn't read that part. But it seemed like my name should be there with theirs. I had everything going for me that they did. I had that "drive" they talked about. That determination. That fire fueled by the confidence that I could do it. That image of myself high on the platform, silver trunks sparkling in the sun. Yes.

But it was reading about Marshall Wayne that sat me straight up and sent Lou almost off the edge of the bed.

Marshall Wayne was 24 when he won the platforming title in Berlin in 1936.

No *big* deal—except that when he started training, every coach told him he was too tall, too skinny, too awkward to be a diver. He didn't care. He went for it. And he won.

I tossed *Tales* somewhere in the direction of my bag and scrambled for the phone. *Hey, Dad, old buddy, old pal of mine, want to buy me a trampoline? Extra lessons on Saturdays and Sundays? Whatever it takes. Man, whatever it takes.*

Meg answered the phone on the fifth ring gasping.

"Where were you?" I said. "Running a marathon?"

"I just got in. You caught me at the front door with three bags of groceries. Wait—I've got a loaf of sourdough poking up my nose—"

But I didn't hear the rest. "Dad's not there?"

"No. Oh, Josh, I'm sorry. He's out of town again. How do you feel about that?"

"Don't start sounding like a family therapist. I'm not going to go on drugs because he isn't in. I just wanted to ask him something. I'll get back to him."

"Right. Have your secretary call his and you two can do lunch. Oh, yuck."

"What's the matter?"

"This avocado I got is soft, and I just put my finger through it—right through the bag."

"If Dad isn't there, what are you doing with three bags of groceries?"

Matter of fact, even if Dad was there, what was she doing with three bags of groceries? Neither one of them could cook. Without order-out Chinese and pizza they'd both starve.

"I'm cooking dinner."

"*What?*"

"For Carl."

"Grab the Alka Seltzer. Listen, what's his phone number? I gotta call this guy and let him know you can't make microwave popcorn without burning down half the block."

"Thank you, Orville Redenbacher. And there's no need. He knows already. He's teaching me. Tonight is Lesson Number Three."

"What is it?"

"Chicken sautéed with mushrooms and garlic. Fettucine. Baby carrots."

"You're going to cook all this?"

"*We* are."

I snickered. "What were Lessons One and Two?"

"One was B.L.T.s."

"And?"

"They turned out to be L.T.s."

"You burned the B."

"Yeah."

"And Two?"

"Omelettes."

"I'm afraid to ask."

"Good." She laughed wickedly. "But it's such fun getting there."

"Spare me the details."

"Hey—" I could hear her shifting the bags, and I could

almost see her dimples turning to craters. "Why don't you hop on a train and come over here and join us?"

"No—thank you."

"What, you don't like baby carrots?"

"No, I don't like young love."

"Imagine—a kid sixteen years old who still hates kissing on TV."

"See ya, Sis," I said and hung up.

Actually she was wrong. I didn't mind kissing on TV. Matter of fact, the few times I'd done it, I didn't mind kissing in real life. But all the other strings chicks attached to it—*those* I did object to. I had other things on my mind.

Well, so much for hitting Dad up until he got back from Timbuktu. He'd help me out. He wanted this for me.

I decided to do double duty at the health club and slipped into some sweats.

"So long, Lou, my man," I said.

He switched his tail indignantly from his sprawled-out position on the bed.

"Hey, it's okay, guy. When I go to the Olympics, I'll take you with me."

He blinked.

◆　　◆　　◆

I was only about two blocks from home when they got me. One of them came charging from behind and pulled my legs right up over his head. The other two came at me from the sides and hooked my arms around their necks. All I could see was a black, curly head between my feet as they carried me like a harpoon to the pick-up truck, speared me into the cab, and crawled in around me.

When he got into the driver's seat, Nathan grinned at me. "Thought you were going to get away from us, didn't you?"

"What the—"

"This is an official kidnapping," he said. "Brain, show him the ransom note."

On the other side of me, my feet propped against his arm, was Brain. Wordlessly he unfolded a piece of paper bearing a message of taped-together words from magazines.

WE HAVE YOUR SON. HE'S GOING TO A PARTY WITH US. AFTERWARDS WE WILL PROBABLY WANT TO PAY YOU TO TAKE HIM BACK, BUT UNTIL THEN, DON'T WORRY ABOUT HIM.

Terrific. Just the kind of thing my mother loved. She'd have it posted on the bulletin board in the teen room at church.

"Hey, come on, guys, don't—" I said. But I might as well have been asking the history teacher not to give the final exam. Brain got out and stuck the note on our front door. Then, with him firmly back in place and Jon Ricco under me in the middle, loving the heck out of clapping his hand over my mouth at intervals, we squealed off toward Zondra Shannon's.

"Par-ty!" Nathan yelled out the window to an elderly couple teetering toward their Mercedes. Probably stopped the old dude's pacemaker.

"Josh Daniels is going to party with us!" Young Jon yelled, purple-faced, out the other window. His yell was less effective, seeing how he had to shout past Brain. Most of it resounded against my right eardrum.

"I told you guys, I'm not going to this party."

Nathan looked blankly at the other two. "Looks like he's going to me, doesn't it to you, Brain?"

Brain nodded.

"You, Jon?"

"Yeah!" Jon's face started to go magenta, so I put up my hands—one to Nathan, one to my right ear. "Okay, okay, I'll go."

Nathan smiled slyly. "I know you will."

"For fifteen minutes."

"Half hour," Nathan said. "Then if you aren't having any fun, we'll leave."

Jon's head jerked.

"And take you to another party!" Nathan banged the steering wheel like he'd just out-Johnny-Carsoned Johnny Carson, and Young Jon banged on me.

"Man—" I said.

"You promised," Nathan said. "Tell him he promised, Brain."

Brain just lifted his eyebrows at me and went back to looking out the window. I groaned.

"He said yes!" Nathan jabbed Young Jon with his elbow. "The dude said yes. You heard him."

"You said yes," Jon told me.

"Thanks," I said.

The party was about the way I remembered the ones I'd been to before—the ones that had made me decide to give the things up for life.

Zondra's parents were ensconced in another part of the house—like maybe in the private sitting room adjacent to their bedroom upstairs or something. There was no need to heavily chaperone a party like this. These were all Christian kids.

And they sure seemed like it. Squeaky-clean faces—right off the cover of *Campus Life* magazine. Top grades. Bible verses engraved in most of their brains. Christian songs that would roll out of their mouths at the mere passing of a collection plate.

Acted like it too. When I got past Zondra's hanging on me at the door, I saw all the usual trappings. Bowl after bowl of chips on the dining room table. Coolers full of pop in the kitchen. Board games all over the living room. Nobody ever ate any of the dips except the sour cream and onion. "Clam? Gross me out!" was like the password for getting in.

I soon noticed that nobody was playing Clue or Monopoly. They were too busy dodging into the hallways to make out without making it look like they were dodging into the hallways to make out. And the pop? Here's how it was done. You picked up a Diet Slice, strolled casually out onto the back deck with it, then stayed gone for twenty minutes—or however long it took you to empty a Diet Slice into the petunia bed and refill the can from the supply of beer stashed under the steps, down it, and pop the Certs you were careful to put in your pocket before you left home.

Who'd have thought Kim Barnes was already on her third Coors? She was sitting demurely on the couch, letting Steve Barber hold her hand and listening while he told her what Bible college he was getting a scholarship to. Both of them had the cleanest-smelling breath in town.

"Josh Daniels! Wait, catch me, I'm going to faint."

"Catch her, Josh!" Nathan shoved me toward Jill Pronk and dragged Jon off with him. "I'll get you a drink."

"7-Up," I called after him. "Diet. Plain."

"Gripe, gripe, gripe," Jon flung back at me.

Jill sidled up, a cluster of potato chips poised in one hand. These chicks even held junk food like they'd practiced for hours. "What are *you* doing here?" she said. "You never come to parties anymore."

"It wasn't by choice."

"Well, excuse me!" she said. But she laughed and put a chip into her mouth without letting it touch her lips. We wouldn't want to mess up our gloss now, would we?

"Hi, Josh." Kim came up beside her and flashed her smile, but I immediately focused on her eyes. Nobody's eyes were really like that. I mean, who grew blue eyelashes and had irises the color of the Gulf of Mexico? The rest of her eyes were so bloodshot from the contact lenses—or from the brew—

"Gee, you came to a party. Did somebody die or something?"

"Brute force," Jill said.

"Oh . . . Nathan and Jon. They said they were going to do that." Kim took a Dorito out of Jill's hand and put it in my face. "Chip?"

"No, thanks," I said.

"Oh, go ahead," she said, giggling and prying open my lips with one triangular corner. "It isn't going to kill you."

"Man—" I started to say. Big mistake. Kim stuffed the chip right in. She was so close I could smell the strawberry stuff on her hair. Why did girls always reek like a fruit salad?

"Hey, Josh—pssst!"

Nathan had poked his head out of the dining room and was motioning me toward the French doors that led outside. I showed my teeth at Kim. "Gotta go," I said.

"Bye-bye," she said.

I disappeared into the dining room, then dodged the door Nathan had already gone out of, and went down a hallway. There was an empty den there—or at least empty for the moment. A half-eaten bowl of popcorn and a half-played game of Scrabble said somebody had recently vacated. It'd do for now.

There was a couch facing away from the door. I leaned on the back of it and tried to swallow the lump of Dorito in my throat.

Man, I hated these parties so much. It seemed like everybody was trying to impress everybody else with how cool they could dress, how much of their parents' money they could show off, how long they could kiss, how much they could drink without anybody finding out. As far as I was concerned, everybody there ought to be wearing peel-off tags that said HELLO, MY NAME IS HYPOCRITE. Sunday morning they'd all be in my mother's Sunday school class, saying all the right things about their commitment to Christ. Maybe I hadn't always been the greatest Christian, but I still knew that what I was seeing here just didn't make it.

"Nathan's looking for you."

I jerked my head up. Brain was filling up the doorway. "Is my half hour up?" I said.

He shrugged and came to lean on the couch beside me.

"How many have you had?" I said.

He shook his head.

"None?" I said.

"*Nada.*"

"How come?"

"D.D."

I raised an eyebrow at him. Actually this talking without saying anything was pretty easy.

"Designated driver," he said.

"So what does Nathan want?"

"He's got a drink for you."

"He'll wait."

So, apparently, would Brain. He folded his arms across his big chest and crossed his ankles like he was staying a while. I folded mine too.

"You still diving?" he said.

I looked at him in surprise. "You could say that."

"That why you don't drink?"

I was still staring at him. "Partly," I said slowly. "Why?"

He shrugged and comfortably surveyed the room. When he glanced at the couch behind us, he chuckled. His elbow nudged mine.

I followed his glance. Below us, a couple entwined in a horizontal position was just becoming aware of our presence. Through the tangle of arms and legs, I couldn't even tell who they were.

"Just leaving," Brain said.

"Man, don't they ever come up for air?" I said when we were back out in the hall.

"Never," Brain said.

He wandered off down the hall, and I decided to look for a bathroom. Naturally when I found one the door was locked and the sound of hairspray and giggling oozed out from under the door.

I leaned against the wall to wait. How long could it take to make your hair stick out like you'd just gotten out of bed?

I really wasn't trying to hear what they were saying. Frankly I couldn't have cared less. But when you hear your name, tuning in is as natural as sniffing when you smell steaks cooking.

"I can't believe Josh Daniels is here," one girl said.

"He's so fine," another one said.

"Oh yeah—he's a babe," said another one.

"But he knows it," said still another.

Man, how many women were in there?

"So?"

"I hate it when a guy knows he's good looking."

"Jon Ricco knows he's cute, and I don't hate that." There was a wave of giggles I'm surprised didn't knock the door down. I almost walked away so I could locate the Pepto-Bismol. I wish I had.

"Jon *knows* he's cute," one of them went on, "and he knows *you* know he's cute, and it's, like, no big deal. With Josh it's—"

Another one picked it up. "'I'm a hunk. *I* know I'm a hunk. *You* probably *don't* know I'm a hunk because you're too stupid—'"

"'—and you aren't worth the time it's going to take to *show* you what a hunk I am!'" a third one finished.

They really liked that one. It set them all off into new realms. Now I knew why women went to the bathroom in groups—so they could slice you open with their fingernails without your ever knowing it.

But as I walked away I knew I'd been sliced.

"Josh. Where the Hades you been, man?"

I turned around and curled my lip at Nathan. That was another thing I hated about this group. Nobody swore—hey, that wasn't Christian. But they sure found ways to do the same thing.

"Let's get out of here," I said.

"Yeah—this one's a drag. We'll take you over to—"

"No, man, I want to go home."

Nathan wiggled his eyebrows. "Okay. We'll grab a couple chicks and a six-pack and party at your place. Those wedding showers can go on for hours."

"How did you know about that?"

"Denise Stahl has a big mouth."

At least Nathan and I could agree on something.

"Drink this," he said, handing me a Diet Slice, "while I round up some—companions."

For a minute his half-mast eyes almost opened all the way and then, mouth comfortably slanted into a practiced sneer, he slunk off down the hall, prying Young Jon Ricco away from a clench with Justine Johnson en route.

I shuddered. Suddenly I couldn't stand the sight of my best friend. I was just starting to lift the Slice to my lips when Jill shimmied by and did a double take.

"I'll beat you at a game of Aggravation, Josh," she said.

Funny how you can rip me apart in the bathroom and then come out and fall all over me.

"What are you drinking?" she said.

She grabbed the can from me, took a drag, and smiled like she'd just figured out the puzzle on "Wheel of Fortune."

"Come on, one round," she said.

"I don't play games."

"You said you didn't drink either."

"It looks like I don't," I said, taking the can back from her. I got it almost to my lips again when Kim joined her. "Come on, Jill," she said. "Ooh whatchoo got?"

I didn't dare dodge her grasp. She was so drunk she'd have hooked into anything, including my face, and with the talons she had, I'd be a prime candidate for plastic surgery.

She downed about half of it, looked at Jill, and threw herself into hysterical laughter. Soda drooled down her chin.

"Very attractive," I muttered.

"Here." She waved the can at me, spilling another several swallows' worth on Zondra's parents' pale-blue carpeting.

"Keep it," I said in disgust.

"No, it's yours!"

"Let the lady buy you a drink, Josh," Nathan said behind me. He had a weaving Young Jon in tow, but no girls. "You two want to come to a private party?" he said to Jill and Kim.

I snatched my soda can from Kim and wiped her lipstick off the top so I could take a mouthful. A second later I was spewing it—all over Jon Ricco.

"What the—"

"Hey!"

"Do you *mind*? My parents are going to kill me!"

Suddenly everybody at the party was crammed into the hallway with us, watching Jon Ricco smear rum-laced Diet Slice off a face that was growing redder and madder by the millisecond.

"You know I didn't want that stuff—I told you I wanted it plain!" I said to Nathan.

He shrugged. "You don't know what you want, man," he said.

"What I want is out of here!"

"You aren't going anyplace until I get an apologee."

At least I think that's what Jon Ricco said. He was drunk. He was mad. He was out of control. I dodged a fist that suddenly came flying out of nowhere.

"Hey—"

"Ricco—man, don't!"

There was a general roar as Jon flung out again, then a sharp silence, and then Zondra's father's voice from upstairs.

"Is everything okay, Zon?" he called.

"No problem, Mr. Shannon," Nathan called up to him. "Just some crazy kids messing around."

Jutting his lower teeth at me, Nathan grabbed both of Jon's arms from behind and wrestled him toward the front door.

"Feisty little fella, aren't ya?" he said, feigning a grin and winking at Zondra. "Some people don't know when to quit fooling around, huh, Zon?"

"Let me—" Jon got out before Nathan clapped a hand over his mouth and said, "Anybody got a Certs?"

In the midst of the laughter and the scuffle to get Jon through the door, Nathan cast a look at me. "Let's go, Josh," he said. "In the truck."

I handed the soda can to Jill and strode across the living room to the door. I could feel cold eyes on me from all sides.

Everybody else stayed in the house. Once outside, Nathan gave Jon a shove toward the truck.

"Have you lost it?" he said to him. "Man, you don't start a fight in some chick's house!"

"You don't spit in somebody's face either." Young Jon came for me again, but Nathan stopped him with one hand, and he went limp. The ladies' man was a noodle after a six-pack of Bud.

"I'm putting him in the back," Nathan said to me. "Get in the cab."

"Since when do you give me orders?" I started to say, but Nathan turned his back.

"Hey."

It was said so softly I wasn't sure I heard it. But I knew I felt Brain behind me. I turned around.

"Come on," he said, watching Nathan struggle with Jon Ricco.

I didn't say anything but followed him through the hedge he'd obviously just come out of and down along a cement gutter that bordered Zondra's parents' property and led off into the trees. He stopped me just as the party noises started to fade behind us.

"Through there's the side street that leads out to the main drag," he said. "You got money for a cab?"

"Yeah. Thanks, Brain."

"Hey."

"What?"

He stood there for a minute, hands stuffed into his jeans pockets, his big shoulders hunched. His silhouette reminded me of a sheepish Incredible Hulk.

"Nathan's really ticked," he said.

"Yeah. So?"

"He's gonna get more ticked."

I puffed out some air.

"Save yourself the hassle," he said. "Don't go home."

And he disappeared back up the gutter.

7

By the time the cab dropped me off at my dad's place, Dr. Carl was gone and Meg met me at the door wearing one of his lab coats over her clothes and carrying the rose he'd brought her. If I hadn't been so bummed out, I'd have gagged for her benefit.

But, man, she looked happy.

Until I spilled my story, that is. When I was through regaling her with the details of good little Christian girls ripping me apart from behind a closed bathroom door and my best friend dragging me to a beer bust under duress and my second best friend getting drunk and trying to rearrange my face with his fist, she turned around from warming up her fettucine in the microwave and gaped at me.

"These are your *Christian* friends?" she said.

"Yeah. What a bunch of hypocrites. I know not everybody in the whole school's like that, but everybody I used to call a bud is."

She pushed a plate across the counter and pulled a bread knife out. "So what are you going to do about it?"

"Nothing."

She stopped with the knife poised over a half-loaf of sourdough, gaping again. "Nothing?"

"What do you want me to do? I don't need them."

"But it sounds like they need you."

"They aren't my problem."

"Oh, now there's a Christian attitude!"

"Who died and left you in charge?"

She dropped the knife completely.

"Meg, if you don't stop hanging your mouth open like that, your jaw's going to come off the hinges."

"You gravy-sucking pig," she said.

A little something special she picked up on the streetcar, no doubt.

"I don't need them," I said again. "If you want to talk Christian—"

"I do."

"Then I look at it this way. God's got a plan for all of us."

"Okay. I'll buy that."

"Those kids don't know from dog droppings what it is for them. They're not even asking yet."

"Probably not, no. But—"

"Well, I've already asked, and I know what mine is."

She deepened her dimples and waited.

"Maybe tonight was supposed to happen," I said. "I mean, it's like it proved to me what I've been thinking for a long time. Girls aren't where it's at. Parties aren't either. All the stupid high-school stuff—it just doesn't get it for me. Everything has to go into diving. That's where I'm going." I stuffed a forkful of fettucine into my mouth and kept talking. "Nathan and Jon Ricco'll probably never speak to me again—if I'm lucky—and, see, that kind of lets me off the hook. That hassle's out of the way. I don't have to deal with it anymore."

Meg pulled a hunk of bread out of the loaf and nibbled at it. "So you're going to just let them go down the tubes while you go through the rest of high school with no friends, no girl-friends, no parties, no fun—*no life*!"

"Diving's my life."

She opened her mouth—to say something, I thought. But she pushed a piece of bread into it instead.

"Hey, did you make this?" I said, motioning to my almost empty plate. "It's almost edible."

She ignored that.

"Do you think you can squeeze your family in?"

"Sure," I said magnanimously. "You and Dad—"

"Ha!" She jabbed her next piece of bread back into the loaf. "Dad—the phantom father. How long has it been since he's seen you?"

"Man, Meg, don't start."

"Has he been to one of your practices with your coach?"

"Not yet. But he will."

"Does he know how intense you are about diving?"

"Yeah," I lied. Actually it wasn't completely a lie. If he didn't, why would he have set me up with Mouse?

"What does he say?"

I sighed. "Nothing. I mean, come on, he'd understand. He's driven. Nothing stands in his way either when he wants something."

Meg twitched her ponytail. "That's for sure. I don't think, though, Joshua, that he'd understand about your party attitude."

"He'd back me."

"A-a-a-a-agh!" She stood up and leaned right into the remains of my fettucine. "You're sitting here talking hard-line Christian. Then you look at Dad—he hasn't darkened the door of a church since before he left Mom—and yet you worship the ground he walks on."

I pulled my face out of her glaring range. "Dad loves us. He'd give us anything." Frankly the whole conversation was making me feel like I was teetering on a precipice, and I wanted her to lighten up big-time. *Man, I thought this was the place to come when the rest of the world was scrambled.*

"You know what?" Meg pulled back from my plate abruptly and darted for the refrigerator. "Carl made a chocolate and strawberry torte that's to die for. You're having a piece with whipped cream. You're way too skinny."

She pulled the thing out of the fridge and stopped to look at me over whipped cream and strawberries.

"You're a big boy, Joshua," she said. "You don't need me in your face."

Thank you.

"Now," she said, dumping a piece of torte onto a plate and shoving it at me, "the day of reckoning has come. I have to make a decision, and you have to help me."

"Gee, let's see, what'll it be for this year's vacation? White-water-rafting down the Colorado? Camel ride across Death Valley?"

"Put a lid on it, dipstick. I'm not planning a trip—I'm planning my life."

She reached into the pocket of the lab coat and pulled out a small box. I stared at the contents and then back at her.

"Diamond," I said.

"No joke."

"He *did* ask you to marry him." No wonder she'd been glowing like she had a radium implant when I came in. I felt a little stupid. I'd been rattling on for the past hour about my problems and hadn't even asked her why her face had added another 500 watts.

"That's just it—he didn't ask me."

"He just *told* you? This guy's a trip. I better fill him in on a few things about you before he blunders on any further."

"Would you shut up! He didn't *say* anything. He just asked me if I wanted one of his old lab coats to wear around the house. He knows I like to schlep around."

"What was his first clue?" I said, nodding to the baggy jeans she was currently schlepping in.

"So of course I said sure. When he left I put it on and stuck my hand in the pocket and there was this box."

"He's going to wonder where it is when he proposes to his real girlfriend," I said.

"Slime."

But she didn't look worried. To tell you the truth, I'd have killed for a fourth of her confidence. But she did look confused. You don't see that often on Meg, so I let up on her.

"Weird," I said.

"It is. I don't know if he was going to ask me and changed his mind and forgot it was in there—"

"Well, in the first place, you don't 'forget' a ring that cost what that thing must have cost. Besides, I'm sure he wasn't going to pop the question wearing his lab coat. 'Hey, Meg, let's just slip over here behind the test tubes—I've got something to ask you.'"

She laughed and smacked me. "So you think he intended for me to find it?"

"Uh, yeah. The only surer way was to throw it at you."

"But why?"

"I don't know!"

"To give me time to think!"

"Okay—"

"He didn't want me to have to *say*, give me some time to think it over. Is he the sweetest, most considerate—"

"Man, where are the barf bags?"

She danced around the counter and threw her arms around me. "Thank you for helping me figure this out." She kissed me sloppily on the cheek.

"You haven't figured anything out yet. What are you going to tell him?"

Her face clouded over. "I don't know," she said. "Marriage. Wow. Kids."

"Kids! Forget it!"

"Little nieces and nephews for you, Joshua!"

"No thanks. I hate kids."

"More whipped cream, Joshua?"

I dodged and let it spurt all over Dad's kitchen wall.

◆　　◆　　◆

On the bus Monday afternoon I decided I'd been right one thing—no, two things.

athan and Young Jon Ricco were definitely not speak-
e. For obvious reasons I didn't go to the courtyard

before school. During lunch they sat a table over in the cafeteria and stared menacingly at me, but didn't say a word. Brain, too, had been right. Nathan *was* angry—really angry!

But that was fine. At least they weren't hassling me about going out with them this weekend or spending too much time diving. The only problem was, that left enough space on the bench for Denise to plop down beside me.

"I heard what happened at Zondra's Friday night," she said.

"Hi, Denise," I said numbly into my milk carton.

"Did Jon Ricco really, like, try to hit you?"

"Uh-huh."

"Why?"

"He didn't like my face. He thought he'd push some things around on it."

She looked at me solemnly and nodded. "Y' know, you're just, like, too modest to say you were trying to get him to stop drinking and he got mad at you."

"Oh." I stuffed the straw down into the milk carton and got up. "Is that what happened?"

"You try to be, like, so cool, Josh," she said, braces gleaming under the fluorescent lights. "But you are, like, the *best* Christian."

For some reason that made my stomach lining peel off. I wanted to get away from her more than ever.

The other thing I'd been right about, when I'd been talking to Meg, was that I did hate kids. I didn't remember that until a Chinese—or something—woman got on the bus two stops before I got off with a round-faced kid under her arm with no visible eyes. It was a wonder those Oriental kids could even see before they lost their baby fat. Anyway, that's when I remembered that Phong was going to be waiting for me at the fence, pawing at the sidewalk to go to the pool with me.

How Mouse was going to react when I appeared with Bruce Lee, Jr. in tow was anybody's guess, but it was probably going to be something like, "If you really want to make it as a diver, you can't be picking up strays on the street and bringing them to practice with you. You have to concentrate."

My only hope was that the kid would get bored watching me have all the "fun" and go home after ten minutes. Matter of fact, I decided to offer him that as an option.

Just to make the day unforgettable, Acapulco Al *and* Big Black Foot *and* No Teeth were all in evidence when I got to the lot. So, of course, was the kid. But it was so strange to see him on the outside of the fence that their jeering faded into the background for a minute or two.

He looked younger and more vulnerable without the pattern of metal diamonds across his face. He was just a little guy, with baby-fine skin and eyes that at this point were glittering with anticipation.

Lighten up, kid. We're just going to the pool.

"I'm ready."

No kidding! What was my first clue? The runner's crouch at the starting line? The panting tongue maybe?

"I'm going with him," he said proudly to the trio positioned on the other side of the fence.

Terrific. Hey, why don't we all go? We'll make it a quintet and break into five-part harmony between here and the unemployment office.

"Where to, kid?" said No Teeth. He leaned over the fence like he was going to reach for him.

But I was too quick for him. I slapped my arm around Phong's shoulder and catapulted us both down the sidewalk.

"See ya, fellas," I called back to them. "Sorry we have to go, but I'll make it up to you later with a smashing game of squash or something."

"You're a stupid honkie," Big Foot yelled.

I looked down at the kid tucked under my arm. *For once, Big Foot, we agree.*

It was still weird to me that they never came over the fence after me or tried to do anything beyond humiliate me, which they were good enough at. It was even weirder that out of it I'd ended up baby-sitting this little Vietnamese victrola needle. Even after I let go of him his mouth was going 90 miles an hour.

"I never been to the pool. My sister, she swims. Not me. I know it's right around this corner and by that health place."

"How do you know if you've never been there?" I had made a silent vow not to answer any of his questions or respond to him in any way, but you either answered this kid or the interrogation kept up into eternity. It was like he carried an invisible naked light bulb.

"I followed you." He said it as naturally as if he'd been reporting his grade on the last spelling test.

"You little—dweeb!"

"What's a dweeb?"

"It's what you are. Hey—"

I stopped and grabbed him by both shoulders. "Did you tell those three orangutans where I go?"

His smile slivered open. "No. Why? You afraid of them?"

I hissed and started walking again. He had to run to keep up.

"They won't come after you," he said.

"Great. I'll sleep better tonight."

I pushed open the door and nudged him inside the pool building.

"What's that smell?" he said.

"Nothing. Look—"

"Smells like something to me."

His face was drawn up into a question mark, and he was already investigating the potted plants. Overbite Betty leaned over the counter with interest.

"Okay, it's chlorine, all right?" I said. "Now look, you can't be—"

"What's chlorine?"

I grabbed him as he headed for the locker room. "It's what I'm going to soak in a washcloth and put over your face if you don't shut up and listen to me."

Actually it was more chloroform I had in mind, but it

stopped him long enough for me to take him by the scruff of the neck and get him up onto the counter.

"Hi," I said, smiling at O.B. Betty.

If it struck her that this was the first friendly word I'd ever said to her, she didn't show it. She just sucked harder on her lower lip.

"This is Phong. He's going to be observing me today. Could he just sit here while I get changed? Thanks, lady. I owe you."

"So, lady, what's your real name?" I heard him say as I made for the locker room before she could knock him off the counter at me.

She laughed. I actually heard her *laugh*.

I made the change in record time and was still tying a knot in the string on my trunks when I went back out to the lobby. Phong, however, was not sitting on the counter.

"Where—"

Overbite pointed toward the pool door.

"What? Man, he doesn't swim! What'd you let him—"

"He's with Tulley."

"Oh."

"Don't mention it," she said.

"Thanks."

"Don't forget—you owe me."

"Right." *Just call me the walking National Debt.*

I was almost afraid to open the door to the pool, but twice as afraid not to. Mouse was probably writing his letter of resignation even then—with Phong dictating.

What I found was even more bizarre than that. Mouse had obviously just executed a dive, and Phong was standing poolside, legs apart, arms folded, like he was about to flip his scorecard over. Mouse swam to the edge and grinned up at him.

Not just a pleasant ripple across his face. A grin.

"So what did you think?"

"That's the way they do it on TV," Phong said.

"What more can I ask for?" Mouse hoisted himself out of

the pool and saw me. "You brought us a judge, huh, Josh? That's one way to keep us honest."

I stared. In fact, my mouth was open so wide, a small Vietnamese family could've climbed inside and taken up residence. Mouse was *smiling. Laughing* even. Next thing I knew he'd be giving out hugs.

"He seems to think I'm good enough for 'Wide World of Sports,'" Mouse said. "Show him what *you* can do. Let's—"

"I know, I know, 'warm up,'" I said.

There wasn't time during the warm-up to see what Phong was doing. I had to concentrate on what *I* was doing—and I had to concentrate on not concentrating on him. He was bound to get under Mouse's skin sooner or later, or maybe with any luck he'd be bored by now and would be bugging Overbite Betty and she'd be in the process of booting him out into the street. Shoot, I'd forgotten to tell him he could leave anytime.

But at the end of the warm-up Phong was settled in beside Mouse at the edge of the pool, pants rolled up, shoes and socks off, feet dangling in the water. Big sister wasn't going to be happy. Neither was I. I'd really expected my first observer to be my dad, not some Vietnamese candidate for juvenile hall.

"All right, let's show my man Phong some real diving, Josh," Mouse said.

"You did *real* diving," Phong said to Mouse.

"My *real* diving days were yesterday," Mouse said. "Josh's are tomorrow. With any luck, maybe they'll even be today."

Luck. Is that what we're hoping for now?

"Josh, we're going to hone in on your somersault technique."

Since when do you use my first name every other word? When did we become friends?

"Do you have a cat, Phong?"

Oh, now that *follows.*

"Nope. No pets allowed in our building." He giggled. "Except my sister."

Mouse laughed and smothered Phong's head under his arm. "You have a cat, Josh?"

Oh, yes, how did you guess? And a goldfish, and a white picket fence. Call me Beaver Cleaver. "Yeah," I said.

"Okay—" Mouse crouched on the edge of the pool and started explaining to both of us. Phong listened as if it were the story hour.

"You know how when a cat's dropped upside-down, he turns himself over to land on his feet?"

I envisioned Lou tumbling off my water bed after a piece of dental floss and nodded.

"When he does that, he's using the same technique a diver like Josh uses to twist in the air. See, if a cat twists his upper body around, then according to the action-reaction principle the lower body will twist in the opposite direction, and he'll go nowhere. So he instinctively works it so they'll twist together and he'll land on all fours."

I could've had that run by me a few more times, but the kid was nodding like he had it in the bag already.

"If Josh does this right," Mouse said to him, "he'll twist exactly like his cat does when he turns himself over in the air, and he'll come out the right way."

Phong looked at me, his almond eyes fizzing like two soda pops. "Let's see it," he said. "I want to see you be a diving cat."

"Do a couple one and a halfs for openers," Mouse called to me as I headed for the board. "Then let's try that forward two and a half."

"Not long ago," he'd told me last week, "most people thought a forward two and a half somersault in the pike position from the one meter board was impossible, but now most collegiate divers use it in their repertoire." It was in mine now.

A diving cat. Terrific. Lou would be laughing in his paws if he were here.

I steadied for my approach.

What's with Mouse and the kid? Suddenly he's Mr. Rogers because a little boy shows up?

I closed my eyes and saw the dive. The steps. A nice lift. A twist circumducting my arms—

What the heck is the difference?

I took the dive. An easy one and a half. A slice right through the curtains to the bottom. No evidence of a splash when I got to the surface.

"Good save," Mouse said.

Save? What in blazes was there to save?

"All right! Nice cat! Nice cat!"

I stared at Phong. The little wise guy was grinning like he was on his way to Disneyland—and clapping. *Clapping.* And there wasn't a trace of the smart mouth on his lips.

"That was good!" he said to Mouse.

Mouse grinned—again. He was working facial muscles I'd never seen him use before.

"He can do better," Mouse said. "Show him, Josh."

I will. I'll knock the little kid's kimono off.

Man, I thought as I climbed to the board again, *what am I saying? I'm showing off for this Mini Mao Tse-tung.*

And it felt good. That was the difference.

I skipped the one and a half and went right to the two and a half. I impressed Phong's slants right into American circles. That didn't stop Mouse from critiquing it to death.

"Don't let go of your rotation too soon. That tuck is everything—you have to use it to get that spin with your height."

But after fifteen more and a pretty good stab at a three, he didn't have much to say. Least of all "but—"

And Phong didn't go home. Not even while I cooled down with some laps and took a shower. He and Mouse were sitting side by side in the lobby when I came out. For a minute Mouse looked like a person instead of a coaching machine.

"Did you get ahold of a trampoline?" he said when I walked up to them.

I shook my head.

"Oh. I thought you had. It'll still help your form, but you're coming along." He looked down at Phong. "Speaking of coming along—you do it anytime—*any*time. Where did you two fellas meet?"

At a bar. Come on.

"You got some kind of exchange program at your church or something?" Mouse asked me.

"No—I—"

How am I going to explain this one?

"We met around the corner," Phong said. "I been protecting him from this street gang down there."

Mouse nodded seriously. "Oh. Well, keep it up. Josh has his mind on diving. He doesn't think about a whole lot else. He needs friends to protect him."

Phong couldn't sit still any longer, obviously. He got up and went for another bench where he proceeded to practice an approach.

"Another Sammy Lee," Mouse said. "What is he, Korean?"

"Vietnamese," I said, trying not to sound too much like I hadn't known that myself right off. And who, pray tell, was Sammy Lee?

"I meant what I said. Bring him along anytime. He's—" He stopped and looked at me for a second. "He doesn't get in the way."

He got up then and lunged for Phong, who was about to do a one and a half gainer off the end of the bench. Mouse scooped him up into—my worst fears were realized—a *hug*.

"Good-bye, buddy," Mouse said.

"No. So-Long Phong," Phong said. His voice went up in that singsong thing, and Mouse howled. Good grief, the man howled.

◆　　◆　　◆

I hadn't realized how late it was until we got outside and saw it was already getting dark. We must have practiced at least an hour overtime. I wondered if my dad would get a bill for time and a half.

I looked down at Phong, who was leading the way in the direction of the fence. I slowed down. Just the thought of meeting up with No Teeth and Company in the gathering darkness put the lead right in my Nikes.

"Hey, kid," I said.

"What?"

"Is your sister going to be freaked because you're getting home after dark?"

"I guess so."

"You're really afraid, aren't you?" I said sarcastically.

"I'm not afraid of anybody."

"I believe that."

But I am.

"Okay, look, I'll take you home and catch a bus from your neighborhood. Where do you live?"

"You don't have to. Nobody's gonna kidnap me."

"If they did, they'd bring you right back and pay somebody to take you off their hands." I knocked at him with my bag. "Come on, where do you live? I can probably get you off the hook with your sister."

Phong gave me a look that read *Want to make a bet?* "What is she, some kind of dragon lady?" I said.

"Dragon Chinese. Phong Vietnamese."

"I know—I know—where's your house?"

He didn't tell me, of course. He just broke loose and took off on an obstacle course that would've had Bruce Jenner panting. We climbed at least two chain-links, ducked down a couple alleys that made me wish I'd opted for Al and the fence, and led me through a store that had a door in front and one in back so fast the manager didn't have time to yell. Not that he would have. Everybody from the greasy-smelling pizza parlor to the fire department seemed to know him. Even a guy poking his head out of a manhole in a barricaded alley said, "'How ya doin', Phong?"

Through the whole thing I could barely keep up. When we went through the outside produce section of a run-down market, I almost knocked over a whole bin of bananas.

We finally stopped on a sidewalk in front of an apartment building with a locked gate. It was a puzzle of broken windows and out-of-control vines. At least three families had their laundry hanging out on their balconies.

"Hey, don't you have a key?" I said.

Phong had just climbed the gate like a spider monkey and was headed for a set of buzzers inside the entryway.

"Yeah, but just climb over."

"I climbed two fences and a brick wall to get this far," I said. "Let me in, you little—"

"Dweeb," he said.

Grinning his eyes into slits, he swung the gate open for me.

"We can wait for this one," he said, nodding his head toward the second gate which barred the steps going up to the apartments. He pushed a large nectarine toward me. "Want a bite?"

"Sure—hey!" I snatched it out of his hand. "Where'd you get that?"

"Market."

"When?"

He grinned again. "Just now."

I glanced, panicked, over my shoulder. "You stole it?"

"I told you, the old guy's a 'tard," he said. He took a chomp and let the juice run down his arm.

Man, get me outa here. I don't think they let you in the Olympics with a police record.

"Where have you been?"

I almost shot my hands up in surrender—until I realized the words had come from an hour-glass-shaped Oriental person behind the gate.

"With J.D.," Phong said.

The woman swung open the gate as Phong leapt onto it and swung out with it, leaving me face to face with her.

It was all but dark now, and all I really saw was a head of dark, thick hair which she shook impatiently away from her face and back from her shoulders. It wasn't too dark to see her eyes glittering, though. She wasn't too happy—and I got right away that it was *me* she wasn't too happy *with*.

"J.D.," said Phong, singsonging it for all he was worth, "this is my—"

"I'm sorry, Mrs. Truong," I said, stretching my hand toward her. As much as my mother got under my epidermal layer, I was glad she'd taught me some manners. This *was* the dragon lady. I'd have rather been turned over to the cops for being an accomplice in a nectarine rip-off.

"I'm not 'Mrs. Truong,'" she said, ignoring my hand.

"She's Tram," Phong said. "She's my sister."

I looked at Phong, but he jumped off the gate like he was getting off the merry-go-round and slipped past her.

"Come on," he said and disappeared up the stairs.

No way!

Tram—or had Phong said Tramp? Trump? Train? Who could tell when he was chortling it out of his throat like he did? Anyway, the dragon-lady sister was still just looking at me, eyes leveled. Even in the dark I could tell they were definitely not amused. She sure didn't have his gift of gab either. So far she'd only said four words.

"Well, look—" I started to say.

"I didn't know you were going to be so late," she said.

Ah, so you can *talk. You have the same voice teacher as your brother.* Actually the words were sharp, but the voice itself was soft. "Yeah, well, we got—" I started to say.

"He's supposed to be in before dark."

Well, excuse me for living. You know, I didn't hire on as the kid's baby-sitter.

"He might run the streets and he may be a 'foreigner,' but we do have rules."

I stared at her. My eyes were getting used to the dark, and I could see her face better. She was about my age, and yet she

was looking at me like a vice principal calling down a sophomore for leaving spit wads in the water fountain.

"I never said you didn't have rules," I said coldly.

"Hey, J.D.—man, come up!"

Phong's voice trailed down from several floors up. Tram
looked hard at me. She didn't say it, but her eyes spelled out
Don't you dare.

"Guess he wants me to see where he lives," I said. "Excuse
me?"

If her eyes had been lasers, I'd now have two large holes
in my back. As for me—I smiled at her as I brushed past and up
the stairs.

Phong had the front door open and was choking the doorknob when I got to the top of two flights, almost breaking my
neck on a broken concrete step en route.

"Come on," he said for the third time.

"Take a pill," I said. But for some reason I stuck out a hand
and batted at his hair.

I followed him into the apartment. The living room was
basically furnished with cushions and more plants than even my
mother had. The only other furniture, and I use the term loosely,
was a cement block and plank bookshelf bearing a tiny TV and
more paperbacks than your basic yard sale. It was so hospital-
corner neat I had to blink to be sure I was still in the building
with the broken windows.

"Living room," Phong announced before flitting off to the
kitchen.

"No joke," I said.

"No joke!"

"Don't tell me," I said, glancing at the garage-sale vintage
dinette table bearing a bowl of oranges. "This is the kitchen."

"No joke!"

I looked around curiously. There was something so familiar about this whole place. It wasn't the decor. Unlike our house,
which had baskets, paintings, and needlepoint nailed to every
square inch of wall space, this place was bare except for a water-

color of a lemon hanging above the table. It looked a little lumpy, but it sort of had a style about it.

Phong took a huge snuff. "Pizza!"

I sniffed too. Somebody had indeed been making pizza, but I smelled something else along with the pepperoni, and the something else was what was familiar: Everything smelled like pine. Like somebody from my mother's school of housekeeping scrubbed this place down on a daily basis.

"J.D., do you want—"

"No, he can't stay for dinner," Tram said from behind me. She looked coolly at me. "Phong has homework. He can't have a guest."

Thank you, Simon Legree.

It didn't faze Phong. He flung open what I thought was a closet and pointed madly into it. "My room—no joke!" he said.

I didn't have a whole lot of choice but to go in, and I wouldn't have refused anyway with the dragon lady standing there silently ordering me not to cross the threshold.

The "room" he led me into was no more than a cubicle containing a cot covered with a bright blue blanket, a trunk painted fingernail-polish red, and walls papered with more watercolors like the one I'd seen in the kitchen. It was weird though—

"How old are you?" I said.

"None of your business," he said.

"What?"

He grinned and flopped down on the cot. His hands went behind his head, and he crossed his feet.

"Eleven," he said.

I'd had him pegged for about nine, but still I wanted to ask where the Legos were and the Tonka trucks and the Transformers. There were neat stacks of worn paperbacks everywhere—everything from *Chronicles of Narnia* to *Encyclopedia Brown*—but nothing that said an eleven-year-old kid lived there. And like the rest of the house, it was squeaky-clean.

Phong was lying there waiting for comment, and I could

feel Tram drilling a new set of puncture wounds on either side of my backbone, so I started examining the watercolors on the walls. What I know about art would fit on your thumbnail, but this stuff looked pretty good. Dogs, war scenes, a couple of things that looked more like the Teenage Mutant Ninja Turtles than what I'd seen on a lot of lunch boxes. They were all kind of lumpy like the lemon in the kitchen, but they also said that whoever did them had an imagination that wouldn't quit. I looked at Phong, whose eyebrows were raised in expectation.

"Who did these for you?" I said.

"Nobody."

"Did you steal these too?"

"I did them!" He stood up indignantly on the cot, ignoring the clearing of Tram's throat from the doorway.

"You want one? Pick one."

I'd learned by now not to protest when he made statements like that. I could practically feel Tram drumming her fingernails on the doorjamb, but I perused the wall carefully.

I poked my finger at a seal poised at the edge of a very lopsided cliff.

"Is he getting ready to take a dive?" I said.

"No joke?" Phong said.

"I'll take that one, I guess," I said.

He whipped it off the wall, but almost before he got it into my hand, he was off again. "I'll show you my paints!" He scrambled past me and then Tram and headed for the kitchen.

"Look, So-Long, I've really got to go."

"He's really got to go," Tram chimed in.

"But I can stay long enough to see your paints."

I gave Tram the Sugar-Twin smile. Two tiny lines appeared between her eyebrows, but other than that her face didn't betray the fact that she probably wanted to smack me one.

"Tram, help me," Phong said. It was not a request by any stretch of the imagination.

"Na-na-na-na-na," Tram said.

"Yes!"

Tram sighed and went toward him.

"They're up there," he said, pointing to an upper cabinet. Without another word from his sister—although I wasn't sure na-na-na-na-na could be classified as a word—he climbed up onto the counter and from there straddled her shoulders. She maneuvered him into place to reach the highest cabinet. I realized she looked taller than she really was. She couldn't have been over five foot one, but she had a kind of willowy look.

"Here. See?"

Phong handed me a single metal case from his perch on Tram's shoulders. Good grief—I'd been expecting at least one of those big old honking palettes and an easel or something.

"Why do you keep it up there?" I said, turning it over in my hands.

"Because I make messes and paint under my pillow at night," he said.

"Oh—you're a pig, huh?"

Big Sister cleared her throat. What—did she have a permanent frog in there or something?

I flipped open the case and examined the paints. Just like everything else in the house, each little paint square was clean and shiny—not like the paints I'd occasionally used as a kid where all the colors looked the same after one session—mud-brown.

I looked at Phong. Freaky. He could lie, steal, and wise-guy worse than Eddie Murphy. And then you go into his house and find out he's a budding Michelangelo.

"Want to see where Tram and my mother sleep?"

I actually considered it for a second—but only as long as it took Tram to say, "No, he *doesn't*."

What? Not na-na-na-na-na?

Oh well, enough was probably too much already. "No, I don't," I said. "I've really gotta jam."

"I'll meet you at the fence tomorrow."

Phong said it with such finality that I was surprised at the trembly look in his eyes. This kid didn't cry, that was a cinch. But if I said no, it looked like it could be a first.

"I'll be waiting for you," he said. "We'll go to the pool."

Tram cleared her throat more adamantly this time, but I'd sooner have flipped her a Vick's than back down.

"I'll be there. Mouse said you can come anytime." I looked openly at Tram. "That is, if it's okay with you."

She wanted to say na-na-na-na-na. I knew it. But Phong jumped up on her back and curled his arms around her neck.

She said something to him in Vietnamese. It sounded like you-chung-king-fooey. He laughed at it and squeezed harder.

"Be home before dark," she said.

"Yes, *ma'am*," I said.

◆   ◆   ◆

That's how it started—the routine of Phong waiting for me at the fence every day and going with me to the pool. Once the bus was five minutes late, and he was pacing like a tiger cub. I'd have sworn from a distance I saw him chewing on his nails as he searched the sidewalk for my arrival, but as soon as I came into focus he put his hands on his negligible hips and started spewing.

"Where you *been*, white boy? Man, I could grow into a new shoe size while I'm waitin' here for you."

No Teeth hissed gleefully.

"Give me a break," I said. "The bus got in a traffic jam." *Why in blazes am I explaining this to you?*

"You could've jumped out the bus window or somethin'. Man, I got places to go, things to do—"

"Honkies to see," Big Black Foot put in.

Phong broke out of his Arsenio Hall imitation and grinned proudly.

Suddenly it got weird. Suddenly I didn't want Phong talking like those three losers. Matter of fact, I didn't want him talking like I talked to those three losers.

I grabbed his shoulder and started to steer him off. Acapulco Al stopped in mid-spit. "Where you takin' the baby-san?"

"None of your business," Phong and I said in unison. I poked him.

"You don't want to go with him," the Mexican said to Phong.

"Stay wif us, Chinky," Big Black Foot said.

"I'm sure he'd love to hang out here in Disneyland," I said, steering Phong in earnest. "But he's got an executive board meeting."

Al did spit then, but we plowed on. I had to disguise the fact that my stomach was turning itself inside out.

"You okay, J.D.?" Phong said when we were down the block.

I looked down at him. "You know something?" I said. "My name's Josh."

"J . . . Josh. What's the D for?"

"Dingbat," I said.

What got even weirder was how Mouse reacted to the kid. I know he spent the whole time I was changing into my trunks every day jacking his jaws with Phong and doing funky Peewee Herman type dives for him. Overbite Betty told me.

"I never saw Tulley crack a smile before that kid came along," she said one day. Unfortunately she'd gotten real friendly since the first day when Phong had sat on her counter. I guess that was part of what I "owed" her. "They sit out there and chew the fat every day," she said. "He'll have the kid diving himself before you know it."

Yeah, and then they'll have to drain the pool to get the germs out of it. The way that kid hangs out all over town, no telling what he's got crawling on him.

It didn't bother me any, though. Ever since I'd started bringing Phong—okay, ever since he'd started insinuating himself into my diving lessons—Mouse had had a whole lot less to gripe about in my diving. Even the day I started on the platform.

That day I wasn't exactly steady in my Nikes. I'd passed up my mother's blueberry waffles for breakfast and the French bread pizza they served for lunch, and I still threw up in the bathroom after school. I wouldn't even have known Big Black

Foot called me a particularly unprintable word if So-Long Phong hadn't told me later he thought I was cool for not answering back. I even *looked* at Overbite Betty when she said, "Hey, platform today, huh? Piece of cake, guy." That's how nervous I was.

Of course, no way was I letting Mouse know I had sweat balls the size of birds' eggs in my armpits. I strolled out to the pool, put a hand on a hip, and watched him do a handstand dive right off the thing and didn't even blink myself.

No need to show off, fella. I can do that. I mean, what's the big deal? So you risk whacking your head and possibly ending up a turnip green the rest of your life. I mean, worse things could happen to you.

I got in the pool and started warming up before he told me to. The less he saw of the perspiration on my upper lip, the better. I could just hear him saying, "An Olympic diver can't be a bundle of nerves. If you really want to do this—"

"You're going to go off that," Phong said to me when I swam to the side of the pool.

"Yeah," I said. I couldn't even think of a sarcastic reply.

"You scared?"

I took my time vaulting myself out of the pool.

"No way you could get me up on that thing," he said, shaking his head. "No way."

"I could get you up there," Mouse said. He picked Phong up and started to cart him in the direction of the platform, with the kid screaming singsong style the whole way.

"Put me down!"

"Where? In the pool? No problem!"

There was a string of na-na-na-na-na's which by now I'd figured out was the Vietnamese equivalent to "You do, you die."

"That thing's too high for you, huh?" Mouse said, putting him down beside me.

"No joke."

"It was too high for Kent Ferguson too. Kid had a terrible fear of heights when he started diving."

My head snapped up involuntarily. I knew about Kent

Ferguson hurting his shoulder doing a platform dive in the '88 Olympics.

"They told him he'd never be an Olympian because of that." Mouse chuckled. "Nothing tickles Kent Ferguson more than to be told he *can't*—and then go on and do it."

Mouse looked right at me, and I looked right back. *Don't even try that technique. I'm not afraid in the first place.*

"You ready?" he said.

"Yeah."

"Then let's do it."

I stood up slowly, though probably not half as slowly as I felt like I was moving. Suddenly everything was going at half-speed.

Phong squirmed ecstatically on the side of the pool. "You gonna be great, J.D." He stopped both squirming and talking, and his face got deadly serious. "Josh," he said, "you really not scared?"

"None of your business," I said. And then I messed up his hair and followed Mouse toward the platform. *If I am, you'll never know it, kid. You'd be the last person. You'd think I was a wimp. And then you'd think you were a wimp for ever thinking I wasn't a wimp.*

Man, what was I thinking? Since when did I become the surrogate father?

I followed Mouse up the ladder.

"We've already talked about the disadvantages of the platform," he said as we gazed together into the water which, as far as I was concerned, was a good four stories down. "But you've got some good news coming to you too. Every springboard is different, and that affects your timing. Every platform is the same. You can always count on it. If you get the hang of it and aren't afraid of it, you could possibly use it as your strong suit in competition."

"I'm not afraid of it," I said, strolling back and forth at the edge.

"Then you're the first," he said. "Now, the safest distance is three to four feet out. Even if you come out of your dive at the wrong time, you won't hit. You know to get that distance you need to lean forward ten degrees at your center of gravity, but after a while that just gets to be a feel—"

I listened to the rest of what he said, but most of my mind was on the black and beige spot that made up Phong at the edge of the pool, so far below. Waiting for me to perform. Expecting me to conquer the cement monster that had been looming over me ever since I'd started coming here. Knowing I was going to out-Louganis Greg with my first handstand.

I gave one last look at Phong. He waved—and something went through me.

So I did it. That day, my first time on the platform, I did it.

We started with a simple front dive and layout—until I could get control of my body, Mouse said. It might as well have been a quadruple flip the way I felt standing there. But I did it. Almost in slow motion I approached, and at the edge of the platform I hopped. "You have to generate energy yourself," Mouse had said. "There's no spring from the platform." But there was spring in *me*. And I was up. And I was away. And I was in the water.

I did forwards and inwards and reverse and back dives, all in layout and then pike and then tuck positions. At first my feet were stinging from trying to press the platform into bouncing for me. But by the eighth dive it was there—the feel I was looking for.

Phong was practically doing a one-man wave when I finally finished the round and got to him.

"You did it! You did it, man! Josh, you did it!"

"Come on, guy, you sound like there was some doubt or something," I said.

He looked right at me, and I saw it in his big almond eyes. He'd known all along I was scared spitless. And the little dweeb hadn't said a word. He'd just been scared for me. He'd taken a good part of my fear on himself.

I scooped him up, plastering my wet self all over the crummy T-shirt he was wearing.

"You know what people get when they doubt me, man?"

"No! What?"

"They get to go swimming!"

In spite of the images of the dragon sister drumming her fingernails when I brought her precious brother home dripping wet, I was about to jump in the pool with him. But his body went stiff in my arms.

"I can't swim!" he said.

"I'm going in with you, dweeb."

"No—please!"

I put him down. It wasn't only the fact that he'd said "please"—a word I didn't even think was in his vocabulary. It was more that there was no singsong in his voice. It was straining in the pre-freak mode.

"Okay—not today," I said. "Your sister'll rip off my arms if I bring you home soaked."

"No joke," he said. He tried to smile.

"But someday we'll get in the shallow end, and I'll teach you. Man, you're missing out if you can't swim."

He nodded solemnly, but he was pressing his lips together so tight all the color had gone out of them. It was nice to know he could be afraid of something.

◆　　　◆　　　◆

That afternoon when I took him home, he made me sit on the floor of his cubicle and split the banana he'd slipped away from the "'tard" at the market on the way.

"You have to stop doing that," I said to him.

"Why?"

"It's stealing, brainless. Don't you know it's wrong to steal?"

"Not really stealing," he said. "It's—"

"It's stealing, and you've got to knock it off. And another thing—you can't go around calling people 'tards. That stinks."

He looked at me and took the banana peel. "I have to throw this away."

*Right. Or dragon lady does the Chinese . . . oh, excuse me
. . . Vietnamese water torture on you.*

While he was in the kitchen I looked around the room, to
the extent of lifting up the blanket and looking under the cot.
There really weren't any toys in the place. No wonder the kid
roamed the streets. I probably would have too, if it hadn't been
for my toy lawn mower and all that stuff. Most of us middle-
class types owed our sense of being to Fischer-Price.

◆　　　◆　　　◆

I guess that's where I got the idea to give him a present. I
was lying on my back, feet on wallpaper, that night when it came
to me: Buy him something. Shoot, playing with one G.I. Joe is
better than getting locked up for grand theft fruit.

Of course, what to get him was something else again. I
racked my brain, asked Lou, who opted for about three thousand dollars worth of cat toys, and finally decided to get Meg on
the phone. She'd have some ideas—once she stopped squealing
over how wonderful I was to be doing this generous thing for
an underprivileged child.

A woman answered the phone.

"Oh—is Meg there?" I said.

"No, she isn't."

This lady sounded like the voice-over in a men's cologne
commercial.

"How about my—is T.R. there?"

There was a smooth laugh. "Mr. Daniels isn't here either.
May I help you?"

No, I have my year's supply of Polo, thank you.

"No. No thanks. I'll get back to them later."

After I hung up, I stared at the ceiling a little while longer.
Okay, who was this woman hanging out at my dad's place? She
could've been a friend of Meg's, although I doubted it. My sister would have said anybody with a voice like that needed to get
some lessons in Real immediately. The lady could've been a

business acquaintance of my dad's too, but why would she be there by herself?

I shook off any other thoughts that might creep in and went downstairs. There was no way I could concentrate on homework. Mom wasn't home, and a raid on the refrigerator might give me some ideas.

I almost had a coronary when I found Denise doing her homework at the counter in the kitchen.

"Ah!"

She shrieked back. "You scared me to death!" she said. "What's the matter?"

"What are you doing? I didn't even know anybody was here."

"Your mom's at a meeting, and things are, like, y' know, weird at my house, so she gave me a key and said I could work on my term paper over here."

"I'm glad somebody told me," I muttered as I stuck my head into the refrigerator.

"She said not to disturb you."

For that you'd have to have a personality transplant.

"Do you know anything about Vietnam?" she said.

I almost banged my head on the fruit compartment.

"Why?"

"I'm doing my term paper on Vietnam, and I can't even, like, narrow down the topic."

So what do I look like, Time *magazine?*

"I'm learning a lot of neat stuff about the culture and everything. Did you know their kids aren't even allowed to date until they're, like, old enough to get married or something?" She sighed. "But I can't do a term paper on that."

"Why not?" I said. "Sanderson would drop her bifocals and never find them again."

"Sure she would. She wears them on a chain around her neck, remember?"

"Why do old women do that? Do they think they're going to, like, get away or something?"

I stopped and put my head back in the refrigerator. Was I losing it? I was having a conversation with Denise Stahl.

"They're, like, y' know, really big on education," she went on.

I was going to have to watch myself. *Terrific. Why don't you go over there and go to school?* That was better.

I pulled a covered casserole out of the fridge and examined it.

"Your mom said if we got hungry there was quiche in there."

I curled my lip. She did a mini-shriek.

"That's what *I* thought, but I didn't want to hurt her feelings." She dug her hand into her canvas bag, knocking *Vietnam: The Whole Story* onto the linoleum. "Want some of these?" she said, producing a bag of peanut M&M's.

Oh, goody. Candy for you and me. Shall we eat them on the swings?

Even for me that was pretty low. I held out my hand and perched on the stool next to hers. She dumped half the bag into my palm and another quarter all over the counter.

"Forget it," I said as she scurried to pick them up.

She gave a tinselly smile, then looked back down at her books. "I really have to find a topic," she said.

What—no shriek? No "Joshua, let's be best friends"?

Man, that was low too. I popped a red M&M into my mouth and leaned back on the stool.

"I know a Vietnamese kid," I said.

"A real one?"

I snorted. "No, he's a phony. He tapes up his eyes every morning so they'll look slanted and sprays egg-roll scent on his clothes before he goes to school."

She shrieked, but just a little. "No—I mean, like, y' know, was he born in Vietnam or does he just have one or two parents who are Vietnamese?"

You got me by the nose. I didn't ask to see his pedigree.

"I don't know. He speaks pretty good English. So does his sister." *Unfortunately.* "And she's our age."

"A Vietnamese teenager. Does she go to school?"

I don't know. I don't care even.

"I wonder what it's like to be a Vietnamese teenager in an American high school," she said. "I bet other kids, like, give her grief all the time."

I bet they don't if they want to live to graduate.

Suddenly she shrieked. Since she'd barely done it all evening, this one was a biggie. She'd been saving up.

"Man—what?" I said.

"I could do my paper on Vietnamese teenagers in American schools! You know, what it's like to be a foreigner. What it was like to live in Vietnam and have to readjust to here—how it's different. Whoa—Ms. Sanderson will choke on her bifocals over this one."

"Don't mention it," I said.

"What?"

"I gave you the idea. But don't mention it. I mean, it's okay."

"Well, you kind of did."

"So now you owe me."

"Oh."

For a second Denise looked weird—I mean, weirder than usual. It was like she was afraid of me for a minute.

Get a clue, chick. I'm not going to jump you.

I sighed. "You know so much about this stuff—tell me what to buy an eleven-year-old Vietnamese boy who doesn't have any toys."

She blinked at me for a second. "Don't buy him toys," she said finally.

"That makes sense. He's hungry—but don't buy him food."

"No, really . . . If he wanted toys, he'd have them. See, with the Vietnamese, their kids come first. His parents could be, like, starving, and if he wanted toys he'd have some. They don't spoil them exactly, y' know, like the kids we know. But their kids are, y' know, like, everything to them."

"Oh. Okay. So what do I do—get him a tie? Some cologne?"

Sure. Call T.R. He knows somebody who sells it.

"How do you know this little boy? I mean, what's your relationship like?"

"What difference does that make?"

"It makes a big difference to them. He might not even be allowed to accept a gift if you aren't, like, really good friends or something."

I stared at Denise, a brown M&M halfway to my mouth. She was actually making sense. A twentieth-century miracle. Next they'd be finding a cure for cancer.

"How do you know him?" she said again.

"He's just this little kid who follows me to the pool and watches me dive and then I take him home." I shrugged. "He thinks I'm Superman or something."

She cupped her chin in her hand. "You want to know what I think?" she said.

Do I have a choice? Oh, shut up, man. You asked her, didn't you?

"What?" I said.

"I don't know *exactly* what you should give him, but I think it should be something that's a part of you. That's what he'll want."

"I'm not cutting off my ear for the kid," I said.

But I would. I mean, at least a finger or something. It was weird, but I already knew I would.

I actually thought about what Denise said that night when I had my feet up on the wallpaper. Another twentieth-century miracle.

What must it be like to be a Vietnamese teenager in an American high school, especially in the neighborhood Tram lived in? Kids anywhere could be vipers, but down there they were probably boa constrictors.

It wouldn't hurt me to turn on the charm a little. I'd been halfway decent to Denise, and she hadn't tried to worm a marriage proposal out of me.

Besides, Tram was probably only the Asian answer to King Kong to me because I'd been kind of a cad to her. The real Tram was probably like the Oriental women you saw on the late movies—bowing and looking at the floor and nodding in agreement like a dashboard animal.

I fell asleep with long black hair and almond eyes mingling with platform dives and Phong screaming "Please." No more peanut M&M's before bed for me.

The next day on our way to the apartment, I stopped Phong in front of the market and dug into my bag.

"Go in and *buy* three Snickers bars," I said, handing him a five-dollar bill.

"I can get 'em at a discount from the—old guy."

"*Pay* for them," I said. "I want to see a receipt."

It obviously wasn't half as much fun as ripping the old man off, but having a candy bar instead of a pear seemed to take the sting out of being deprived of the thrill of larceny. Phong had his wolfed down before we got to his place. I'd stuffed the other two in my sweats pocket. It didn't occur to me I hadn't got any change back.

Tram was in the kitchen spreading cream cheese on a bagel when we got there. I slid away the paper towel it was on.

"Don't eat that, it's too healthy," I said, and wafted a Snickers bar in its place.

I was leaning close to her. Close enough to notice that her hair didn't smell like strawberry shortcake or something.

She glanced up at me for a second. No blue stuff on her eyelids either—

"I *like* to eat healthy—*thank* you," she said. In spite of the singsong thing that was even liltier in her voice than in Phong's, the words came out tight and stiff. She pulled the bagel back to her and slid the Snickers toward the edge of the table.

"I'll eat yours!" Phong said.

"Na-na-na! You don't eat candy."

I grinned sheepishly. "He does now."

She didn't grin back. Matter of fact, her face couldn't have been further from a smile as she looked hard at me. "No—he—doesn't," she said. "Phong, do you have homework?"

"No."

"Phong!"

"Yes."

I nudged the kid. "You little liar!"

"I don't lie," Phong said. "I just—stretch."

"Well, stretch yourself in there and get it done," I said. "Or you don't go to the pool tomorrow. What is it?"

"Spelling."

Whiz kid that I was in school, I said, "I'll help you. Get in there and get your book out."

I watched him dance into his cubicle. Man, I was starting to feel like Bill Cosby. It was kind of neat.

One glance back at Tram, however, revealed that she saw me more as the Charles Manson type.

"*I* can help him," she said evenly. Those non-Maybelline eyes were glittering. "I do spell. I can even read."

"Bet you can write too," I said. My teeth were starting to grit.

"Yes. So, really, you can go now. I can handle it."

So much for the late-night Oriental movies.

"Your sister's gonna help you," I called to Phong. "She probably spells better than I do anyway."

"Probably," she said very quietly. Man, she was giving new meaning to the word *shrew*.

"Get that done and I'll catch you tomorrow," I said to Phong. I still didn't go into his room. He'd have caught the sparks in my eyes in a second.

I really did not understand women, I decided on my way to the bus stop. If you ignored them, they gathered in bathrooms and said you were a jerk. But if you tried to be nice to them, they also said you were a jerk, practically to your face. Forget it.

My mother was on the phone when I got home. She pointed to the receiver and mouthed "Meg" when I went into the kitchen. She also shook her head and deepened her concern-dimples when I spread peanut butter on a hunk of celery, then pointed to the stuffed mushrooms she had swirled on an *hors d'oeuvres* plate. I ignored her.

"Honey, you know you'll make the right decision—in time," she said into the phone. "But please, be sure you give yourself that time."

Ah. The Dr. Carl Avery Question. Sounded like Meg was still playing eeny-meeny-miney-mo with the diamond. At least she hadn't thrown it back at him and told him he was a jerk. Maybe if more girls were like Meg—

"Of *course* you can!" Mom leaned toward me: "Meg's coming up—" Back to Meg: "Now listen, your father's place may be your mailing address, but this is your home, too—" To me: "this weekend—" Now Meg: "I have to teach a seminar all day Saturday, but you and Josh—yes, he's right here—" To me: "she wants to—"

It was like a tennis match. The score was forty all, and I was getting nauseous. I took the phone she waved at me.

"I'm running away from home this weekend," Meg said into my ear. "You free to hang out Saturday?"

"You're not going to cook anything here are you?" I said.

"No way. You're taking me to lunch."

"On what, my good looks?" With the response I was getting to those lately, that would get us each a glass of water.

"You're right, we could starve. My treat."

Gee. Thanks. So much for my self-esteem. "Hey," I said casually, "is Dad there?"

"Do chickens have lips?"

"Is—anybody else there?"

"Uh—no. Just me and the contestants on 'Jeopardy.' Josh, that's a weird question."

"Forget it," I said.

"So, sweet thing," my mother said when I hung up, "what do you want for dinner?"

"Bread and water," I said. "In isolation."

It was weird how that Oriental chick's snubbing me hung on me like a cobweb you walk into without knowing it. I thought about it all through my workout at the club, all the way home, and unfortunately all the way through reading Chapter One of *The Scarlet Letter* for English. I usually couldn't have cared less what girls thought of me. I mean, who needed them?

Hey, you know what, Josh, my man? Girls can be jerks too. Sure, she's good-looking. She has this air of something most girls you know couldn't even think about having. But she acts like she knows it. That's it. She acts like she knows it. She doesn't have to bother to take the time to find out what I might be like—

Yeah. That was it. I tossed Hester Prynne aside and propped my feet on the wallpaper. Lou walked up my chest and blinked into my face.

"Lou, my man, you ought to thank me for making you an inside cat. You don't even have to go out there in the world and ever see a female feline." He hunkered down and started washing a paw. "It's the whole male/female thing that messes up people's lives. Look at Meg. The most together chick you ever saw—until the doctor comes into her life. Now she's running home to Mommy to figure out what the blazes to do. And look at me."

Lou's sandpaper tongue missed and hit my chin. "I said 'look', not 'lick.' I'm minding my own business. Concentrating on the Olympics. Steering clear of chicks because none of them knows there's anything in life that doesn't have a designer label on it. Just once I try to be nice to one because she's, like, a stranger and her little brother is kind of like my protégé or something, and I figure for him I could be friendly to his sister—and she blows me off."

Lou looked at me, eyes drooping with boredom.

"You're right, guy. Why am I doing this to myself? Let's get down to business. Okay—"

Eyes closed.

Every springboard is different, but every platform is the same. Use that to your advantage.

Don't let it scare you. It isn't going to move. Only you are. You can depend on *you*.

You can depend on God. He wants this for you. He isn't going to let you down.

Concentrate.

Approach.

Easy glide out over the water.

Head down.

Rip entry.

Not a sound. Not a splash.

Just the kid dancing on the side of the pool.

"You were *great*, Josh Dingbat. You were *smooth*, man."

I opened my eyes and grinned at Lou. Yeah. That was more like it.

Until the next day—when Mrs. Sanderson gave a pop quiz on Chapter One of *The Scarlet Letter* last hour. So much for ever using my college fund. I knew I flunked it. She really didn't have to grade them during class and call me up after the bell rang to inform me.

She tapped the paper with the big red zero on it and looked up at me through her bifocals. "Josh, you aren't my *best* student, but it isn't like you to totally blow a quiz. Anything wrong?"

"No—ma'am," I added quickly. Thanks to Mom, I did know when to throw in a nicety to take the edge off.

"Sit down," she said.

Great. Lady, I've got a bus to catch. I have an Olympic coach waiting for me—and an eleven-year-old who keeps time better than Greenwich Mean.

But I scraped up a chair. She let her glasses fall on their chain leash and sighed. "I only ask because I'm becoming increasingly aware that a lot of our kids are in trouble—I mean, socially. It's affecting their work, and I feel like it's part of my responsibility to pay attention to that. That's got to be more important than whether they walk out of here knowing Nathaniel Hawthorne."

Anything's got to be more important than knowing Nathaniel Hawthorne.

She was looking at me closely, even sans glasses. "I don't think you fall into that category, but I thought I'd ask. Contrary to popular belief, I do care about you bozos."

"I guess a lot of other things are more important to me right now," I said. "I tried to read it, but I couldn't get into it."

"Perfectly understandable. If it weren't on the required curriculum—" She frowned at the curriculum guide. "Well, be that as it may, you're no slouch, Josh. You could get Hawthorne if you wanted to. The point is, what *could* you get into—I mean, if you had a choice of any book?"

I glanced at my watch.

"Am I keeping you?" she said drily.

"No, ma'am." I could picture Phong pacing, and I squirmed. "*Tales of Gold,*" I said.

"Beg pardon?"

"*Tales of Gold*. It's about people who've won gold medals all through the history of the Olympics."

"A biography of sorts."

"Yeah—yes, ma'am." *So much for the first bus. Come to think of it, was there a second one?*

"Have you already read it?"

Take a cab? Right. You'd have to hock your watch, your Nikes, and your—

"Josh?"

"Ma'am?"

"Have you already read it—this *Tales of Gold*?"

"Only parts of it."

She tapped the curriculum guide, her copy of *The Scarlet Letter*, and my offensive pop quiz. Then the glasses went back on. All we needed was a drumroll to complete the suspense.

"All right," she said. "You bring the book in Monday and I'll take a look at it. If I think it's appropriate, I'll let you do an independent study project on it instead of reading Hawthorne, but—"

The glasses bounced down on the leash again for effect.

"Tell anyone and I'll have to hurt you."

"Okay. Yes, ma'am," I said.

"Now would you please go meet the girl or do whatever it is that you're so anxious to get to?"

"Thanks," I said—and I was out of there.

It was way too late to catch the bus by then, and I wasn't even sure there was another one that would get me to the pool before Mouse gave up and went home. Not to mention what Phong would do. He'd probably join No Teeth's gang and hurl epithets at me through the fence.

I couldn't decide whether to call the pool or dig out my bus schedule. I did neither. Instead I did the insane thing and took off running.

I was putting the sidewalk behind me at a pretty good pace—going who knows where—when I felt a car pull up beside me. I didn't look. I just kept going. It stayed with me.

"Hey!"

I ignored that and kept going. Maybe if I got to the church, Mom could—

"Daniels!"

I only slowed down enough to look over my shoulder. A big head and industrial-size shoulders emerged through the driver's window, all beige.

"Brain! Hey, look, I'm in a hurry."

"Where you headed?"

"I've got to get to the pool, man. I've really got to go."

"Get in. I'll take you."

I stopped. "It's all the way to downtown Oakland, man."

"Get in," he said.

You don't argue with six foot three, one-eighty. You just get in.

It was an old royal blue car, from the fifties I guessed, but it was in better condition than most of the ones people bought last year. Brain snapped off the radio, and we cruised away from the curb. You didn't do anything else in a car like that. You just cruised.

"It's down on—oh, man, I don't know the name of the street," I said. "It's by the health department and the unemployment office—do you know?"

"Yeah," he said. "I used to live downtown."

"You?" I said. I didn't think anybody else from CCA had ever even been downtown except to eat at an expensive restaurant or something. He'd actually lived there? In an apartment like the rattrap Phong lived in?

"In my other life," he said.

"Your other—"

"You going to see your coach?"

Okay—you don't want to talk about it. I get your drift.

"Yeah," I said. "So—neat car. What year is it?"

He looked at me the way I probably looked at people who asked who Greg Louganis was. "Fifty-seven Chevy," he said.

"I never knew you were into cars."

"You never asked," he said.

We didn't talk much the rest of the way downtown. Brain

just eased himself down in the seat, propped his arm outside the window, and *cruised*. Which was fine with me, because I was nervously trying to figure out how I was going to meet Phong.

"Look," I said as we took the freeway exit into downtown. "You really don't have to take me all the way. It's a hassle down there with the traffic and everything. Why don't you just drop me at the corner of—well, where that vacant fenced-in lot is, you know? I have a short-cut I take from there."

Okay, so I lied. Cutting through the newsstand wasn't exactly a short-cut. But it was close—

"I can take you to the pool."

"No!"

Brain slowly swung his eyes toward me, and for a minute I felt like Phong getting caught with a piece of hot fruit. Only I wasn't nearly as cool.

"Look, man, I've got to meet somebody there, okay?" I said.

"On *that* corner? You got a death wish?"

"Okay, so my elevator doesn't go all the way to the top floor. Just—it's all right. It's safe."

"Right."

Brain took the turns with no directions from me. I opened the window and craned my neck to look for Phong. As soon as we rounded the corner to the lot, I saw him. Standing outside the fence. Arms crossed. Legs planted. With Big Black Foot dangling above him, and Acapulco Al pacing on the outside of the fence in front of him.

As Brain pulled the Chevy to the curb at the end of the fence, I saw No Teeth take a swing at the chain-link from the inside with his fist—just about a foot from Phong's head. Phong flinched, but he stayed there.

"Stop!" I said. I had the door open before we'd rolled to a halt. I'm not sure I even closed the car door. I was digging into the pavement with my Nikes, and I was yelling.

"Get away from him!" I screamed.

All four of them looked up. No Teeth looked back over his shoulder.

"Leave him alone," I said. I hardly recognized my own voice. In spite of the huge gulps of air I was taking in, it sounded cold and hard. "Just back off from the kid."

There were no jeers and no snide remarks. There was only hate hardening in every eye that looked back at me, except Phong's.

"Come on, kid," I said. I held out my hand, and he ducked under it and behind me.

"These dudes harassing me, Jo—"

"Don't worry about it. Let's just go."

I swung my bag over one shoulder and pulled him to my side with my other hand. But when I tried to take a step, the Mexican kid blocked our path. A vise grip started grabbing my stomach.

"This school bus needs to find another route, *gringo*," he said.

"Fine," I said. "I'll redraw the map. Let us get by."

Don't puke, Josh. Whatever you do, don't wimp out and throw up right in front of the kid.

"Today," said Big Foot above us.

No Teeth made a hissing sound, and Big Foot scrambled—but not before Acapulco made a bad move.

"You remember what I said, Chinky San," he said to Phong.

"Chinky Chinese—" Phong started in.

"Shut up!" The Mexican kid cocked his arm back and elaborately clenched his fist. The windup gave me enough time to realize he was going to hit Phong. When he jerked his fist forward, I caught it in midair.

"Don't you touch him," a stranger's voice said. It was mine.

No Teeth hissed again, and this time Big Black Foot hissed with him. Acapulco Al backed toward the fence, but he didn't take his eyes off me. I didn't even want to throw up. I just wanted to belt him.

"Find another way to go," he said. And as he vaulted back over the fence, Phong and I moved on.

"You could have taken him, Josh Dingbat," Phong said singsong style when we'd gotten as far as the newsstand.

"Man—you little dweeb! Why'd you start coming back at him when you knew he was mad?"

"You were there to protect me. You can take those jokers, all three of them."

"Yeah, if they were all in the morgue—as clients!"

But that didn't daunt the little dingbat. He just grinned worshipfully up at me and swore.

"Don't be a trash mouth, okay?"

He looked up again. That hero-worship on his face scared me. But it was weird. It brought out the best in me too.

I only looked back over my shoulder once. None of them followed us, per usual. But I did think I saw a royal blue fin disappear around the corner. I didn't have time to wonder how much Brain had seen.

Just to be on the safe side, I turned Phong over to Overbite and told her not to let him out of her sight.

"That's two you owe me," she said, leaning her bowling-ball body against the counter. "And you're going to owe Tulley a lot more than that. He's been waiting a while."

So sue me for having another life.

Timing was everything, I thought as I changed into my trunks. As long as Phong and I left the fence at a certain time, they wouldn't bother us. Just as long as we moved along before—

Before what? You barely had to be out of kindergarten to figure out there was something they didn't want us to see. Fine. We'd meet elsewhere from now on. With only a couple weeks left before the Regionals, it wouldn't be that much of a pain to take a long-cut from the bus stop. But, man, wherever it was I had to be there on time. Phong wasn't moving until I got there—I could see that. And if he didn't move . . . it looked like they didn't have special treatment for children under twelve. I shuddered and went out to the pool.

Mouse didn't ask any questions, but just put his hand on

my shoulder when I emerged from the locker room and squeezed it.

"You okay?" he said.

I stared at him for a second.

"Yeah," I said.

"Good. Then let's warm up."

In spite of Phong's being there and Mouse's not getting all over my case about being late, I didn't dive as well as usual. I couldn't concentrate. And it wasn't the fact that if No Teeth hadn't given the final hiss, Acapulco Al would've cleaned up the sidewalk with me. And it wasn't the fact that I had been an almost-witness to something I was sure I didn't want to view.

It was the fact that Phong could get hurt.

Every time I stood at the back of the platform and tried to flip a dive through my mind, I saw No Teeth's fist slamming into the fence above his head. And him wincing, but standing his ground.

Every time I walked through an approach, I saw the Mexican kid's arm slicing through the air toward Phong's face. And Phong sticking out his chin, innocently, sure I'd defend him.

Every time I ripped into the water I tore for the surface to be sure he was still there poolside, body parts all intact.

All right, don't be an idiot. What means the most to you? Diving. So dive. Don't let this other stuff put creases in your road map. Go for it.

"Let's try a handstand," Mouse called to me. "And, Josh— concentrate."

I am concentrating. Do you think I'm up here planning my vacation?

Down to the edge of the platform. Up on your hands. Hold it three seconds.

A fist. Right above Phong's head. Crashing against the metal. He must have been so scared.

I couldn't hold it. My arms wobbled, and I let go. Even before I did I could feel my body going out at an angle. The concrete burned against the tops of my legs.

Mouse had his hand out when I got to the edge of the pool. I wouldn't have taken it except my own was shaking like the rest of me, racking my insides.

"Let me see," he said.

"It's okay. Don't worry about it."

"Let me see." Mouse's voice was tight, so I sat down on the edge of the pool. All three of us looked down at the raw-looking flesh. The skin wasn't broken, but both legs were stinging-red. I glanced at Phong. His eyes were bulging like a Pekinese dog's.

Mouse saw them too.

"All right, Josh. I call the dives—you make them . . . Off the springboard."

"I can—"

"Let's put on a show for Phong."

Our eyes clinked together, and I nodded.

For the rest of practice I was the main attraction at Phong's private circus. Mouse had me doing crazy dives that would have made Ronald McDonald eat his heart out, and Phong never stopped squealing. Mouse didn't fool me though. He made me do it as much for me as he did for the kid.

When I was through, I swam over to the side where Phong was waiting. "I was going to give you a swimming lesson today," I said to him, "but let's go home."

"No joke," he said.

He and Mouse were eating Popsicles in the lobby when I came out of the locker room.

"Your sister says you aren't supposed to have that stuff," I said.

Phong grinned and kept licking.

"What stuff? It's a juice bar," Mouse said.

"You can have one too, if you're a good boy." Overbite Betty snickered at me from behind the counter. "I've got a bunch in the freezer in the back."

"No thanks," I said. Between the near head-smashing in the street and the near head-smashing on the platform, my stomach was being squeezed in a vise that didn't have an off button. Besides, I didn't want to "owe" her any more than I already did.

"Where can I drop you two?" Mouse said.

I looked at him stupidly.

"Phong's been filling me in on what happened today. I don't think you should be back on the street tonight. It's really getting late."

I tried to glare at Phong, but he just grinned at me over his juice bar and kept slurping. At least that explained Mouse's patience with my flubbing up today.

"That's okay," I said. "We'll be all right."

"Why take chances?"

Frankly, I couldn't figure out which was going to be a bigger chance—risking being mugged by the trio, or hauling Phong out of a stranger's car with Tram watching from the apartment window.

"I don't think his sister would like it if he rode with somebody she didn't know," I said.

"Who cares?" Phong said.

"I do." *About my life. I wouldn't be surprised if she knew a little Tae Kwon Do she could get me with.* "We've never even seen those guys between here and Phong's anyway. It'll be okay."

Mouse looked over at Phong. "Go in the locker room and wash that sticky stuff off, guy. You'll be drawing flies."

Phong obeyed without comment. Mouse drew in closer to me. "What do you think it's all about?"

I shrugged. *Who am I—Dick Tracy?* "I guess they're trying to cover up something they don't want anybody to see."

"And they'll obviously go to great lengths to do it." Mouse did something between a grimace and a smile.

"Don't underestimate these street types, Josh. You're in good shape and all that, but you can't handle them. Don't even try."

I wasn't planning on it.

"I wasn't planning on it."

"Good. You're sure I can't take him home and you to your bus?"

I thought about Tram again and shook my head. Nope. She was going to see *me* bringing her little brother home safely. *After* I convinced the little public address system not to tell her what had happened. *If* he hadn't already spilled it to the "Ten O'clock News."

"Why is your hair wet?" Mouse said as Phong appeared, black hair in spikes across his forehead.

"I washed it in the sink so I could try out that hair dryer on the wall."

Mouse and I exchanged blank looks and then guffaws.

"That's a *hand* dryer, dingbat," I said.

"No. Josh Dingbat—that's you. Phong—that's me."

"Ding-dong—that's you," Mouse said. He picked him up and wrestled him around.

◆   ◆   ◆

It would be the understatement of the *decade* to say that Tram was upset when we got to the apartment. It was dark, and she was pacing at the downstairs gate like a starving cougar. The fangs appeared as soon as we did.

"Do you know what time it is?" she said.

"No," Phong said brightly.

"I wasn't talking to you." She looked at me as if she expected me to fall down in some Vietnamese act of contrition. *Does it ever occur to you, chick, to get all the facts before you start playing Ho Chi Minh? What do I look like, a P.O.W.?*

"Go upstairs," she said to Phong. "I want to talk to him."

"So-Long Phong," he sang going up the stairs. "See you Monday."

"I have a couple of things I want to say to Phong before I leave."

I started toward the steps. She stepped right in front of me.

It was the second time that day someone had just flat out blocked my path. I'd almost belted the first one.

"Just a minute," she said. She barely came up to my shoulders, but she had her chin pointed up as far as she could get it, and she was looking me right in the eye. "My brother has always had the run of the streets. I know it isn't so safe, but it's been difficult to stop him. But he has never wandered so far away from home as he has since he met you, and he has never been so late getting back."

"You wrote a note. You gave me 'permission' to take him. Not that you're his mother or anything—"

"I am responsible for him." Her voice and her face grew so cold I almost shivered. "If you can't get him home before dark, you *don't* have my permission."

"Did you ever think about asking me why we were late?" I said.

"Okay." She straightened her shoulders and tossed her hair back over them. I noticed crazily that she didn't have shoulder pads in her sweatshirt. "Why?"

Oh. That's all you need to do—tell her you'd gotten off to just a scosch of a late start because you'd had to rescue her little brother from the street gang that had been harassing you on a regular basis for a month—

"Well?" she said.

"Look," I said. "Stuff happens. But I can take care of the kid."

The two faint lines appeared between her eyes.

"If it'll make you feel any better, I promise he won't be late again."

"No, it doesn't make me feel any better."

"You still down there, J.D.?" Phong's voice rang from above. Tram trumpeted something up to him in Vietnamese, and the door slammed. She looked up there for a minute before her eyes came back to me. "Okay," she said.

What am I supposed to say? Oh, your worshipfulness, I'll be forever in your debt. "I still need to talk to him."

"Why?"

"We're going to plan a liquor store heist, okay?"

She glared at me, but not half as hard as I glared back. "I'll give him a message," she said.

That was it for today. I wasn't getting past her to tell him to meet me someplace else and in the meantime to keep his mouth shut—unless I knocked her down, which did occur to me.

"Tell him I'll see him Monday," I said instead. It was amazing I got it out at all, my teeth were clenched so tight.

"Fine," she said. Hers were clenched even tighter.

Too bad she was so beautiful when she oozed confidence like that.

I was still lying in bed Saturday morning, wondering how much Phong had told Tram about the street gang, when I heard Meg's Audi pull up. My father had bought her the car and a membership in Triple A as congratulations presents when she got her job at the lab. Meg herself would've bought a used Volkswagen and kept it together with Scotch tape.

I knew better than to stay under the covers until she got upstairs. That was grounds for anything from ice water in your shorts to being dragged by your heels down two flights of steps and suffering terminal carpet burn in the process.

"Joshua!" she yelled from the foyer.

"I'm in the shower!" I yelled back, heading for the bathroom while stripping out of my sweatpants. Lou blinked at me from the windowsill as if to say, "Liar!"

"Who died and left you in charge?" I said to him.

"You aren't in the shower. You're barely out of bed!" Meg said from the stairs.

"Thanks, buddy," I said to Lou.

He just blinked back.

"Go away. I'm naked," I said, diving into the bathroom.

"So close the door."

I could hear her rummaging around in my room as I turned on the water. The girl had no shame. None whatsoever.

"*What* were you eating out of this bowl that looks like it's been here for days?" she said.

"Top Ramen."

"Very attractive."

Who knows what else she ransacked while I was in the shower. The only thing I'm really sure of was the watercolor from Phong. She was sprawled on her stomach on my water bed examining it when I came out wrapped in a towel.

"Where'd you get this?" she said.

I tried to look nonchalant as I turned to the closet and moved hangers back and forth. "Oh . . . A kid."

"A child did this? She's good."

"He."

"Really?"

"Yeah, really. Guys can be artistic. We've got feelings."

"All right, all right! I wasn't trying to be sexist. Call off the National Guard."

I shrugged. Actually, I wasn't real sure why I'd gotten so hepped up about it. Man, I was sure getting defensive about the little guy. The little guy I might never see again if he'd spilled his guts to the dragon lady—

"Well, *he*," Meg said, "whoever he is, is really talented. You ought to keep this. Someday you'll be able to say, 'I knew him when.'"

"Might be worth some bucks, huh?" I slid on a T-shirt and took my jeans into the bathroom.

"You sound like your father."

"Oh, now he's *my* father. Did you disown him or something?"

"I'm about to. That man is so—"

There was a silence. I poked my head out the door. "So *what*?"

"Nothing. I promised myself I wasn't going to do this today. You don't want to hear a bunch of dirt about Dad—true as it may be—so I'm not going to dig it up for you."

Thank you.

I ducked back into the bathroom and went at my hair with a towel.

"Except—"

Here it comes.

"You know what scares me, Baby B.?"

"Scares *you*?"

"I've been known to pump some adrenaline, yeah. What scares me is that I might marry Carl just to get away from Dad."

"No way! If you wanted to get away from Dad you'd just—get away from him. Although I don't know why you would want to. You've got it made living there—rent-free, luxury accommodations—"

"That's exactly what I want to get away from—and the attitude that goes with it. The thing is, Josh, I'm beginning to wonder how he exactly comes by all that money."

For some reason the cologne clerk's imaginary face came to mind. I whipped it aside impatiently with the towel. "Come on, are you thinking Dad's dealing drugs or something?"

"No, not drugs."

I came out of the bathroom and looked at her. She was twirling her ponytail with one hand and massaging a cheekful of freckles with the other—a sure sign she was into some heavy thought.

"Not even 'or something.' Knowing Dad, however he's building up his bank accounts it's technically legal. But that doesn't mean it's ethical. Josh, I wasn't going to get into this! I'm just trying to make sure I'm not just going from one male protector to another."

I picked up my hairbrush and snorted. "You never let a male protect you in your life."

"You'd be surprised. Love feels pretty good."

"I wouldn't know."

"Sure you would. Haven't you ever even had a crush on some girl?"

Fortunately by now I had my head in the closet as I dug for a pair of shoes. I just muttered.

"If you haven't it's time you did," she said. "Otherwise your education is being sadly neglected."

"I do *not* need women," I said. I tossed a Reebok over my shoulder.

"Hey! Watch it!"

"I have more important stuff to do right now. Girls are not in the plan." I let the other one go.

"It's a good thing, if you intend to keep throwing shoes at them," she said. She sat up on the bed and watched me while I tied them on. "I guarantee, Baby B., you're going to eat those words someday, and I'm going to be the one to stuff them down your throat."

"If it happens," I said, "I'll hand you the spoon."

Her blue eyes sparkled at me. "Ooh—you've got a deal."

We slapped hands a couple of dozen times, and then she went for the windowsill while I located a jacket.

"King Louis," she said to Lou. He looked at her disdainfully but let her scratch behind his ears anyway. The cat has no pride.

"It isn't Louis," I said.

"Haven't you ever read T. S. Elliot?" she said. "Every cat has to have a proper name. It can't be just 'Lou.'"

"It isn't. It's 'Louganis.'"

She gave me a dial-tone look. "You're putting me on."

"Nope."

"You really do have this diving thing bad. Come on, you need food. Your brain is starving—that's why you're losing it."

While she dragged her overnight bag into the guest room, which my mother insisted on calling "Meggie's Room," I wolfed down two bananas in the kitchen and stuffed an apple into my jacket pocket. Phong was starting to get me hooked on fruit. *Phong—*

Man, I can't believe I let that little vixen sister of his keep me from arranging a new meeting place with him and getting him to keep his lip buttoned about what happened. He'd do it for me. I know he would. There's got to be a way—

"So—" Meg appeared in the doorway, sunglasses perched on her head. "Where to for lunch?"

"Chinatown," I said.

"Downtown Oakland?"

"Hey, I can't get enough of it."

She twitched a dimple at me, then pulled the glasses down over her eyes. "Okay. But I'm telling you—you're losing it."

◆　　◆　　◆

"Okay, take this exit and cut down the second street on the right after you get off."

"You're getting to be quite the cosmopolitan, Joshua," Meg said. "Good grief!"

A silver Daihatsu whipped in front of her and careened down the off-ramp.

"These people drive worse than they do in the City!"

"I love how you people from San Francisco refer to *your* town as *the City*. What do you call this—rural America?"

"Since when did you become a member of the Oakland Chamber of Commerce?" Meg said. "Hey—Bud!"

Another car with a brand name that sounded like a sneeze cut her off on its way into a parking place.

"At least he's *using* a parking space," she said. "Look at these people. Half of them are double-parked!"

I found myself grinning. All the drivers were Oriental. They reminded me of grown-up Phongs, all zipping around like aggressive ants behind their respective wheels. But it was so quiet. Everybody did it without so much as blowing a horn. It was a sure thing nobody was carrying on in their cars the way Meg was.

"These little Chinese are crazy!"

"Not all Chinese," I said. "Some Japanese, some Vietnamese."

"Some Nutso-ese. Where are we going, Josh?"

"Turn here," I said. "Then just a couple of blocks."

How I was going to explain this little detour to a strange apartment building, I hadn't figured out. How about: I was picking up some laundry, but it wasn't ready yet. Or: I had to do some research for a term paper. Uh-uh. None of them sounded the least bit plausible, and even as I had Meg pull up to the curb across the street, I didn't have anything better.

"I know I'm slow, Joshua," she said, "but there are no restaurants on this street. I mean, it's rough back there, but I could've found a parking space."

I took a deep breath. "No—we aren't eating here," I said. "I just have to do something first."

"Oh. Okay. I'll wait here."

That was it. No Twenty Questions. No intense interrogation. Just "I'll wait here."

So what made me open the car door and say, "Why don't you come with me?" Call me a 'tard, I guess.

I was hoping Tram wouldn't answer my buzz at the gate. The woman who *did* answer didn't know me from Charlie Chan and didn't speak enough English to figure out the difference. Our attempt at a conversation went on for about five minutes.

"Hal-lo?" she kept saying over and over.

"Phong!" *I* kept saying over and over. "I am here to see Phong."

"You name?" was also a variation on her end.

"My name is Josh!" I'd say to that one. "Please—I am here to speak to Phong."

It was like an Oriental version of "Who's on first?"

"Hal-lo?"

"Phong!"

"You name?"

"My name is Josh. I am here to see Phong."

"Hal-lo?"

"Phong! I—"

"Josh Dingbat!"

"Phong!" I practically hugged the little squawkbox. "Come down, buddy. I want to talk to you. Phong?"

Dead silence—until a door was flung open two stories above and Phong's tennis shoes thudded happily down the cement stairs.

"I love the way you drop your contractions when you talk to these people," Meg said, nudging me. Her dimples were spasmodic. "And, uh—Josh Dingbat? I'll have to remember that."

"J.D.—no joke!" Phong scrambled up the inside of the gate and dropped to the outside, practically into my arms.

"So-Long Phong!" I said. "Hey, guy, this is my sister." I nudged him in the rib. "Don't judge her by *your* sister—she's good people."

"I'm so glad you made the distinction," a soft voice said from above.

I knew before I looked up that it was Tram looking down from the next level. And I didn't even have to see my reflection to know my face was pretty close to magenta.

Okay, so you didn't mean for her to hear that—but it's the truth, isn't it?

"No," I said to her, "*you* made the distinction."

"She looks like you," Phong said, tugging on my jacket sleeve.

For a second I thought he meant Tram, but he was jerking a thumb toward Meg, who was melting all over the little con artist.

"Call me a plastic surgeon," I said.

Phong twinkled. "Okay. You're a plastic surgeon."

"I love it!" Meg said.

"Phong," Tram said. "Do—re—mi—fa—so."

That's what it sounded like anyway, and I was pretty sure it meant, "Get your butt up here before I repossess your paint set." He didn't, of course.

"Come up," he said, grabbing Meg's hand.

"No!" I said quickly. His moon-face fell. "I mean, we've got to go—Meg wants to—"

"It's okay, Josh," Meg said. "We aren't on a schedule. We can go up if he wants."

"I want," Phong said.

As usual, what Phong wanted, he got. He scrambled over the gate, pushed it open for us, and took a wide lead up the steps. Meg followed him, chatting like he was showing her to her hotel room. I brought up the rear and tried to avoid Tram on the way up. It was tough since she was taking up two-thirds of a three-foot-wide landing when I got to her. She had *How dare you!* in her eyes.

"It's not my fault," I said. "Your little brother takes over. What am I supposed to do, wimp out on him?"

The more I talked, the harder my heart pounded. If Phong hadn't told her about the gang, she had a serious case of indigestion. Her face was nut-hard and ready to crack.

"My mother is here," she said. "Please be polite to her."

I stared. "Thank you, Amy Vanderbilt, but I think I know how to use manners."

"Do you?" she said. She turned and walked up the steps.

"Do *you?*" I said, and followed her.

Phong was already giving Meg the grand tour of his art gallery when I got inside. Tram disappeared, and I stood in the kitchen doorway feeling about as comfortable as a cowboy in a lingerie shop, staring at the back of a tiny black-haired woman who looked like she was trying to scour the pattern right off the counter. When she turned around I stuck out my hand and said eloquently, "Hi."

"*Chao*," she said. She didn't shake my hand. In fact, she left me standing there with my palm extended over the linoleum. But she did smile and bob her head about a hundred times. She looked tired and uncertain, but there was a twinkle in there somewhere—like Phong's. At least she didn't have Tram's temperament.

"I am Josh Daniels," I said. Meg was right—I did drop the contractions. I also talked three times louder than usual and pronounced every syllable like a robot. I felt stupid.

"Mr. J.D.," she said, smiling and bobbing some more.

"Right!" Wow. Communication. All right. Now where the blazes were Meg and Phong—

"Ba My," she said, pointing to herself. She laughed soundlessly.

Okay, great. Now I'm completely confused. Phong and Tram's last name is Truong. Yours is My. Phong never mentioned having a stepfather—

"Nice to meet you, Mrs. Ba My," I said. I didn't stick out my hand this time, and I found myself nodding for all I was worth. It was contagious. Still, I decided I liked this lady. She was soft or safe or something. I couldn't imagine her trying to push cauliflower quiche on me the way my mother did.

"You stay for lunch?" she said.

Okay, so I'm not such a good judge of character.

"We really—" "Can't" was what I started to say—or maybe "cannot." But Tram appeared in the doorway and shook her head at me. If she'd been mad before, you could probably call her livid now.

"It's impolite to refuse an invitation to share a meal," she said. "Vietnamese manners."

I could barely keep from bursting into an ear-to-ear grin. "I wouldn't want to violate Vietnamese manners," I said. "Yes, please," I said to Mrs. Ba My.

I grinned away at Tram, who sent me back an almond-eyed message I decided not to interpret. Man, she hated me. Which, okay, was fine with me.

Mrs. My singsonged something to her in Vietnamese, and Tram went obediently to the sink. I watched her go and then nearly choked. She headed right for a dishpan full of black ugly mushrooms which were soaking in water. Maybe she was going to get her revenge on me through food. Come to think of it, I had heard stories about Vietnamese eating cat meat—

"I'm going to talk to Phong," I said, bolting for his cubicle.

Meg and Phong were side by side on Phong's cot, backs against the wall, feet hanging over the side. Meg was staring at the wall full of paintings, and Phong was staring at Meg.

"I can't decide," Meg said, "between the purple dinosaur and the giraffe family flying their kites."

"Take two!" Phong said.

"What is this, an art auction?" I motioned for Meg to scoot over and joined them. "We're staying for lunch. Evidently it's bad manners to say no when they ask you." I looked at Phong, but he shrugged. "I hope you like *black* 'shrooms," I said to Meg out of the side of my mouth.

But of course she got that *Oh wow!—a new experience* look in her eye and bounded out into the kitchen to see if she could help. I toyed with the idea of warning Mrs. My about Meg's minimal culinary talents, but I had more important matters to take care of.

"Phong, my man," I said. I thought I'd try a big-buddy approach, but he blinked at me suspiciously. I got up and closed the door. "Okay, no games," I said. He nodded and moved closer to me. "Did you tell—anybody—about what happened to us yesterday, when that punk tried to hit you?"

Phong crossed his arms and shook his head at me. "You kidding?" he said. "You think I'm crazy?"

I choked back a whole throat full of relief and laughter.

"So you didn't tell your mom—or your sister?"

He let out a derisive hiss. "I would be locked in here the rest of my life! No way, man!"

I buried his whole head under my armpit and mouthed thank you at the ceiling. "Good," I said. "What do you say we keep it that way? It's safe—I mean, those guys aren't going to bother us anymore because we aren't going to meet there anymore. So the only people who need to ever know about it are you and me."

"And the Mouse."

"Yeah," I said. I'd forgotten about him. Child Advocate of the Year. He was likely to send a social worker over here. But okay, just three of us. And Brain. Nah, Brain was—Well, Brain was Brain. If he had seen anything, it wasn't going to be a problem.

"So where we gonna meet now, Josh Dingbat?" Phong said singsong style. All three of them had that, especially his mother when she spoke Vietnamese. It was like they were constantly in an opera or something.

"You know that place around the corner from where we used to meet," I said, "where the guy sells magazines and newspapers and stuff?"

Phong nodded. Of course he knew. He could probably get a job as an Oakland tour guide.

"Okay, from now on you meet me there. And, Phong . . ."

"What?" His eyes were innocent.

"Don't steal anything, okay?"

He grinned. "Comic books easy."

There was a tap on the door, and I jumped. It had to be the juvenile authorities, after me for contributing to the shoplifting career of a minor.

"Lunch is ready," Tram said. She didn't add, "I hope you choke on it," but I knew the thought was there.

I was almost afraid to look at what was on the table. I'd already decided if it even slightly resembled something with whiskers and a tail I was out of there.

"Did you ever have a cat?" I whispered to Phong as we sat down.

"No," he said.

Meg kicked me under the table. She must have heard those stories too.

I sat down in front of a huge bowl of what at first glance looked like the parts my mother throws out when she makes a salad, all floating in saltwater. Meg gurgled over it like it was filet mignon and dug in with a porcelain spoon with a flat bottom. I looked doubtfully into the bowl and was about to pass when I glanced up and found Tram watching me. I smiled at her, trying to get my dimples to do whatever it is dimples are supposed to do to girls, and picked up my spoon.

I hated to admit it, but it was good. I bobbed my head at Mrs. My, who bobbed back and then ducked her face modestly. Her daughter could learn some of those tricks from her.

I barely got halfway through my bowl—it took me a

while to master the flat-bottomed spoon—before Mrs. My was loading up the table with a bunch of other stuff.

"Where is the pizza?" Phong said, getting up on his knees on his chair and surveying the table with his brow in a knot. "Josh and I like *pizza!*"

"Josh will eat anything," Meg said. She gave me a big-sister look.

"Yeah," I said. And I bobbed my head.

"What are all these goodies?" Meg asked Tram.

Tram ticked off the names as she and her mother put the dishes on the table, then translated. "Vietnamese meatballs. Shredded chicken cabbage salad. Rice."

Except for the rice, you could've fooled me.

"And *nuoc man!*" Phong said, grabbing a large bottle of dark liquid I wouldn't have used on a dare.

His mother said something to him in Vietnamese which I interpreted as "Do you want to lose a finger? Drop the bottle."

He did, amazingly enough. But he wrinkled his face at her playfully, and she wrinkled hers back.

Meg picked up the bottle. *Here we go. Soon she's going to be trying to feed it to Dad on his Raisin Bran.*

"*Nuoc man?*" she said.

Tram nodded. "Fish sauce. We use it on everything—like you'd use salt."

"How interesting."

Dr. Carl might even get some on his next fettucine.

"What's it made out of?"

"It's just fish and salt, fermented."

I stifled a gag. Meg opened the bottle and sniffed. Her eyes doubled in size.

Tram laughed softly. "Strong."

"Uh—you could say that, yes! Josh, smell."

I shot her a look and took a quick sniff. I'd detected better smells on a bad day at Fisherman's Wharf.

"Great," I said.

"Now," Meg said, "why are the noodles transparent?"

Terrific. Just let me eat this stuff, Meg, okay? If I have to know what it all is, I might never get a bite down. I could starve.

"Cellophane noodles," Tram said. "They're made from *mung* beans."

I shoved those aside on my plate with my fork.

That's about the time I noticed everybody else, including Meg, was using chopsticks. I glanced at Phong, but it didn't seem to matter to him. Since it was clear we weren't having pizza, he was digging into his meatballs like there was no tomorrow. I stabbed one and put it in my mouth. My tongue immediately started to sizzle, and I grabbed for my glass.

I thought you people were Vietnamese, not Mexican. I'd tasted salsa that was milder than that.

I dabbed at my mouth with a napkin and was about to go for the tears in my eyes when I caught Tram looking at me. Her mouth twitched, and she pushed the large plate of meatballs toward me.

"More?" she said.

"Yeah," I said. I locked my eyes right into hers. "They're great."

Meg must have asked three thousand questions while I was trying to get through the lunch. Thanks to her, I found out I was consuming lemon grass, eating spring rolls wrapped in *lumpia*   thank heaven she didn't ask for a translation of that—and drinking what turned out to actually be tea. It tasted the way baby lotion smelled.

Since there was nothing that looked like it might have been one of Lou's relatives—and since the black mushrooms were obviously being soaked for dinner—I managed to eat most of it, including two more helpings of meatballs. After a while my mouth was just numb.

"More?" Mrs. My said, waving a bottle of what they told me was lemon and soda over my empty glass.

"Please," I said.

"That's your fifth glass, Joshua," Meg said.

I glanced at Tram. She lifted a subtle eyebrow.

"I like it," I said.

She looked away.

When Tram and her mother got up to clear the table, Meg stood up too.

"No, no," Tram said to her.

Don't you mean na-na-na-na-na?

"Please let me help. This was so good."

"You're our guest. We wait on you."

How come I never got that treatment?

"Thank you," Meg said. One thing about Meg—she knew how to be gracious. Tram could learn a thing or two from her.

Although, Tram's a lot different with her mother around. So's Phong for that matter. For somebody that robs grocery stores and plans newsstand rip-offs, he sure acts like he loves his mother.

I almost literally shook my head. I hadn't had a wise-guy thought for about an hour. I was thinking positive stuff. Those meatballs must have destroyed some of my brain cells.

Mrs. My put a bowl of fruit that looked like one of Phong's paintings on the table. He wasn't impressed.

"Ice cream!" he said.

His mother just looked at him, and he backed down. She poured more tea and settled quietly into her chair.

That was Meg's cue to settle in too. I was about to protest, but one look at Tram and I changed my mind. She wanted me out of there, so I was staying.

"How did you come to be here in the United States?" Meg asked Mrs. My.

She nodded to Tram.

"My mother can understand most English, but she doesn't speak it well yet."

"I think you do great!" Meg said to her.

Mrs. My bobbed, of course.

"We're from South Vietnam," Tram said.

No joke?

"I was born there—not Phong," Tram said.

"Really?" Meg massaged her teacup. She was warming up to the subject. "Do you remember anything about it?"

"I was only six years old when we left, but I do remember

some things. People don't know—even with the war, it was a beautiful place."

"I've heard that," Meg said.

"Green—just thick with green. And we were happy. My parents had a store. We lived—you know—well." She looked around the sparsely furnished room with the cracked walls. "Not like this."

Mrs. My singsonged something, as she did from time to time through the rest of the conversation.

"But that was before the communism," Tram said for her. "That's what I remember most. My father coming home and telling us they had taken our store." She smiled at Meg, maybe the first time I'd ever seen her smile. But it wasn't like Phong's smile. It was confused, bordering on bitter. "They would still allow him to work there, but it wasn't his anymore. And they had worked so hard—my parents. My father is an educated man—and my mother is a fine businesswoman in her own country."

I looked at Mrs. My, who was looking humbly at the tabletop. Shrewd business exec, huh? No wonder she could make Phong toe the line.

"Until then my father was loyal to Vietnam, you know? No matter what, he wanted to stay there. It was—home."

That word settled over the table like a warm blanket. Meg looked like she wanted to reach over and touch Tram, but she didn't. It was probably a good thing. These weren't touchy-feely people like we were.

"But that changed everything. I heard them talking—my older brother and I did."

I looked around. I hadn't seen any other brothers lurking in the corners. Where would they put him?

"My father knew soon we would lose our house too. I remember it—it seemed big to me. Of course, I was little."

"I'm sure it was a beautiful place," Meg said. "You've made this apartment nice."

Tram looked at her mother, and I did too. The lady's face softened, and she nodded again to Tram. There was something about Meg. She could get people to talk about themselves. I could have come there for the rest of my life and probably never gotten the story. From Tram? Ha!

"But it was 1979. You didn't just—leave. Most of the people like us—of our class—had already gone. My father was stubborn."

Oh, so that's where you get it.

"It wasn't like just getting a plane ticket and a passport and getting out of there—I know," Meg said. "I've heard horror stories."

"You're going to hear another one," Tram said. "If you want to—"

"I'm interested," Meg said.

Yeah, me too. I was—I really was.

Suddenly I felt Tram looking at me. I guess she was waiting for me to say or do something sarcastic. I didn't.

"My parents sat us down, my older brother Huyen and me, and told us we were going to do something dangerous. I never knew the details, but my father had turned all his money to gold and buried it."

"Like a pirate!" Phong said. The kid must have been told this story a thousand times, but he was up on his knees, leaning on the table like he'd never heard it before.

"He used that to pay a man to help us escape." Tram gave that bitter smile again. "You think—oh, lots of gold—a boat for our family and food."

"No?" Meg said.

"No. We could only take the clothes we were wearing. Huyen and I had on four sets of clothes. We looked like penguins. And that evening we went to a festival in Nha Trang. That way we could mingle with a crowd. Only, I noticed a lot of children wearing three pairs of pants!"

"Me!" Phong said. "You forgot about me."

"Wait," Tram said. "When the time came, we had to go down to the water in the total darkness and hide. That's another reason we went that night—there was no moon. When we got there, there were *hundreds* of us. And only four boats."

"You'd paid all that money?"

"To be stuffed into a boat—three hundred in a boat."

"You must have been scared."

"I was terrified. They were dividing us into smaller groups so we would be harder to detect. My father said, 'Hold on to your brother,' and he told Huyen, 'Hold on to your mother.'" She looked at her mother, and the two lines appeared sadly between her eyes. "Someone should have said to my father, 'Hold on to somebody.' He didn't. When we got on the boat— Huyen, my mother, and I—my father wasn't with us. I remember crying and screaming for him, but we couldn't get off and look for him. My mother said he was probably on one of the other boats. She seemed so sure, and we believed her."

Suddenly I wasn't so sure I wanted to hear the rest of the story. It was already heading for an unhappy ending.

"The problem was, there was so much time to think about it. We sat on that boat for five days and six nights. I was too little to count them, but my brother did."

"How old was he?" Meg said.

"Ten."

Almost the age Phong was now. I couldn't imagine *him* sitting still for five days and six nights.

"We were arm to arm on that boat, you know? For all that time. And after only two days there was no more food."

"Three days without food?" I said. I could barely go three hours.

"I remember crying and drinking dirty water. And I remember the sea was so rough and so many people were seasick. You can imagine—"

Meg nodded ruefully. I was turning green myself.

"The sickest person of all was my mother. She—"

Phong couldn't stand it any longer. "She was going to have me!"

Meg looked incredulously at Mrs. My. "You went through all of that pregnant?"

Mrs. My bobbed. "I find out two days. Two days. Too late."

"She found out two days before we left, and then it was too late to change our plans. We had heard stories, but we really didn't think it was going to be that hard. And knowing there was going to be a baby was good news, you know? We needed some good news."

I looked at Phong, who was beaming like a kid on a cereal commercial. He obviously liked being "good news."

"She was so very sick. She looked like a dead body. I was scared—out of my mind."

"And you were headed for where at this point?" Meg said.

"Indonesia. That's where the camps were where the people could stay until they could get a sponsor to come into the United States."

"Of course. The refugee camps."

I saw Tram wince. It was subtle, like everything else she did. But I knew she didn't like that word.

"The fifth day," she went on, "when we could see the beach at Malaysia, when we could almost touch it, our boat sank. It was like we were being swallowed by the sea."

"You must have been so weak from hunger by that time," Meg said.

"The thing that saved us was that Huyen and I always swam, from when we were babies almost. We got to shore, and somehow we got my mother to shore. She just laid there on the beach and I knew she was going to die. But Huyen—he never gave up. He said, 'Come on.' And we practically carried her the rest of the way.

"The people—the Malaysians—wouldn't let us stay there. It wasn't a camp. So after a few days they gave us another boat."

"I bet about the last thing you wanted to do was get on a boat again!"

"I screamed! But we got on, and we landed on an island where there was no one. And we just had to wait there until the Indonesians gave us instructions."

"Our life," Mrs. My said, "no more ours."

"It was obvious that all control over what was going to happen to us had completely slipped out of our hands. I didn't really put that together then, but I kept looking for my father to come. I just kept thinking if he were there, everything would be all right."

I thought I knew the feeling.

"We could stay there, where there was no one and nothing, or we could join another group already settled on another island. But for that, we had to pay them."

"*More* money? That's criminal!" Meg was ready to lobby, I could tell.

"Of course we had no money. So we gave them all our jewelry. They even took my silver cross I wore."

A cross! Huh? I thought you Vietnamese were all Buddhists or something.

"So we lived on Behala for five months. Huyen built us a house out of bamboo and leaves."

"And he was only ten years old?"

That didn't surprise me. I bet Phong could have made it totally on his own on the streets. Fruit diet.

"Each day he swam to another village to get drinking water, and I washed our clothes in the sea."

"For people like you, that must have been grueling—humiliating!" Meg said.

Tram shook her head. "You just do it, you know? But it was filthy, I remember. We weren't used to—the waste—of fifteen hundred people. You can imagine—"

Yes, I can, so don't go into detail, okay?

"Tell about the storms," Phong said. He was practically up on the table by now.

"That was the thing that scared me the most. They were like hurricanes, you know? Knocking down trees. Hundreds of people would be killed in every storm. One night the winds even tore down our hut. Huyen had to build it again."

Meg looked at Mrs. My. "And all this time you were pregnant. You must have been so frightened for the baby."

"I worrying all the time. Baby be—uh—"

"She was worried that the baby wasn't going to be normal," Tram said.

"He isn't!" I said, swatting at Phong.

"When the time came, some other women on the island came to help."

"You were there?" Meg said softly.

Tram did something miraculous then, as far as I was concerned. *She smiled.* And it was a real smile. No bitterness. Just a smile.

"I was the first one to hold him," she said. "And he was normal," she said, shooting me a look. "But my mother was very sick, for a long time, and I had to take care of Phong."

"Good mother," Mrs. My said, smiling at Tram.

"By then almost five and a half months had gone by, and we were moved to a main camp where we were finally cleared for entrance into the United States. A month and a half later they found people to sponsor us—a church—in Palo Alto. We were lucky. We were only on our journey eight months. Some people it now takes over a year, we've heard."

"Eight months is long enough not to have a home," Meg said.

Tram nodded. "Especially when my father wasn't with us. You know, we made our hut our home, but he wasn't with us, so it wasn't the same."

Once again I thought I knew the feeling. Several sentences later I knew I didn't. Not really.

"We thought when we got to the main camp, we would find my father. We still thought he was just on another boat and he would join us there—or somewhere. But it was time to leave for the United States, and we hadn't found him. Huyen and I went to a different part of the camp every day, looking and asking questions—have you seen a man about this tall, you know?"

I guess they don't all look alike.

Tram looked at her mother and sighed. "You sure you want to hear it all?" she said to Meg.

"If you want to tell it."

No, Tram, don't tell it. I'm not going to like this, I know.

"Two days before we were going to leave, we went out to look just once more." She swallowed—hard. "I had Phong strapped to my back, and I took him with us so my mother could rest. There was a whole group of people on the other side of the camp who told us they saw our father. The way we described him, they said yes—he had just left on a boat full of people who were all assigned to go to the United States. We ran to the beach, and we could see it. It was like a speck out in the water. We had come so close—and now he was so far away. We knew if he came to the United States, not with us, we might never find him."

There was a sad silence. Meg was pretty close to tears, and even Phong was holding his breath—and *he* knew the ending.

"I told you Huyen never gave up. Before I could stop him—he dove into the water and tried to swim after the boat. It was so far away, but he tried. I cried and screamed and jumped up and down, but he kept going. I think, finally, he knew he couldn't catch the boat, and he turned back. But he was so far away. He was so tired. He was so thin by then, and he was only eleven." She looked at Phong. We all did, as if he were the only way we could get a grasp of how small Huyen must have been.

"He was such a good swimmer. But on his way back to me, he went under, and then he came back up. Then he went under again."

"He was in trouble," Meg said.

"Yes, and so I went after him. But then Phong started to cry. I remembered he was on my back. I couldn't go any further, and I couldn't see Huyen anymore." She looked right at Meg and shook her head.

"I'm so sorry," Meg said.

"We didn't ask anyone to look for his body. There was no place to bury it. We just prayed for his soul."

"I'm sure God took care of the rest, aren't you?" Meg said.

Yeah, I thought to myself. "Yeah."

Tram looked quickly at me. I hadn't been real sure I'd said it until her eyes clinked with mine.

"Lost one son. Got one more son." Mrs. My smiled at Phong. He grinned. I wondered how much like Huyen he was. No wonder they treated him like a little prince.

"So a church group in Palo Alto sponsored you?" Meg prompted Tram.

"Right. They also found out for us, after we got here, that the night we left Nha Trang our father was captured by the Communist police before he could get on the boat with us. All that we went through—and he was still in South Vietnam."

"Then that wasn't him on the boat your brother went after?" Meg said.

"No."

Another silence. *Don't ask, Meg. Please don't ask.*

"And now?"

Tram looked down into her teacup, and Mrs. My looked into hers.

"He's still there," she said. "He spent five months in prison. Then he tried to escape twice more, but was caught and went back to prison, five months each time. Illegal escape is impossible now. He's being watched too closely."

"Is there such a thing as *legal* escape?" Meg said.

"Oh, sure," Tram said. The bitter smile again. "For ten thousand dollars."

I whistled. "Ten thou—"

"For an exit permit," she said.

"We'll get it." Phong said it as if it were as easy as lifting a couple of oranges. I wanted to laugh, but when Tram looked around the table at all of us, I choked it back.

"Yes, we will," she said. She lifted her chin, and her almond eyes steadied. "We will do it."

And I believed her.

11

Even though Phong whined—Tram gave him a look that would have withered *my* backbone—we left a short time after that. Mrs. My sent us off with all the leftovers wrapped in aluminum foil.

"Enjoy the rest of the meatballs," Tram said to me.

"I will," I said. *Vietnamese vixen.*

Meg bobbed her head a lot to Mrs. My and promised Phong his pictures were going up on the wall in her room the minute she got back to San Francisco. But when she got to Tram, she couldn't control herself. She pulled her into a hug.

"You're great," she said. "Don't ever forget how great you are."

"Na-na-na-na-na," Tram said.

Phong followed us all the way down to the gate and hung on it as we walked to Meg's car. "See you Monday, Josh Dingbat," he called.

"Newsstand," I called back. "And no comic books."

He just sparkled a grin at me and kept swinging.

Meg didn't even wait until we were out of downtown to start cross-examining me.

"All right, Joshua," she said, wheeling the Audi back into the double-parked traffic. "Spill your guts. Who are these people to you?"

"The girl isn't anything to me," I said.

She cocked an eyebrow. "Right. I've got my spoon ready."

"And until today I never laid eyes on the mother."

"That poor woman. Can you believe what she's been through? What they've all been through. So, go on."

"I would if you'd cut with the bleeding heart."

"You know them through Phong. How?"

I laughed uneasily. "You aren't going to believe it, but, okay—"

"After today I'd believe anything."

"I just kind of picked him up on the street."

"I don't believe it!"

"Man—"

She reached over and squeezed my leg. "I'm just kidding! What—he was lost and you took him home?"

"Uh, are you high? Phong doesn't get lost. It was more like *him* showing *me* the way—" I looked at her. She was alternating between watching the road so she could dodge Chinese maniacs and glancing at me to scope out the expression on my face. She wanted to know. She really did.

Aw, heck.

So I told her the story. Most of it. I omitted the stuff about the three punks. I mean, that was immaterial. Mrs. Sanderson would've red-penciled it out of any paper as being off the topic.

Meg just listened to it all and nodded her head a lot. She looked like Mrs. My bobbing.

"That little boy really loves you, Josh," she said when I was through.

"Nah, he just—"

"He *does*. And I think all the more because he doesn't have a big brother *or* a father right now."

"Man, Meg, don't start telling me I'm a father figure!"

"I'm serious, and don't try to fake me out, Baby B., 'cause I know you see it too. All the trust and respect he would be heaping on a father, he's heaping on you. I mean, yeah, those two women are strong. You know, they seem so gentle and soft—"

I thought of Tram and snorted. *They do?*

"—and they're really made of steel. But he still needs masculine energy in his life—and I think he's found it in you."

I looked at her sharply. Yeah, I'd thought about it. But it went through me like one of those cold chills you get out of nowhere.

Phong's father substitute. His own father had the guts to try to escape from Vietnam. His own father had spent fifteen months in prison for trying to get to his family. His own father had sold everything and buried the profits in the backyard so he could save his kids.

You expect to measure up to that, Josh? Good luck.

"Joshua? Are you okay?" Meg said.

What if I fall short?

"Josh?"

I won't. God's got plans for me. Phong's going to be able to look up to me. He'll see a man in me too.

"Baby B.—"

"*What?*"

"Back to earth, guy." We were at a red light, so she could look at me long and hard. When it changed she drove on, dimples working. "You know what's one of the saddest things about what they told us?"

"Man, where do you start?"

"I think it's what Tram said right before we got up from the table."

"About getting their dad out?"

"You know, don't you, that there's no way they're going to raise that kind of money for an exit permit?"

"She said her mother's working two jobs."

"As a stock person in a grocery store and as a manicurist. I bet they can hardly *live* on that. You know, those slumlords will charge up the nose even for a dump like that. And it is a dump. I mean, they're trying to make a clean, decent life out of nothing, but—well, they'll never save ten thousand dollars."

"She said they'd do it!" *Good grief, what are you saying?*

"It's naive, Joshua. That makes me so sad for them. I wish

there was something we could do. If only we knew more about this kind of thing."

We were back in our neighborhood by then. I looked out the window at the line of manicured condos. And suddenly I felt like scum. Total scum.

◆　　◆　　◆

We both smelled rhubarb cobbler the minute we got in the front door. We looked at each other. "Mom's home," we said simultaneously.

Then—of course—there was a shriek from the direction of the kitchen. We looked at each other again. "Denise," we said.

"Wonder why she's here," Meg said. She started to take off her jacket.

"She lives here," I said.

Meg stopped in mid-sleeve. "Oh, no—Mom's taken in another 'foster child.'"

I just groaned.

"Poor baby." Meg tweaked my nose and laughed. "So what's Denise's problem?"

"You got me," I said. I headed for the stairs. "She says things are, 'like, weird' at her house—whatever that means—and she comes over here for, y' know, 'space' so she can get her homework done, and—whoa—"

I stopped three steps up and looked down at Meg.

"What?" she said.

"Believe it or not, she might actually know something."

There was another shriek from the kitchen, and Meg chuckled. "About what? Hyenas?"

"No." I went for the kitchen door. "Vietnam."

Of course Denise had to fall all over Meg, and Mom had to slobber all over Meg, and then, just on general principle, Mom had to drool all over me, and then when I handed her the authentic Vietnamese leftovers it had to start all over again. I didn't think I'd ever get Denise alone. Weird. I hadn't thought I'd ever *want* to.

While Mom was popping the Vietnamese spring rolls and killer meatballs into the microwave, I dragged Denise into the living room.

"Sit," I said.

She did.

"I have to ask you something."

"Okay."

She was cross-legged on the couch, her big eyes bulging, her braces gleaming, and even her hair standing on end in expectation. Mom had been wrong about that perm ever settling down. She still looked like a surprised poodle. Suddenly I couldn't picture myself saying, "Denise, tell me how to get somebody out of South Vietnam." She'd be shrieking for days.

"So," I said instead, "how's the term paper coming?"

She didn't even look suspicious. If somebody had treated me like I was infested with lice for the last two years and then out of the blue took an undying interest in my schoolwork, I'd have at least wanted to know why. She didn't even blink.

"Great! I'm finding out so much stuff! Is your friend really smart?"

"What friend?" I said. *I thought I was supposed to be asking the questions.*

"The Vietnamese girl."

"Oh. Smart?" I didn't even have to think about it. "Probably," I said. "Why?"

"Because Asian-Americans are practically setting the pace in education for the rest of us now." Her hair was almost crackling, she was so excited. "Did you know that, like, 25 percent of the freshman class at Berkeley is Oriental?"

"No—"

"They don't take just anybody at Berkeley."

"Yeah, I know—"

"They're just, like, tearing up the math on the S.A.T.'s—"

"Okay, okay—" *Maybe I should get into this slowly,*

before she throws a rod or something. "What do you know about how the names work?"

Shriek. "It can get really confusing."

"Then let me ask you some questions," I said quickly. "Their mother's name is Mrs. Ba My—"

Double-shriek—if that's possible. "No, it isn't! Ba *means* Mrs."

Great. Tram now thinks you're a real whiz kid.

Denise went on, "My is her maiden name, but she's called Ba My—Mrs. My."

"But the kids have the father's name?"

"Yeah—and when they say it they, like, put the last name first and the first name last. Only here they reverse it, so we don't, y' know, get confused."

"Too late," I said. But I was mentally translating: Truong Something Tram. Truong Something Phong. Daniels David Joshua. It sounded like Mrs. Sanderson calling roll. "Are they taught to respect their parents under penalty of death or something?"

"Well, not *death*. But respect is, like, a big deal. That's why their manners are so polite. And they're, like, different from ours, y' know. Like, they don't shake hands—"

Terrific.

"They hardly ever make eye contact."

They do now.

"And it's really rude, according to their customs, to point or crook your finger like you're saying 'come here.' That's how they call dogs."

I couldn't remember having pointed or crooked. *At least you're not a total 'tard.*

"They just really hate to be, y' know, criticized and humiliated, and they'll, like, go out of their way not to offend you."

Ha.

"But if you hurt their feelings—they'll remember it for a long time."

Oops.

"They're known to be cheerful, romantic, resourceful, and can stand almost any hardship—"

Romantic? Sure. "Enough with the Boy Scout promise," I said. "Do you know anything about—"

"The food!" Meg said. She sailed in with a plate of steaming spring rolls and set it on the coffee table. "Tell me more about the food!"

Denise dove for the spring rolls and stuffed an entire one into her mouth. She kept talking as the braces went to work on it.

"Very attractive," I muttered. Meg poked me.

"I know . . . I love it," Denise said. "*And*—this will kill you—"

It might.

"Boys aren't even allowed in the kitchen in most houses."

"Josh wouldn't survive," my mother said from the doorway. She put a bowl of chicken-cabbage salad on the table and beside it the leftover meatballs on rice. I held up my fingers in a cross.

"What's the matter?" Mom said.

"Don't eat those meatballs unless you want to get rid of the lining of your mouth," I said.

"Josh Dingbat, you little faker!" Meg said. "You ate three helpings at their house!"

"You ate at their house?" Denise said. The poodle-look grew incredulous. "They must really like you or, like, want to repay you for something. They just don't do that." She nodded seriously. "They really wanted you to enjoy it."

Meg laughed. "Oh, he did."

"I can see why," Mom said. "These spring rolls are superb."

Meg nodded. "I watched her make them. No oil."

"Really?"

"I knew you'd like that."

"Do you have their address, Joshua?" Mom said. "I want to write a thank you note *and* get some of these recipes."

There goes the rest of my gums and stomach lining.

But I got up and found a pencil and pad. It was obvious I wasn't going to get the info I really wanted. This whole discussion was turning into a tribute to Betty Crocker.

"Why do you know so much about Vietnamese culture, Den'?" Meg said.

"I'm doing a term paper on, like, y' know, how their teenagers fit into American high schools."

Meg shot me a disappointed look. Everything on Denise drooped. "You don't think that's a good topic?"

"I think it's a great topic," Meg said. "I just—I was hoping you'd know something about exit permits. You know, how you can get people out of South Vietnam and into the United States."

Denise shook her head slowly. *I almost felt sorry for her.*

"If that's what you want to know," Mom said, "I think I may be able to find out some things. I get information all the time about sponsoring a family. I'm sure I could follow up—"

Her voice trailed off. I looked up to find her watching me. For once I wasn't sure she "understood" what I was thinking. "I can do that if you want me to," she said.

I shrugged. Meg flashed her eyes at me.

"Do that, would you, Mom?" Meg said. "It wouldn't hurt anything."

"Josh?" Mom said.

"Sure," I said.

◆　　　◆　　　◆

"Why did you hesitate so long when Mom said she'd find out about getting Phong and Tram's dad out?" Meg asked me later when Mom had gone to bed and we were eating the last of the spring rolls in the hot tub.

"Because I'm a dweeb," I said.

"You *are*."

I aborted the bite I was about to take out of a roll and stared at her through the steam. She wasn't kidding.

"I know you're sixteen and it's in your contract to be rude and obnoxious, but Mom really does try. She's not like a lot of mothers who yell and tell you how horrible you are all the time."

I finished off the spring roll. "Once in a while I wish she would."

"So do I! You're such a wise guy sometimes."

"She 'understands' me!" I said with mock drama.

"Look what she does for a living, though."

"I'm not one of her youth-group problem children. Let her 'understand' Denise. I'm her kid!"

"Ah." Meg leaned back in the bubbles. "So you want her to stop understanding you and treat you the way Dad does—which is *laissez faire*."

I knew I'd heard that expression in history class or something, but like most things I heard in classrooms, it hadn't sunk in. And Meg knew it.

"That means 'hands off.' But I'll tell you, I'd have loved to have some of that understanding when I was your age—"

"When you were my age, Mom was going through a divorce."

"And she didn't understand anything, I know. But she's trying to make up for it with me now. Give her a break. She went through a lot with Dad."

"Poor baby," I muttered.

Meg sat up with a jerk. "Mom may understand you, Joshua, but I don't—not all the time." Her dimples had momentarily turned into stern lines that elongated her freckles. "The last couple of times we've been together you've been talking about God's plan for *you* and how *you're* going where He's leading you and all that stuff—which is fine—"

"I'm glad you approve," I said drily.

"What I don't get is how you can be so into Christ when it comes to your *own* life and then totally forget about Him when it comes to everybody else." She was by now inches from my nose. "How can you be such a good Christian about *diving* for Pete's sake and then such a jerk about people?"

"What people?"

"Denise. Mom. Nathan and that other kid." She smacked me on the shoulder. "Tram."

"Those 'people' don't have anything to do with me and God and where I'm going!" I said.

"Does *Dad*? Oh, yeah—I forgot—he's paying your way."

"That's not fair!"

"I don't mean to lecture you—"

"It's too late. You already are." I hoisted up onto the side of the tub. "Man, Meg, get off my case."

"Not in this lifetime. Because I think you're salvageable."

"Thank you, spiritual bag lady," I said. I could feel the sarcasm coating my tongue.

"The whole thing is, you think the only way you can be somebody is to wipe everybody up with your diving. You've gotten so into thinking that's the only way that you've also gotten selective about your Christianity. It's turned you into a narrow-minded—"

"I thought you said I was salvageable," I snapped.

"You are. Because if you weren't—you wouldn't care about Phong and his family."

We both stopped, nose to nose, chins jutting out at each other like javelins.

I swung my legs out of the tub and made my angry escape.

◆　　◆　　◆

I stood in the shower for twenty minutes and thought about nothing. Even my attitude was numb.

When I was drying off, I thought I heard somebody in my room. Probably my mother bringing in the warm milk. There I was—understanding that I hated Mom's understanding me. That I wanted more of Dad in my life. That I wanted to be a championship diver more than anything in the world so he'd be proud of me. That I wanted to do what God wanted me to do and was confused that nobody else saw it that way. That I was hooked on a relationship with an eleven-year-old refugee and couldn't for a second figure out why. That I was beginning to feel something weird for a girl I couldn't stand.

But there was no milk on a tray. There was only Lou.

I jabbed my legs into some sweats and flopped down bare-chested on the bed beside him, sliding my arms under the pillows. There was something there.

"Man—" I jerked up and pulled it out. Lou watched me as I unfolded a note.

"Why'd you let somebody come in my room?" I said to him.

He blinked and waited. He wanted me to lie down so he could get into my armpit. I did, holding the note up in the light from the hall so I could read it.

It was from Meg.

"Sorry I got on your case, Baby B.," it read. "I care, but I shouldn't try so hard. Maybe you ought to talk to God some more. You don't seem to get so bent out of shape when He gives you advice." The next sentence was in huge letters. "ONLY THIS TIME, LET HIM DO THE TALKING!"

I flipped over the note. On the back she'd written "Matthew 2:1-12."

"Okay, so I'm not so subtle," the note continued in smaller letters. "I love you. Meg."

No, you're not subtle at all. I don't need this. I already know where I'm going and how to get there.

I got up and went to the closet. My Bible was on the top shelf.

I'm also a jerk. I heard some stuff today that made my life seem pretty wimpy.

I let the Bible sigh open on the bed and thumbed for Matthew.

It's not all how you thought it was, Josh, my man.

I sank back on the bed beside Lou and started perusing.

Question is—if it's not how you thought it was, how is it?

My feet went up on the wallpaper, and I stared at the page. One and a half gainer.

Josh Dingbat. So-Long Phong.
Tram saying, "We will do it."
Christ saying, "Come on—I have plans for you."
The Bible saying, "There came wise men from the east to
Jerusalem."

MONDAY morning I put *Tales of Gold* on Mrs. Sanderson's desk before school.

"Good, Josh," she said, giving it the once-over through her bifocals. "I'll have a chance to check it out before last hour and let you know."

She smiled up like she expected me to bolt out of there. I didn't.

"Unless, of course, you want me to sit here and go through the whole thing right now. This isn't a One-Hour, We Peruse While U Wait—"

"No," I said. "I just wondered if you had something else I could read too—maybe something on Vietnam."

She let the specs fall on their leash and looked at me sans lenses. "There's a sudden rash of interest in Southeast Asia around here. First Denise Stahl, then Brian—"

"Bra—Brian? Brian Bibee?"

"Contrary to popular belief, he does know how to read. But you surprise me, Josh."

Why? Because I too know how to read?

"I thought if it didn't have something to do with a pool and a diving board, it wasn't worth your time."

Funny thing. So did I.

"Okay, we've gone from Hawthorne to Sammy Lee. We

might as well throw in Ho Chi Minh. What aspect of Nam are you interested in?"

"The people who are still over there, the ones that have family here. How do they get out?" I was trying to sound casual, as if I'd toyed with ideas like food, dating customs, and religious festivals, and come up with this.

"You've definitely narrowed it down," she said. "I'll see what I can find."

"Thanks," I said. I turned to get out of there. My next move was to find Brain—and find out a couple of things.

"I'll see you last hour," Mrs. Sanderson said. "Josh?"

Lady, come on.

"There's a lot in that head of yours. I'm glad to see you're not putting it all in one place."

I am. It's diving or nothing. Right.

I swung out the door and headed down the hall.

I careened around the corner and pushed the double doors that led out to the courtyard. I hadn't been there since the blowup at Zondra's party. It was like going into a scene from *Back to the Future.*

It was early enough that Nathan and Young Jon wouldn't even be out of bed yet, but I might find Brain out there trying to wake up.

The place was still empty, so I headed for a bench. The minute I sat on it, the leaves behind me started to rustle. I jerked around to meet Nathan nose to nose through an azalea bush.

"What the—what are you doing?" he said.

I forgot for a minute we weren't speaking to each other. "What do you mean 'what the—what am *I* doing?'" I said. "'What the' are *you* doing?"

Eyes slitted in disgust, Nathan pushed the branches apart and climbed out over the bench. "If you hung out here anymore you'd know I meet somebody here. This was going to be a surprise."

I widened my eyes at him. "You were going to surprise Jon Ricco and Brain?"

"No, not Jon Ricco and Brain." He glanced at the double doors. "Get a clue, Daniels."

"I wish I had one."

"So do I." Nathan flipped some hair out of his eyes and looked down at me. I looked back. It wasn't like two friends anymore. It was like two guys competing in a contest for one-upmanship—both of them too chicken to say what they were really thinking.

"Okay. I'll give you a clue," he said finally. "You've changed, man. And I tried to say, okay, I can deal with that. There's got to be some of the old Josh still in there." He hissed out of the side of his mouth. "But there wasn't anything of the old Josh. So I quit trying. You change back—okay, fine, I'll still be here."

I could almost feel my mouth dropping open. It took me a minute to get it to function. "I'm not the only one who's changed, man," I said.

"I didn't change."

He glanced up at the double doors again. Jill was standing on the other side, peering through the glass with *what's he doing here?* in her eyes. So much for *me* being the babe, the hunk.

"I stayed with the way we said things were going to be since junior high," he said. "You're the one who got off. You're takin' another way—and far as I'm concerned, it's *way* off the original track."

He looked up at Jill again and jerked his head almost imperceptibly. She swept in and I swept out.

"Did you walk in on the morning ron-day-voo?" I looked up at Brain who was suddenly just there, hulking beside me. I wouldn't have believed he knew any words with that many syllables.

"How long has that been going on?" I said. "Ah—never mind. I don't really want to know. Where you going now?"

"Nowhere. I was looking for you."

"Oh."

"Let's go out to my car," he said.

As I climbed into the blue '57 I looked it over. Everything

in it was either polished or shined or buffed until it screamed "I belong in Harrah's Automobile Collection!" I'd never thought of Brain with his hand in a can of Turtle Wax. In fact, I'd never thought of Brain any way at all until recently. And now I had to find out some things. Like how much he'd seen on Friday. And whether or not he was going to tell anybody.

I glanced at my watch. There was still time to slide into it gradually. "I asked you this the other day," I said. "How come I never saw you with this car before?"

"They just decided I'd earned it."

"They?"

"Hey, Josh, man—what are you into?"

I blinked. *So much for sliding into it gradually.*

"I wasn't spying on you or nothin'—anything," he said. "I just saw you get into it with those three punks downtown."

That answers that question.

"I was just ready to get out and help you clean their clocks," he said, "but then they backed off. I stuck around, and they didn't follow you."

"They never do."

I hadn't really meant to say that. Brain looked straight out the windshield, his bulky arms hunkered down over the steering wheel like he was waiting for something to clear. He wasn't used to doing this much talking.

"Look," he said, "if this was Nathan or Ricco, I'd just let them do their thing—hang themselves—you know what I mean?"

I didn't, but I nodded.

"But, see, you got something you want to do with yourself and you could mess it up real easy. That's why I tried to get you away from that stupid party we took you to."

I kept nodding.

"See, I'm from downtown."

"You told me that."

"I know what it's like down there. Punks like that, they'll sell you bad stuff and next thing you know you're jumping off a roof instead of a diving board."

I almost laughed. "They're not selling me anything, Brain. What—do you think they're dealing drugs?"

"I know they are. I know those kind—"

"Well, I'm not buying them—"

"They try to take anybody—"

"Brain—okay—I don't want to know. All I'm doing—"

"When you don't pay up or something, they want to mop up the street with you—"

I was really laughing by then. "I don't owe them—"

"They'll even try to use kids, like that little Vietnamese dude "

I froze. An image of Phong clutching a syringe came sharply into view.

"How?" The words snapped out like snakebites. "How do they use kids?"

"Front. Who's gonna suspect they're dealing drugs if they got a little kid with them?"

"He's eleven," I muttered stupidly.

"He's their cover."

"Does he—would he know it?"

"Not if they could help it."

It was my turn to stare out the windshield. *Man, are you stupid or what? It never occurred to you, did it, that Phong was there with them for a reason? That they were getting their kicks from something besides harassing you. Josh—talk about a 'tard.*

But that wasn't the important thing. The important thing was Phong—and how much danger he was in now.

"I messed things up by getting the kid on my side, didn't I?" I said.

Brain shrugged. "Could be. Don't worry about him, though. Those street kids are tough—even that age."

"He isn't a street kid!" I said savagely.

Brain raised both hands in surrender.

"Man, I'm sorry." I sighed and shifted miserably in the seat. "I'm not into drugs, okay? And the kid isn't either. I just went by there on my way to the pool and then I got hooked into kind of baby-sitting—he's got a family, the whole thing."

Brain nodded. There was something besides beige in his cheeks, so I knew he was relieved. "I knew you weren't into that. Really. But, see—you might not be *taking* drugs, but you're involved in their scene now. And they don't take chances with outsiders."

"I never saw anything!"

"They'll figure you saw them get violent, you'll put it together."

I spat out a laugh. "I didn't put it together."

"They don't know that."

"Well, hey—" I sat up straighter in the seat. "It's no big thing now because Phong and I—the kid—aren't meeting there anymore. We won't have to deal with them."

"I told you," Brain said, "I lived downtown. I *know* how it is. I know." He looked at me, beige face hard with what he "knew." "You go down there every day?"

"Yeah."

"From now on I'll take you."

It wasn't an offer—it was a command. "Is Phong—my kid—the kid—is he in trouble with them now?" I said. "Even if he doesn't know anything?"

"Could be."

I nodded slowly. "I'll meet you out here at 2:30."

Brain turned up a thumb.

◆　　◆　　◆

"Hey," I said to him that afternoon as we cruised toward downtown Oakland, "how did you know the kid was Vietnamese just seeing him one time from the car? I always thought they all looked alike, the Asian types."

"Got pictures of Vietnamese kids all over my bedroom," he said.

I stared at him. "Why?"

"Guy that lived there before me was a photographer in the war. Won prizes for some of them."

The guy that lived in your house, before you, left his prize-winning photography collection there and you still have it. O-kay—

That made about as much sense as Brain coming from a dump in downtown Oakland, knowing about drug dealers on street corners, and now going to a fancy Christian school and driving a vintage 1957 Chevrolet. But we were pulling up to the newsstand, and I craned my neck for Phong.

He was flipping through a Batman comic book under the scowling scrutiny of the manager. I got out, put the comic back in its rack in the guy's full view, and gently shoved Phong into the front seat.

"I wasn't going to take it, Josh!" he said. "I'm clean. Wow!"

His eyes sparkled around the inside of the Chevy, and his black, shiny hair practically trembled as his head darted from tuck and roll to dashboard and back again.

"Like it?" Brain said.

"Cool!" Phong said.

A formal introduction was obviously unnecessary, but Tram wouldn't have approved if I'd forgotten my manners.

"Phong—this is Bra—"

"Bri-an," Brain said emphatically. His eyes met mine.

That was the last day I called him Brain.

◆   ◆   ◆

Matter of fact, that was the last day for a lot of things.

It was the last day I was scared of diving off the platform, even though I did a handstand dive that day.

But I didn't just do it to raise my scores. I did it because Phong was there. Thanks to Brian he was safe now. He needed me to be his hero, and I was.

It was also the last day I hated Mouse Tulley. When I made my final dive of the day, he pulled me out of the pool and said, "I think you're a diver." I didn't love him, mind you. There were a lot of other things he could have said, including, "I know you're going to the Olympics." But least there was no "but" in his voice. And with him and Phong standing there grinning at me—yeah, it felt kind of good.

But it was a first for a couple of things too.

"Since I was so magnificent today," I said to Phong when Mouse had gone off to change, "I'm done early. We've got time for your first swimming lesson."

I had not known it was possible for an Asian face to turn grey. Phong's did.

"No swimming suit," he said too quickly.

"Use one of my Speedos," I said. I laughed. "You barely have any butt, but one size fits all."

He didn't laugh with me. He wasn't even considering the possible thrill of wearing my swimsuit. He was scared.

"Come on, man," I said, nudging him softly in the ribs. "I'm not going to let you drown. Don't you trust me?"

I'd meant it as a joke, but he didn't take it that way. His eyes got huge, and he shook his head almost violently. "I do trust you! I do!"

"Okay—then what's the problem?"

Of course I already knew, and I felt mean making him admit it.

"It's no shame being scared," I said. "You knew I was scared when I got up on that platform, right?"

"You said you weren't."

"I lied."

I almost got a grin, but his face was still drawn and ashy.

"Let me ask you a question," I said.

He nodded miserably. This was killing him, being afraid in front of me. Suddenly it meant everything to help him save face.

"What would have happened if your sister never learned to swim?"

The black, elfin eyebrows shot up.

"Right. She would have drowned, and then your mother would've drowned, and there would have been no Phong."

It was heavy stuff, and he considered it long and hard. His

usually impish face was working, and for a minute I thought he was going to cry. Maybe I was pushing him too far—

"But Huyen did know how to swim," he said finally. "And he drowned anyway."

Yeah. Yeah. "Yeah, he did."

Now what?

"But, see, he wasn't healthy like you are now. And he was desperate. You aren't."

This isn't what you should be telling the kid. There's got to be a better reason—

"That was a dangerous ocean," I plowed on. "This is a nice, safe pool."

Come on, you can do better than this, Josh.

Phong was in agony. He was twisting his hands and chewing on his lip and talking all kinds of body language I'd never seen him use before.

Okay—wait—

I took a breath. "Huyen took a risk even though he was scared. That's courage. He'd be proud of you for trying even though you're scared."

Man—Bill Cosby, Dr. James Dobson, all you Professional Fathers—eat your hearts out!

"Okay," Phong said. He stuck out his chin, just the way I'd seen Tram do on Saturday. "We will do it."

One thing I'd learned by now. When these people said "We will do it"—they would.

I helped him change into one of my suits and cinched it up tight. The seat bagged, but he didn't say a word. He just followed me to the shallow end of the pool, which was still about a foot over his head.

"I'll just hold you," I said. "I won't let go. We'll get used to the water—that'll be the first step."

"First step" ha! It looked like that might be the only step—*if* he took it at all.

I got in the water and reached my arms up for him. He put his hands out like steel tongs about to go into a furnace.

"Good," I said. "Now I'll just lift you in—"

The tongs retracted.

"I swear, So-Long," I said, "I will *not* let you go under. If I do, even for a second, I'll flush every Speedo I own down the toilet—"

"Do it here and I'll slap a fine on you," somebody said.

I looked up at Overbite Betty.

She was wearing a swimsuit and looked less like a bowling ball than she did in sweats.

"Gonna learn to swim, huh, Phong?" she said.

Phong just nodded, and she looked quickly at me. When Phong didn't have an answer, he was either scared spitless or he'd had his voice box removed.

"Well, I'm just glad you're not being a wimp about it," she said, slipping into the pool. "I was so scared of the water when I was your age I wet my pants every time I put on a bathing suit."

Very attractive. And you're lying—thanks.

Phong was starting to smile.

"But just in case you get a little nervous—first time and all—Josh and I are *both* here. I don't even have to promise to—" she glared at me—"flush my swimsuit down the toilet because *I* will not let you go under under any circumstances."

That's how we got Phong into the water. It didn't even bother me that I needed her expert help. I saw the Swim Instructor patch on her suit. She knew what she was doing.

And besides—it was me Phong clung to when his shoulders were submerged in the pool and he was choking back sobs.

"You're doing great, guy!" she said after about three minutes. "I think that's plenty for today."

We're just getting started. Come on, Overbite.

She looked hard at me and nodded her head toward the side.

"It was a good start," she whispered to me later when Phong was busy with a juice bar, "but we're really going to have to take it slow with him. He's had some kind of trauma with water in his life."

"His brother drowned," I said.

"That could be it. But as terrified as he is, I think it's in his own experience." She shrugged. "Anyway—not to worry. We'll get him hooked."

I looked at Phong, who was accepting his second juice bar from her and grinning like his old self.

I mentally decided not to think of her as Overbite Betty anymore.

◆　　◆　　◆

"It's been a good day, Josh Dingbat," Phong said on the way to his apartment.

"How come?" I said.

"Number one—we gave those thugs the slip."

I choked. "What?"

"I read that," he said, grinning. "But it's true."

"Yeah, it is." *You don't know how true.*

"Number two—I got to ride in a big, fancy car."

Something occurred to me. "You guys don't have a car, do you?" I said.

"Nope. Gotta save money for my father."

"They'll never raise ten thousand dollars," Meg had said.

"Is there a number three?" I said.

He sliced open a smile that hung happily on his earlobes. "I went in the water. I was a little scared—"

"A little."

"But I did it!"

I looked down at him, swinging along the sidewalk, holding his chin up and walking like he owned Greater Oakland. For a minute I actually thought *I* was going to cry.

"Yeah, you did it," I said. "I think that calls for a celebration."

"What?" His eyes danced.

"Well, it ain't gonna be fruit, I can tell you that. Come on—we have to go by your place and tell your sister we aren't coming straight home."

"Don't have to."

"Yeah, and I don't have to continue to live either."

"She's right there."

I followed the jut of his chin. He didn't point. Right—Denise had said that meant something about a dog. Tram was ramming toward us, riding her bike the way her older counterparts drove cars, her dark hair shimmering behind her like a shiny satin flag. The air and the exercise made her cheeks pink and her eyes shine.

Whoa, Bucko. Time to regroup. Remember, you are not interested.

Phong singsonged something to her, and without smiling she stopped. He ran up to her, and I followed. She was wearing red shorts, and her toes were pointed perfectly over the pedals. I'd never seen her outside her apartment before. She looked smaller and somehow more vulnerable, just the way Phong had the first time I'd seen him on my side of the fence.

Guardedly I said, "Hi."

"Hi," she said back. She was being guarded too, but at least it wasn't, "What's it to you?" or something.

"We're going to celebrate," Phong said.

"Celebrate what?"

"Learning to swim," he said matter-of-factly.

Tram's eyes darted to me.

"Don' t worry, I won' t let him drown," I said.

She kept her face smooth.

Maybe it was the fact that she didn't haul Phong away on the bike that very instant that made me do it. Or maybe I was just on such a high I lost my head. Anyway, I said, "Want to come with us?"

She cocked her head to one side and looked down at the pavement. Not at me. Not through me. Just down—like suddenly she was shy.

Shy? Mrs. Ho Chi-Minh? No way!

"Where are you going?" she said.

"City Square!" Phong announced.

"Oh *really*?" I said.

"For ice cream!"

Tram shook her hair back over her shoulders. "Make it frozen yogurt and okay," she said.

Phong opened his mouth. I clapped my hand over it.

"Lock your bike to that rack and let's go," I said to her. And then added, "Okay?"

Who'd have thought? Monday afternoon. Tram the dragon lady, So-Long Phong, and Josh Dingbat heading from Chinatown to City Square in City Center. Phong running ahead and running his mouth. Tram padding demurely a step or two in front of me in her little red shorts. Me following and noticing the way the sun haloed her hair. Trying to remember she hated my guts.

I'd never even been to City Square before. Phong obviously had, which didn't surprise me.

It was a different place from the rest of the downtown Oakland I'd seen—clean and shiny with soup-salad-and-baked-potato places where three-piece-suited executives don't even sit down to eat lunch. There were toy stores your average kid couldn't touch with a year's worth of allowance, which reminded me that I still wanted to buy Phong a present. But although I wasn't the average kid, I wasn't shopping there. Even the candy store looked like the proprietor bought bags of the stuff at K-mart, dumped them into fancy jars, and upped the price 300 percent.

But Phong was fascinated—like he'd never seen any of it before. He was an artist scoping out the symmetry and the bright splashes of color as if it were a gallery. Tram was hard-put to pry him away from the sculpture that stood in the middle of the square, fanning up spikes of fluorescent colors against the drabness of the city.

"It's called *There!*," I said, reading the plaque.

"Gertrude Stein," Tram said.

"Who?"

She looked at me without expression, but I knew there was disdain in there somewhere. I was learning to read what wasn't written in her face.

"She was an American writer who lived in Paris in the twenties," she said.

"I knew that," I lied.

"She was from Oakland. When she came back to visit, she said, 'There isn't any *there* there.'"

"This artist thinks there is, huh?" I said, looking up at the happy pinks and greens and oranges that pointed everywhere like a stack of big toothpicks.

"To some people it must be home," she said.

I wanted to ask her if it was to her. But I figured there could never be a home without her father, so I didn't say anything. I wanted to ask her that and a lot of other things, but—

She thinks you're scum. And you aren't interested. Remember that.

I looked around for Phong. He was examining a stairway that had water cascading down it.

"If they're yuppies, I guess it's home," I said. "This is like a center of yuppiness."

She didn't answer but just looked at me steadily.

Good grief. Isn't there any kind of emotion in these people? No anger? No ecstasy?

I looked back at her. There was only the fine little line etched subtly between her eyes.

"I don't think it's a—what did you call it?" she said.

"Center of yuppiness?" I said.

"Look at the gardens and the waterfall. My mother says she always wishes we could have remembered the flowers and the butterflies in Vietnam instead of the fear and the war. When we ended up here, it was almost worse in that way. Then Phong discovered this and dragged me here."

She shrugged suddenly, as if she were ashamed she'd said that much.

"He's an artist," she said, brushing the whole thing off with her words. "This gives him something to paint." She tossed her hair and barked something staccato at Phong.

So much for that conversation.

But in spite of that, the rest of the afternoon was actually kind of fun.

We took one of Phong's shortcuts and on the way counted how many different kinds of restaurants we could pass—espresso delis, pasta joints, every Oriental persuasion. Tram actually laughed a couple of times. Funny. It was the first time I noticed she didn't really have eyelids but instead these soft folds of skin around her eyes. I found myself wanting to touch them.

Back off, Dingbat. She is not interested. Neither are you. Remember that.

We also climbed a board fence and looked at a new skyscraper going up, and then I bought frozen yogurt which we ate sitting on the steps of the Tribune Tower just before dark. I'd been using it for a frame of reference all this time, but I'd never even been close to it before.

"Funky old building," Phong said.

I choked for about the hundredth time that day at the things that bubbled from his mouth.

"Funky?" I said.

"It isn't," Tram said. "It has a kind of warm dignity in the middle of all this sternness."

I stared at her. I couldn't imagine Kim or Jill coming out with things like "warm dignity" or "sternness." In fact, the thought almost made me want to laugh.

"What?" Tram said. She was looking at me.

"Nothing," I said.

"You think we 'think funny'?"

I'd have protested, but she wouldn't have believed me anyway.

"I think funny," Phong said. "I think funny things all the time."

"You're a dingbat," I said, pawing at his hair.

"No. *You're* Dingbat."

"And you're puppy meat," I said.

He jumped on my shoulders then, and I tore down the steps with him astride, whipping me with his yogurt spoon. I didn't notice until we got back to the top, with me gasping like Darth Vader, that Tram was laughing—hard.

"Awesome horse," Phong told her. "Bet I could make him go faster if I had spurs."

"Uh, you get spurs and my horse days are over!"

"But you're an awesome horse," Tram said. There was nothing on her face, but she didn't look away fast enough for me to miss the almost-teasing twinkle in her eyes.

Do that again and I'll carry the kid all the way home.

Okay, so I lost my head. Fortunately, she didn't do it again because Phong out-Phonged himself leading us on an obstacle course he guaranteed would get us home before it got all the way dark.

Who'd have thought I'd be waltzing through Chinatown Oakland in the evening grey with two Vietnamese kids. And who'd have thought the smell of fried rice and the sound of Oriental tires on wet pavement and the reassuring sight of the Tribune Tower hovering over us would make me feel at home.

I got so crazy with the whole thing, I slung my arm around Phong's shoulder the last block. I guess that's when it came to me what I wanted his present to be. I wanted him to be at the Regionals to watch me dive. Yeah, that thought felt good.

For an insane second I almost slung my arm around Tram too. She must have read my mind, because she slanted a *don't even think about it* look at me.

It was a good thing, because—I wasn't interested.

MEG was obviously the one to pick up Phong and take him to the Regionals on Saturday. He was crazy about her, the little Don Juan San. But I waited until the Monday before to call her and ask her. Stupid move.

Actually, it really wasn't all that stupid. In the first place, I hadn't talked to her since our argument in the hot tub. It could be a scosch awkward to suddenly get on the phone to ask her for a favor. Besides, I did try to call her over the weekend, but all I got was the cologne saleslady.

"Could you tell her her brother called?" I said testily after the woman finished oozing into the receiver the information that neither Meg nor my father were there.

"Are you T. R.'s *son?*" she said, as if I'd just announced I was Tom Cruise.

No, lady, just because Meg is my sister, I mean, why would I be his son?

"Yes," I said.

"Are you as good-looking as he is?"

Yeah, compared to me, sweetheart, he's the Elephant Man. Get a clue—

"I had no idea he had a son!" she said.

That one went through me. Okay, so maybe it wasn't cool to tell your scent consultant you had offspring—

I hung up. I'm not sure I even said good-bye.

It was a sure thing I wasn't calling back until I knew Meg was going to be there. Dinnertime on Monday night seemed like a safe bet. When Meg answered, I didn't refer to our hot-tub debate, nor did I ask her about the woman. I just plunged right in about Phong.

I knew when she wailed, "Oh, Joshua," she couldn't do it.

"I wish you'd called me sooner, darn it. I'm going out of town this weekend—and I can't back out."

"The good doctor?"

"Yes—and I've been putting him off about the marriage thing for so long, I can't afford to set him off." She gave an exasperated grunt. "You didn't even tell me this was the big weekend. Josh, I've got to be there for you, especially because—" She stopped.

"Especially because what?" I said suspiciously.

"Nothing. But look, maybe I can change my plans—"

"Forget it," I said. "It's no big deal."

"You little fabricator! This is important. It's everything you want—and right or wrong, that's a big deal. I'm calling Carl. I want to be there. The heck with Monterey."

"I said forget it. If you come I'll rip out your nose hairs."

That was also a lie. Except for my father and Phong there was nobody else I wanted there more. Somehow, through this whole weird spring, she and I had gotten closer. Even if she did give me a verbal rap in the mouth once in a while, it wasn't going to seem right not to have her in the bleachers beside Dad, screaming her head off right along with him after every one of my dives, no matter how bad it might be.

"Hey, Baby B.," she said into my silence, "did you ever read that Bible reference I gave you?"

"Yeah," I said. "It's, uh, pretty good."

I was lying again, and she knew it. I had read it—once, but I hadn't gotten the point. I mean, how many times had I heard the story of the three wise men for Pete's sake? What it had to do with me now I didn't have a clue—and Christmas was a good seven months away.

"We'll discuss it next time I see you," she said pointedly.

"And, Josh, no matter what's ahead, remember there are people who love you."

Yeah, yeah, okay, so how am I going to get Phong to the meet?

Mouse and Dad and I were probably going early. It was all the way over in San Jose, so even ten weeks' worth of allowance—even *my* allowance—wasn't going to pay for a cab.

It wasn't until Tuesday that I resigned myself to the fact that I was going to have to ask my mother. Of course . . . she was going. She'd do it, yeah, she would. But I hated asking her. The psychoanalysis would probably go on for days.

She was soaking in the hot tub with her eyes closed that night when I got home from the gym. I actually looked around to see if Denise was there, winding up to shriek from behind a potted plant.

Mom opened her eyes. "What are you looking for?"

"Denise," I said. She dimpled in a wry kind of way.

"I guess you would expect her, wouldn't you? She's become a permanent fixture around here lately. It's because—"

"Yeah, I know," I said impatiently. "Things are 'weird' at her house." I put a hand into the hot tub with a poke that probably matched the expression on my face.

"Well," Mom said, "you know how it is when parents are going through a divorce."

My chin came up. "Denise's parents? The paragons of the church?"

Mom closed her eyes again. "It happens to the best of us."

Her voice was sad, and for the first time I noticed her eyes were too, before she closed them. It hadn't really occurred to me that it was odd for her to be out here soaking in the tub at this hour. Usually she was misting the ferns, concocting tomorrow night's crab quiche—or counseling Denise.

"She's starting to handle it better now," she said. "She's was having a rough go for a while, but I think she'll be all right."

"I didn't even know about it."

She didn't say anything.

Why would you know? When did you ever show the slightest interest in Denise unless it was for your own benefit?

I wasn't sure where that thought had come from. I batted it aside.

"Are you coming to the meet Saturday?" I said.

"I plan to—but only if you want me to. I know how much this means to you."

How could you know? I never told you.

I knocked that thought out of the way too.

"Could you do me a favor then?"

She dimpled again with her eyes closed. "I'm your mother, Joshua. I don't do favors—I do motherly duties."

"This is a favor."

She waved a limp hand at me. "I'm sorry. What is it, honey?"

"There's somebody else I want to go to the meet too. He needs a ride, so I thought—"

A guffaw echoed out of the bubbles. "The Assorted Buddies are *not* getting into my car unless they are hosed down and sheep-dipped—"

"It isn't them," I said.

She opened one eye.

"It's—it's the little Vietnamese kid we were telling you about."

"The one whose daddy is still in-country?"

Here come the questions.

"Yes," I said.

She was quiet for a minute, and something queasy happened in my stomach. It had never really occurred to me that she might say no. She never said no. Man, now what was I going to do? There was always Brian—

"Of course, honey," she said finally.

I exhaled in a rush.

"I have the address already. I'll just put it out there on the counter to remind me."

She closed her eyes again, and the only sounds in the

greenhouse came from the bubbles. She seemed to sink away somewhere, into the misty tendrils of steam.

She wants you to leave her alone, Dingbat. Get out of here.

◆　　◆　　◆

I'd been so hung up on finding a way to get Phong to the meet, it didn't strike me until Wednesday that it was actually happening in just three days.

Everything I'd seen in my head for the past year.

Everything I'd worked my tail off for for the last four months.

Everything that was going to take me over the hump into being the man God intended me to be—the man my dad was going to stand up and bust his Op shirt wide open over.

It was everything, and I wasn't handling it well.

"You got that foot going at about light speed," Brian said in his dial-tone voice when we were driving into Oakland that afternoon. I glanced at my foot. Crossed over my other leg, it was jittering like a leaf about to be blown off a tree.

"Yeah," I said, and held it still with my hand as we pulled up at the newsstand.

My case of nerves didn't escape Mouse either. At least he had the decency to wait until Phong was out of earshot before he said, "I've seen you go through a lot of different emotions since we've been working together."

Totally your imagination, Bucko. I never show my emotions.

"But this is the first time I've seen anxiety."

Anxiety? Okay, anxiety.

He reached for one of my hands, and I watched as he uncurled my fist.

"It's natural to be nervous. This is your chance to get an 'in' into the Olympic community. An outsider doesn't make the Olympic team."

"You told me that," I said. But I didn't grit my teeth. *Face it, Dingbat. He's right.*

"But there's a difference between nerves you can use to put you on your best form and anxiety that freezes you up." He closed his hand around my shivering right arm. "You have to be warm to dive."

I nodded.

"Now we'll talk it all through again on Saturday, about finding your place on the board before each dive to get quiet—"

"—confident, relaxed," I finished for him.

"But right now I'm talking about your head overall. This thing is important to you, but if you don't keep it in perspective, that could ruin you."

I felt my arm stiffen under his grip, and now my teeth were gritting. If he noticed, he didn't let on.

"Is Phong coming to the meet?" he said.

"Uh—yeah," I said. "Why?"

"Nothing. That's just . . . it's good."

"Why?" I said again.

Mouse ran his hand back over his wet hair, a motion I'd seen him do at least two thousand times in the last few months. It meant he was about to say something that was going to make me either clench my teeth—or go home and sweat.

Finally he said, "It's balance. You have to give any sport you're committed to 100 percent—but you have to have another 100 percent of something to balance it with, so it doesn't consume you."

He laughed. "Or it could just be the power of love or some Oriental mystical baloney!"

I stifled a snort and went toward the locker room.

"Take the day off tomorrow," he called after me. "We'll just do a run-through of your dives Friday, but tomorrow I want you to stay loose. Take care of those nerves."

Nerves, I thought as Phong and I walked to the apartment that night, *are not going to get to me.* Warm as a hand in a glove, that would be me. *No ice water anxiety pumping through these veins.*

That must have been precisely why I let Phong get into the apartment without my asking him if he wanted to go to the meet. Yeah, nerves of steel and a mind like a steel trap.

◆　　◆　　◆

"I won't be needing your chauffering this afternoon, guy," I said to Brian in English class Thursday.

"You ain't—aren't—out of the woods with those punks yet," he said.

I almost laughed. The whole thing with Acapulco Al and Big Black Foot and No Teeth seemed almost like a dream to me now. I wasn't even sure I should've let myself make such a big deal out of it. Mouse was right. I probably did have a nerve problem.

"It isn't funny, man," Brian said.

"I know. Look, I don't have to go to the pool today. You can still take me tomorrow if you want."

He grunted and nodded toward my foot, which was vibrating like hummingbird wings. "You're still freaking out."

"I am not!"

"Gentlemen," Mrs. Sanderson said drily, "do you think we could get to work on our book reports, or do we need to return to *The Scarlet Letter*?"

Brian ducked his head into his book like he'd been shot. I took a look at the cover: *Vietnam: A History*. The thing looked like it must be eight hundred pages long. I'd had Brian figured for the type that would use a book like that for a doorstop. I wondered vaguely if the "guy who'd lived in his house before" had left the book behind too.

"Mr. Daniels," Mrs. Sanderson said.

I grinned sheepishly up at the bifocals and retreated into *Tales of Gold*. At this point I could concentrate on reading about as well as I could knit.

But the name Sammy Lee reached up and pulled me in like a hook. Where had I heard it before?

Sammy Lee, the book said, was the first American-born Oriental to win a gold medal for the United States in diving. He took it at age twenty-eight, after he'd already earned his M.D. and was a U.S. Army surgeon.

That must have been the Korean diver Mouse was talking about. "You'll be another Sammy Lee," Mouse had told Phong. I grunted. Not the way the swimming lessons were going. After weeks, Phong was still clinging to my neck like a baby monkey.

I must have grunted right out loud because I could feel Mrs. Sanderson looking at me. I dug further into the book.

In school, Sammy had been student body president and co-valedictorian, but his friends' parents wouldn't let him in the house because he was Korean. His father encouraged him through education to show what kind of person he was, so he picked a dual purpose: to be an Olympic diver and a doctor.

He'd gotten his first big break in diving when he was eighteen. He'd been training on his own because he wasn't allowed in private clubs. He'd swim at Pasadena's Brookside Park on Mondays because that was International Day. Afterwards, the custodians drained the pool so white kids could use it the next day without having to swim in the same water foreigners had been using.

I sat straight up in my desk. Something was pushing right up my backbone.

Coach Jim Ryan saw Sammy at Brookside one Monday, the book went on, and watched him dive. "See that little Chink over there?" he said to somebody. "I'm going to make him the world's greatest diver or I'm going to kill him."

I identified the surge up my spine. It was anger.

◆　　◆　　◆

As it turned out, I didn't have any trouble passing the time, or the nerves, that night. After I stretched out at the gym, I came home and sank into the hot tub with *Tales of Gold*. My mother brought out a protein shake, but except for that, I did nothing but read until I was shriveled.

The fuel for Sammy Lee's competitive drive, the author wrote, was anger.

I believed that. I was about to blow a gasket, and it wasn't even happening to me.

There was so much prejudice, Sammy practically had to be superhuman in order to win. It seemed he was. They called him the Yellow Peril because he did dives never done before in competition. *Atta boy, Sammy*, I thought. Man, times had changed. Now it seemed like if you were in any kind of minority, they gave you the world.

He always prayed, the book said. Frequently it was, "Dear Lord, let me dive to my potential. Just let me do my best, but please let it be the gold medal."

I smirked. Nothing like outlining everything for the Lord.

But as I read on, I saw it must have worked. He won in London in 1948 when he was twenty-eight. He won again in Helsinki in 1952, and he was thirty-two. And I was worried about being too old to start at sixteen! I felt strangely relieved.

Of course, that only lasted until the next paragraph, which said Sammy Lee had started coaching Greg Louganis when he was ten. As much as I knew about Louganis, I'd never heard that. "He was trying to do dives he wasn't strong enough for yet," Lee was quoted as saying, "but you could already see his greatness in the way he sprang off the board, his grace, how he could line up with the water. He had indescribable talent. He was poetry in motion."

I tossed the book out onto the deck and closed my eyes. Man, it was confusing. One minute I felt like I was way ahead of the game, with Christ pulling for me all the way while I gave up just about everything to work with a private coach and work out in the gym and spend practically every waking moment either diving or thinking about diving or wishing I were diving.

And then I had moments when I thought about guys like Louganis and Desjardins and now Sammy Lee who just seemed to have it. Sure, they worked hard, but nobody ever doubted they'd make it. None of their friends ever looked at them like they were nuts because they worked out at the gym Friday nights instead of going to drinking parties. None of their families ever warned them about being consumed by their sport. It was just assumed they would be. They were born for it.

I churned restlessly in the water. I'd thought that about myself too. I'd really thought that was God's plan, the way He came to me when I was doing my feet-on-the-wallpaper thing and seemed to reassure me that, yeah, this was the right direction for me. Mouse had even finally said I was a diver.

But there were the ifs and the buts and my own doubts. Man—

And then He was there, and I wasn't even lying on my water bed. I hadn't even asked for Him. He was just there, dusting off His sandals and holding out a hand.

He didn't say, "Of course this is where I want you. You just have the last-minute jitters. Chill out." He didn't say anything. He was just there. For the moment, I guess that had to be enough. Feeling a lot like I was going to cry, I went up to bed.

◆　◆　◆

By Friday afternoon my head was a little more together. Yeah, I still had a ton to do. I had to invite Phong, get his mother's or at least Tram's permission, and make sure all the arrangements for Mom picking him up were made. It sure would be a lot easier if Meg were going.

But I was going to do this. I wasn't going to let God—or myself—down, no matter what. And I wasn't going to let Phong down. I could almost hear him saying, "We will do it." *I was going to measure up.*

I slammed my locker shut and strode off to meet Brian in the parking lot. A tall form in the doorway squealed my Nikes to a halt.

"Dad?" I said.

"*Son*?" he said, mimicking what I knew must be the question mark contorting my face.

He looked different somehow. More grey in his hair. More paunch around his waist. Less bigness to him all over. He was my own father, but I had to stare at him like he was a suspect in a lineup to be sure it was him.

That's because you haven't seen him in four months, Dingbat. Four months.

He was close enough now that there was no doubt. The same narrow blue eyes. The same sharp features. The same right-on-cue smile. He stuck out his hand to me, and I shook it.

"What's this?" he said. He massaged his palm with exaggerated care. "You've turned into a brute."

I laughed—loud. My dad was here. Yes. "Must be the workouts at the gym," I said.

He grabbed me by the back of the neck and squeezed playfully as we walked toward the front parking lot. "What on earth is the matter with Tulley? I'm paying that—" He glanced around him at the squeaky-clean Christian kids. I nodded that I knew what he meant. "I'm paying him to make you a diver, not a—wrestler."

I mentally filled in the blank there too.

"Well, let's see what this high-class coach is doing for you," he said. He nodded toward the silver Mazda RX-7 parked in the bus loading zone—the one Bus #117 was honking at. I hadn't seen that one before.

"Relax," he barked in the direction of the bus driver. To me he said, "You haven't ridden in this new buggy, have you?"

"No," I said. "But—"

"Get in before this guy in the bus has a hemorrhage. I'll swing you around to the pool."

Call me a slow learner, but it didn't occur to me until then what was going to happen. It was so good to have him *there* with *me* that Brian and Phong had been shoved to some fold in my brain. But, hey, Dad was cool. I could fix it.

"Look, Dad," I said. I was saying it to the back of his suit now because he was already halfway to the Mazda. "Can I meet you there?"

He didn't stop but turned around and shot me a look that was grounds for having me committed. He all but said, "Are you crazy?"

The bus driver leaned on the horn.

"What do you mean, can you meet me there?" Dad shouted. "I came down here to get you because I can't—" There was a final, adamant blast from the bus. "I have to move this thing. Get in."

I did. My mouth felt like it had just been swabbed out with a Q-tip.

Dad swore a string of epithets as he wheeled the Mazda out of the loading zone and started to careen out of the parking lot and onto the street.

Man, say something. You can't leave Brian sitting there in the Chevy. You can't leave Phong—

"I have a ride waiting for me, Dad," I said. The words simpered out like a piece of limp spaghetti.

"Where?"

"Back in the student parking lot."

"Oh." He smiled mechanically at me. "You wanted to meet me *there*."

"Yeah," I lied.

"Okay." He turned the car on two wheels and slid it into the back parking lot. If he'd been one of us kids he'd at that very moment been having his license ripped out of his wallet by the vice principal. "Where's your buddy?" he said. "You can jump out and tell him—or her—your old man's taking you."

"Him," I said. "Right there, in the blue '57."

"Somebody's parents are in a high bracket," he said. I was out of the car before it stopped completely—but then, my father never seemed to stop completely. Brian was leaning back in his seat like a big beige being. But when he saw me get out of the Mazda, he leaned forward and turned the key.

"I won't need a ride today," I shouted over the motor. "My dad's taking me."

Brian looked at the man in the Mazda like he didn't believe me. Did he think everybody in the world was out to kidnap me and give me drugs?

"What about the kid?" he said.

Yeah, what about the kid?

"We'll pick him up," I said. "My dad's cool."

"You sure?"

"Am I sure my dad's cool? I oughta know!"

Yeah, I oughta.

Brian still looked doubtful as I gave the side of the Chevy a rap with the palm of my hand and climbed back in beside my dad. I had the feeling he was going to follow us, but I didn't look back. The words to come out of my father's mouth would block everything else out.

DAD glanced at his watch. The sun glinted off the gold and burned the word Rolex into my forehead.

"I'm glad I could get out of the office for this," he said. "Don't want to miss seeing my man dive." He reached over and squeezed my leg roughly.

"You didn't have to do this, Dad. I mean, I'm glad you did," I added quickly, "but I'm not really working today. We're just running through the dives. You'll see the real thing tomorrow."

"You better show me the real stuff today, my man. I'm not going to make it tomorrow."

Everything in me that had been on fast forward for the past three days flipped to a stop with a jerk that almost snapped it all in two.

Trucks were still whipping by on the freeway. Cabs were still blasting their horns. People were all moving forward to somewhere. But inside the silver Mazda RX-7, the world had slammed to a stop.

"Tomorrow's Saturday," I managed to say. "That's the Regionals."

"And while you're jumping into a nice, cool pool I'll be wiping off the sweat in New York."

"New York City?" I said stupidly.

"I'm not talking about Schenectady."

He looked at me, but I'm sure he saw none of what I was feeling. My face felt like it had been given several shots of Novocain in strategic places. "Hey, this is just a preliminary meet, right?" he said.

"Yeah, but it's the first meet—" My tongue was going numb. "—you know, the first step to making the Olympic team."

There. I'd told him. I waited for realization to dawn across his features.

It didn't.

"It's, like, crucial," I said.

"Piece of quiche! You knock 'em dead there, then you go on to what? Nationals?"

Mechanically I ticked off the process.

"Internationals in Mexico City? You and I'll be there, my man." He slapped the back of his hand against my arm. "Better work on your tan before then though."

I stared.

We'd reached the freeway exit into town by then, and he downshifted the Mazda to take the ramp. As it growled itself down, I could feel myself sinking with it. If he even heard me confide that it was the Olympics I was going for, it was obvious he had no idea what that meant. Or just didn't care.

He glanced at the Rolex again. "You forget what the traffic's like down here when you don't drive in it for a while." He tapped the horn as a Daihatsu darted out of an alley. "Lousy Chinks are worse here than they are in the City." He jammed the gearshift lever impatiently and rolled down his window. "So how long you usually practice with Tulley?"

"Couple hours," I said. My voice was barely there. It seemed to have seeped into the sponge of disappointment that was sopping up everything inside me.

"Give me your best shot off the top then," he said. "I have to catch a plane out of here in an hour and a half—and I want to see if this so-and-so coach is worth the cash I'm laying out for him." He punched his feet at the brake and clutch and shoved the gearshift lever cruelly in its boot. "Go back to China, ya foreigner!" he shouted out the window. The saliva splattered as he yelled, and two bubbles of it stayed on the tip of his nose. I focused on them. I couldn't move my eyes off of them.

"You look great, my man," Dad said to me. "Knocking the women dead yet?"

I watched the bubbles and shook my head. He perused the street and chatted on.

"So how's your mother? She isn't turning you into a vegetarian, is she?"

I didn't even move this time. Neither did the bubbles of spit.

"Now how the—what street do we turn on to get to this place? Do you have any idea or are you on automatic pilot? Come on, Josh! I can't be making sudden turns in this mess."

What street—

Suddenly I pushed the play button, and my mind jolted back on. I snapped my eyes off the bubbles and pointed with my chin. "Turn here," I said. "We have to stop at the newsstand on—"

"What for?" He darted his eyes at me. "Something you have to have for practice?"

Yes. Definitely.

"Not exactly. I just have to pick up this—"

"Listen," he said. His voice sliced my words off. "If you want me to see any of your diving, we haven't got time for detours. I have to catch a plane in an hour and twenty minutes."

He can't make it tomorrow? He barely has time today. I slowed again to thirty-three and a third.

"Okay," I said woodenly. "Just turn here and the pool's around the corner."

The Mazda took the turn with a high whine. I craned my neck until I must've looked like the victim of demon possession, but I could only catch a glimpse of the newsstand. Phong wasn't waiting outside. He knew the '57's purr, and he always timed coming out to the curb with the last roll of Brian's whitewalls. At the moment he was probably tormenting the manager by pawing through his copies of *Rolling Stone*, thinking any minute I was going to show up—

"So where do I park?" Dad said.

◆   ◆   ◆

When I came out of the locker room into the lobby, I could see Dad and Mouse deep in conversation poolside.

"Who's the dude?" Beth said from the counter.

I glanced around. "My father," I said sadly.

"Funny. You don't look like him."

I grunted from the front door where I was peering out into the street.

"You didn't get your dimples from him. Hey, Josh . . ."

"*What*?" I said. Phong was nowhere in sight, and I was contemplating dashing around the corner to the newsstand to grab him before Mouse and my father knew I was even out of the locker room.

"You're acting like a fugitive. What's your problem?"

I slid to the counter and slapped my palms on it. "Have you seen Phong?"

"No. Why isn't he with you?"

That was it. I turned to squeal out of there—but my father caught me from the other side of the glass. He waved me out like he was summoning the *maitre d'*.

"Aw, *man*—"

"What?" Beth said. "You going to run out in the street like that?"

I glanced down at my largely naked body.

She shook her head. "This meet tomorrow is getting to you. Get a grip, guy."

But I grabbed both her wrists in my hands. "Do you have to stay right here at this counter all the time? I mean, can you leave?"

"What—do you want me to run out for pizza? Your old man doesn't look like the pepperoni and mushroom type."

"Would you shut—just listen, okay?" I could hear my own voice quavering. She heard it too.

"What is *wrong* with you?" she said. Her face got serious.

"Look, Phong could be—"

The glass door pushed open, and Mouse put his head in. "Could you hurry it up, Josh? Your father's getting a little impatient."

His eyes held mine for a second before he went back out to the pool. My insides groped to keep it together.

"You know that little newsstand, the one around the corner?"

Beth nodded solemnly.

"Would you just go over there and get Phong? He's inside—probably ripping off comic books or something."

"I'm gone," she said.

I took a split second to watch her come out from behind the counter.

"Get out to the pool," she said. "I'll get the kid."

I went for the door. *It's gonna be okay. She's gonna get Phong. He's probably still there reading* Mad *magazine. The gang doesn't know that's where we meet. They've got better things to do. Phong probably doesn't even know I'm late yet—*

Dad was standing with his hands on his hips, eyeing me narrowly.

"Just give me a second to warm up," I said.

"I haven't got time to watch you do laps, my man."

"He can't dive when he's tight and cold," Mouse said quietly. "It's dangerous."

Dad held up both hands in surrender, but still I cut my warm-up short and went for the springboard.

Take your time at the end of the board. Find a quiet place. Relax. Concentrate. He can't make it tomorrow when you jump into a nice cool pool.

Forward two and a half. Way over. I had to save. When I came up, my father was clapping.

"Nice-looking dive!" he said. "Have you improved!"

"From what?" Mouse said.

The slightly acid tone made me glance at him.

I took the board again.

Quiet. Relax. Concentrate. Three steps. Triple. Here we go. Smooth, like a work of art. Phong would've read everything in the place by now. But he'd see Beth coming. He'd know it couldn't have been helped.

Triple. A sloppy splash like a trout. Dad was reaching his arm out to me from the side, being careful not to get water on his Italian suit.

"That's fantastic!" he said. He slapped me on the bare back and then pulled out his handkerchief to dry his hand. "Anybody else his age around here diving like that?" he said to Mouse.

I looked at Mouse, who just flinched his eyebrows. "Show him what you can do on the platform," he said.

"Yeah. Now that's the biggie, right?"

"You could say that," Mouse said. "Go ahead, Josh."

I climbed the ladder for at least ten years. *Where is Beth with Phong?* I'd never gone off the platform without Phong there, much less without knowing where he even was.

When I got to the top I looked down. Number one no-no. Judges would start subtracting points before I even started my approach if I acted like this tomorrow.

No, Dingbat. Tomorrow Phong will be there. Even if your father isn't.

Business is business. That's what I told myself when I got to the back of the platform—when I should have been flipping through the dive in my head. *How do you think Dad affords this coach and this private pool time and the health club membership and the allowance if he doesn't go wherever business calls? So you show him your stuff now. While you've got the chance.*

Get rid of that fear. It makes you cold. The platform isn't going to move. Only you are. Think it through. Think it through before you go. He's got to catch a plane in less than an hour. Think it through. He doesn't have time for detours. Think it through.

I didn't. With everything on fast forward again I just made

the dive. And as soon as I left the platform I knew it was wrong. I came out of the water a trembling glob of jelly.

"Whoa." My father looked at me and nodded slowly. "Now I have to admit, that scared me. That's a thrill, all right, watching you get so close you almost hit the thing there."

He gave an impressed grunt. I didn't even look at Mouse. I just held on to my shoulders and shivered.

"Well, look, guys, I don't need to see any more. You dive like that tomorrow, my man, and you'll kick tail. Right, Coach?"

If Mouse answered, I didn't hear him. My father massaged and slapped me for about ten seconds, sealed it with a punch, and was off. His gold Rolex glinted against the glass door as it closed behind him.

I felt a towel come across my shoulders, and I clung to it gratefully.

"You okay?" Mouse said.

I shook my head miserably.

"Anything physically wrong?"

I shook my head again. "I was lousy today."

"Yeah. But your dad thought you were the greatest thing since Sammy Lee."

That little Chink? Isn't that what he'd have said?

I shuddered. For the first time in my life I was embarrassed by my father. "He didn't know what he was looking at," I said, sinking onto a bench with the towel.

"He's just like a million other uninformed spectators," Mouse said. But he didn't sound convincing, and I wasn't convinced. *His son's into this. He shouldn't be uninformed about the dives his son is doing.*

I looked suddenly at Mouse. "If you had a kid who did everything but sleep on a diving board, would you make it your business to know something about it?"

For the first time since I'd known him, Mouse looked uncomfortable. He ran his hand back across his hair three times before he answered.

"I would," he said finally.

"He runs this gargantuan corporation," I said. "I mean, he's busy. I could see why he didn't get to my high-school meets, but this one—"

Mouse cleared his throat but didn't say anything.

"I don't know," I said. I tossed the towel aside and started to get up. "I've got work to do."

"Whoa." Mouse put a hand on my arm.

"If I dive like that tomorrow I'll get laughed right out of the pool!"

"You're not going to dive like that tomorrow. This means too much to you. You were just nervous because your dad was here."

I snorted. "You don't think I'm going to be nervous tomorrow?"

"You wouldn't be human if you weren't. But you'll have other reasons to get it under control."

Phong. I looked anxiously toward the lobby, but I didn't see Beth yet. What—did she take the kid out for ice cream?

"I really don't want you to dive any more today," Mouse said. "What I want you to do is go home, take a hot shower, and go to bed. Get up early tomorrow, go through all your dives in your head, and concentrate on the psych. Big psych, Josh. That's all you need now."

I listened, and I nodded. It occurred to me even then that I was actually listening. *Of course you're listening. He cares.*

"Okay, Coach," I said. It sounded a little sappy, but I meant it.

"Atta boy. I'm picking you up in the morning."

I could feel my eyebrows shooting up. "You are?"

"Your father's orders."

"You don't have to—"

"It's in my contract. Be ready to roll at 7 A. M."

"Okay."

His hand closed around my arm for an instant, then he got up. I followed him to the door.

"I'm surprised old Phong wasn't here for your last practice," he said.

I swallowed a glob of guilt.

"The way your dad was ranting about the Oriental drivers, don't guess he'd be too crazy about your sudden interest in the Asian population, huh?"

That wasn't it, exactly. But I couldn't tell him how it exactly *was*. Suddenly I didn't ever want to put disappointment into Mouse Tulley's face.

I got changed without showering or rinsing the chlorine out of my hair. It was still standing up in spikes when I raced back out to the lobby. Beth was just coming in the front door, red-faced and Phong-less.

"That little monkey," she said. "I couldn't find him anywhere."

"Aw, no—"

"Now don't hyperventilate, Daniels." She pulled off the sweatshirt she was wearing over her bathing suit and fanned her face with it. "He had definitely been there at one time. The guy at the newsstand was pretty positive about that."

"I bet he was." I drummed my palms on the counter. "So, what—?"

"So I chased around about four blocks asking people if they'd seen him."

"*Had* anybody? Seen him?"

"*Everybody* had seen him." She slipped back behind the counter and dug around under it, producing her bag. "I followed all the leads, Sarge, but when somebody told me they saw him going just about all the way down to the freeway—you know, where they're doing all that construction, I said forget it. It's almost quitting time for me, and if he can go that far, he can find his way to the pool. What is wrong with you?"

I could feel my face getting pasty.

"Look, he obviously gets around," she said. "I really don't think you need to worry about him too much."

I grabbed my bag off the counter and tore for the door.

"Hey! Daniels!"

"Gotta catch a bus," I said.

"I just wanted to say, good luck tomorrow."

I stopped for a second. Her eyes softened for about that long. "I think you've got what it takes," she said.

"Thanks," I said.

Her eyes glittered again. "Now get out of here. And don't ever come back without that kid again. I lost five pounds, and I'll probably miss *my* bus!"

She may have still been calling stuff after me when I was at the end of the block, which was only a matter of seconds. *Just about all the way down to the freeway.*

I heard tires squeal as I jay-ran across the street and headed up the alley to the newsstand. I didn't even bother to stop. I could see Phong wasn't there, so I took the street at a slant and bulldozed my way down the sidewalk. I had to grab a stroller to keep from mowing down a woman with a baby, but I didn't even say excuse me. I just dug in my heels and churned. If he was at the fence, I had to get there before—

I choked off the thought as I rounded the corner. He wasn't there. Nobody was there. The yard was grey and silent, and the shadows of the chain-link loomed like huge cages on the walls beyond.

I stopped running, but I moved steadily toward the fence, looking for Phong, looking for *them*. It was all so still, it looked unnatural. I'd never been there when there wasn't at least him, at least Phong—blinking over the top at me with those eyes that tried to be tough and macho and still bordered on little-boy fear.

Man, he is just a little boy. He thinks you're a hero. He thinks you're the dad he doesn't get to have. He thinks as long as you're around, there's nothing to be afraid of.

It surged up my backbone again—that anger. I hurled my L.A. Gear bag over the fence and followed it, landing with a dusty thud beside it. But when I reached down for the handle, a shadow fell across it.

The shadow's owner moved closer, but I didn't look up. I didn't have to.

"Drop something, honkie?" he said.

M Y hand froze in mid-reach. A size thirteen foot obliterated the bag.

"This yours, honkie?" he said.

*Don't lose it now, Josh. Just put your mouth in gear. That's
always done it before. Just the right insult—*

"Gee, thanks, pal. It is." I went for the bag again. Big Black
Foot slid it across the vacant lot with the sole of his Adidas in a
smash of dust. I swallowed and stood up slowly.

"Like I said, pal, thanks." I moved toward the bag, which
now lay crumpled at the base of the fence. Big Foot eased non-
chalantly into my path, but the face I looked up into was far
from casual.

"I tol' you to find another route, man," he said.

"I did," I said. "To this side of the fence. And, hey, thanks
for the advice. There's a lot less traffic over here. Now if you
don't mind—" I didn't push him. I hadn't gone *that* far off the
deep end. I just stepped carefully to one side to go around him.
But his arm came out like a railroad signal.

"I do mind, honkie," he said.

*All right, man, you can do it. Think of something. Or bet-
ter yet, just get the heck out of here.*

"Okay, I can take a hint," I said. "I'll get my gear and—
hey—back over the fence, okay?"

I glanced behind him at the chain-link, on the off chance

that he might let me go. No Teeth was just slithering over it and into the yard. The few tusks he did have gleamed gold in the fading light as he sneered at me.

"Too late, honkie," he said. He was carrying something. A chain. He snapped it out, and it wrapped with an ugly clang around the top, gaping pole of the fence. The pole suddenly bore a strong resemblance to my throat.

"Whatchoo doin' here?" he said.

I tried not to put my hand up to my neck. "I'm looking for the kid," I said. "You seen him?"

"The Chink?"

I gritted my teeth. "Yeah. The little Vietnamese guy. You know where he is?"

No Teeth spit like I'd just asked for green slime on toast. "Is that what he is?"

"Look, what do you care? Do you have him?"

As if on cue, both of them took a menacing step toward me. The silhouettes of their hulks in the gathering darkness were suddenly twice human size, and I was getting smaller by the second. *Do something, man, before you disappear altogether.*

"How much it worth to you, honkie?" Big Foot said.

My heart slammed wildly. "No. The question is, how much is it worth to you?"

"Whatchoo talkin' 'bout?"

"I've got bucks. Whatever you want for me to take the kid off your hands, you got it."

"How many bucks?" No Teeth wanted to know.

"Enough to keep you in dental work," I said.

His nostrils widened, if that's possible. Big Foot backed toward my bag.

"Of course I don't have it all on me," I said. I started to go with him, but No Teeth put his fingers squarely into my chest. I stood still.

"My old man's got bucks he hasn't even used yet," I called to Big Foot, who had by now unzipped the Gear bag and was tossing a wet Speedo over his shoulder. "Name your price and give me the kid and I'll be out of here."

"You gonna be out of here anyway."

The voice came from behind me, hard and mean and very definitely Mexican. When I turned around, Acapulco Al's black eyes were narrowed at me like two angry, pointed masses of coal.

Man, you can outtalk the other two—but not this one. You showed him up in front of his playmates. He doesn't want to see your hind parts disappearing around the corner. He wants to see them smeared all over the ground.

"You don't belong here, *gringo*," he said. His mouth was like a piece of jagged glass as he spoke.

"Okay, so finally I got the message," I said. My voice, to my own surprise, sounded deadly calm. "You don't want me around—I'm going. I'll pay you—you give me the kid."

"Ain't enough money in here to pay for no kid if we had one," Big Foot said. He leaned over to pick up my now-limp Gear bag. As he did, something fell from his pocket and plumped softly to the ground. Four pairs of eyes went to it. No Teeth snatched it up, but not before I saw that it was a plastic bag, cinched tight around a lump of powdery white.

I whirled back to face Al. He was so angry he didn't even spit.

"You too late," he said. "You didn't listen, and now you get hurt."

I don't know how the knife got from wherever he'd been keeping it and into the hand that snapped to position over his head. The sight of it stabbed the breath out of me, and I froze.

But only for a second. Al's big weakness was setting himself up with the big flourish. Still staring at the knife, I hurled my right shoulder at him. When he staggered, I took off.

In front of me was a huge wall, camouflaged with graffiti and solid as far as the eye could see.

The dust kicked off my Nikes. Behind me was the machine-gun fire of Acapulco Al's swearing and the pounding of size thirteen Adidas.

They get in here from somewhere. Phong didn't climb over the fence. There's got to be a—

My eyes strained through the dusk as I pounded headlong toward the wall. If I didn't find an opening—

Movement to the left caught my eye. Something was swinging toward me. A gate.

Somebody was pushing it open.

Go for it. Dig, man, or you're taco stuffing. Get there before he closes the gate.

Whoever it was, coming for his drugs, he didn't have a chance. Bless Mouse Tulley. Bless those workouts at the gym. Bless those thousands of laps. I got to the gate with the big feet fading behind me—slid past the form in the opening—and tore blindly to the right. I was outside the lot. And the thing that kept me going was that they didn't have Phong. If they had, they'd have taken money for him, I know.

The only thing I didn't do was close the gate behind me. I could've slowed Big Foot down considerably if I had. But I was new at this business of running from drug-dealing street gangs armed with knives. Stupidly I ran hard, in a straight line, right down the sidewalk under the streetlight. Before I got to the corner I could hear him gaining on me.

God, help me. Please. Help me be fast. Help me.

The prayers came as blindly, as unthinkingly as the way I was running. But in the midst of them came a thought, like a pinpoint of light in the murky fear.

Get out of sight. Make him guess. Make him hesitate.

By some miracle, when I turned the first corner I was only a block from the pool. Phong had taken me on at least six different obstacle courses from that very corner. There were alleys. There were fences. There were shops with doors at both ends.

I took them *all*. Down the alley that always smelled like dead fish. Up a side street barricaded from traffic and dotted with open manholes. Over a low fence that bordered construction.

It wasn't until I got to the street that led to Phong's favorite fruit felony market that I dared look behind me. The street, just after rush hour, was almost quiet. There was no black pursuer shoving through the few people scattered on the sidewalks. I'd have seen him towering over their calm, golden forms. I'd never thought I'd be so glad to be among quiet, unaggressive Asians.

He wasn't there anymore. I slowed to a walk and tried to pull it together. My heart and my breath were both pounding in my ears: *Okay, okay. You're okay.*

Now get to Phong's, fool. He's gone home. He probably thinks you've deserted him completely by now.

I turned and went for the corner. A block ahead, a black mass emerged from a doorway.

Where he came from, I still don't know. I only know I bolted around the corner, burning my soles on the pavement. This time I did not look back.

He couldn't have seen you. He just stepped out. You're cool. Just keep running.

But he *had* seen me. He came around the corner and stopped, head jerking like a mad dog in every direction. I didn't wait for him to spot me again. I dove through the door of the market and shut it behind me with a jarring tangle of bells.

I'd never been inside before. I'd always sent Phong in alone. The place was dingy and smelled like nearly-rotten fruit and too-old cheese. An ancient dude who appeared to be molded to a stool behind the counter gave an annoyed stir and tried to focus his eyes in the direction of my entrance. It must have been "the old 'tard." No wonder Phong got away with what he did in there. The man was more like a lumpy relic than a person. Irritated eyes glared at me from behind glasses the thickness of Coke bottle bottoms, distorted to E.T. proportions.

"Hi," I said. It came out in a wheeze. *Good move, Josh. That doesn't sound like somebody coming in to pick up the Friday night groceries.*

I didn't say anything else but moved quickly to the back of the store. From the cereal-cracker-cookie aisle I could see out the front window. A large black head shone under the streetlight. I had to buy some time.

"What are you doing?" the old man shouted at me. His voice was loud and dull, as if he were deaf as well as half-blind. I moved to the canned goods aisle, still gasping.

"Looking, sir," I said in a voice deliberately too low for him to make out.

"Hah?" he said.

"Just browsing." It was amazing to me that I could speak at all. I was still breathing like a freight train, and my heart was slamming so hard it hurt. I stole another look out the window. No Big Foot.

"If you're not buying, get out! I'm sick of you kids stealing me blind."

Phong would've gotten a kick out of that. I didn't. I snatched up two cans of creamed corn and stuffed them under my arm. "Just need a few things," I said, coming into his view. He scowled fiercely.

He's gonna do worse than scowl when he finds out you don't have any money.

I stopped short. All my cash was in my Gear bag—or at least it had been at one time. Now my brain was starting to throb along with everything else. I slid back into the canned goods aisle and stuck the corn back on the shelf.

"If you're not buying, get out!" he said again.

My eyes darted to the window. The black head was back but across the street this time. Looking over the other heads, scouring the street—for me—the guy who now knew they were dealing drugs out of the vacant lot.

Buy some time, Josh. Or one of those big feet is going to be in your face.

I shoved my hands into my sweats pockets and sauntered to the counter. *You can talk your way out of this, man. You always can.*

"Got any *nuoc man*?" I said.

He snarled. "What do you want that for?" he said.

"It's great stuff!" I tried to laugh. "Once you get past the smell!"

"I don't carry anything Oriental."

I took another glance out the window. *He* was still there.

I leaned casually on the counter. "How do you stay in business in this neighborhood?" I said.

"I carry what I'm told to carry. You want to eat Chink food, you can go down the street. You buyin'?"

Now what? Now what?

"Maybe."

I took another stroll past the cookies and picked up a package of Oreos to examine them. "How much artificial stuff do you think they put in these?" I said.

He spat out an expletive. I almost did too when I saw the price—almost five bucks! Nobody in this neighborhood could afford five bucks for cookies.

"You ain't got that kind of money," the old man barked at me. "Either buy somethin' you can afford, or get out!"

As slowly as I could without giving him a cerebral hemorrhage, I put the package on the shelf and moved back toward the counter. What I was going to do next, I didn't have a clue. But outside Big Foot was pacing further from the store. *Just a little more time, guy. Just a little more.*

I looked around desperately. *Make checks payable to Daniels Market,* the sign above the old man's head read.

"Hey!" I said. "My last name's Daniels! You think we're related somehow?"

His E.T. eyes exploded in anger. "I ain't Daniels! Daniels is the owner—and if I were related to that son of a—"

"Okay, okay," I said. My hands went up in front of me, but his words kept coming out in blows.

"Everybody in that outfit is a crook, from T.R. Daniels himself right on down!"

T.R. Da—

The old man came off the stool. "You related to him?"

I didn't move.

"If you are, you can get out of here—now! Cheap Nazi son of a—Even if you ain't related to him get out! NOW!"

Everything on him shook as he leaned painfully across the counter. But he didn't have to tell me twice. I didn't say a word as I backed to the door and stepped out into the fear again.

Any other time I would've stumbled to the bus stop in a haze, trying to make it make sense that T.R. Daniels would own a store where Oreos cost five dollars and an old man who could barely see or hear was left to manage from a stool he was rotting on.

But just then I could only think about my own survival. And when I didn't see Big Black Foot anywhere, I could only think about Phong. He had to be home by now, fighting to hide the disappointment in his eyes from his mother and Tram. Josh Dingbat had let him down.

I pushed my thoughts about my father into a crevice and glanced around. Still no sign of Big Foot. Even if I had seen him, I think I'd have headed for Phong's. I had to explain to him. I had to. I was the only dad he had.

But I stayed close to the storefronts and kept my head down, glancing up only at intervals to check for giant Africans. When Tram's bike passed me, I almost missed her.

"Tram!"

She wheeled the bike in a deft U-turn. I ran to the curb to meet her.

"Hey, is Phong real—"

But I didn't finish. Her eyes were ripping into me, and within seconds so was her mouth.

"I told you—have him home before dark!"

I felt myself sagging. "Tram—"

"I mean it. You don't know this neighborhood. You don't have to put up with the things that go on around here—not where you live. We want him home. If you can't be responsible for him—"

"Tram." I put both hands on her shoulders, and she was instantly rigid.

"Phong isn't home yet?" I said.

She looked around, stunned, as if she were seeing for the first time that he wasn't with me.

"No," she said.

And then we looked at each other, long and hard. Neither one of us could say the words.

But we were both thinking them. I could see them slowly transforming her anger into fear.

If Phong isn't with you—where is he?

WE stared at each other as if answers were going to pop out of our pores. Then I started talking, before the blame could come into her eyes.

"I couldn't meet him today, but I thought he'd come to the pool. He never showed up."

"He said you *always* meet him!"

I do. Man, I do! "Look," I said, "we don't have time to stand here and argue. It's all but dark, and we need to find him."

It wasn't just the angry words or my own guilt I wanted to stifle. It was the fear flickering in her eyes. I'd wanted to see emotion, but I hadn't wanted to see that.

She looked around helplessly. "He goes everywhere. I don't even know where to start."

I'd suggest the police station, the hospital, the morgue— Trying to look like MacGyver or somebody, I said, "Why don't you go back to your place and camp out there in case he comes home? I'll run around some more. I know some of his hide-outs."

The two lines of doubt puckered her forehead.

"I'll keep checking in with you," I said. "I won't leave you hanging. Besides, the little dweeb is probably already there, eating you out of won-tons or something."

The puckers deepened.

Way to go. Nice time to be funny. Try again.

"He's not lost," I said. "He's just being an eleven-year-old kid."

She didn't believe that any more than I did, which is probably why she unstraddled her bicycle and pushed it toward me.

"Take this then," she said. "You'll be able to hit more places."

I nodded. A pain had started in my chest, like something was stuck there.

"You bring him home the minute you find him."

Two months before I'd have thought, *No, honey, I thought we'd stop off for a beer on the way*. But I just nodded again and swung my leg over the seat. "Not the minute, the *second*—and then we'll both hang the little dweeb up to dry."

Her eyebrows flinched, and she took a step back so I could turn the bike around. She wasn't buying the *Phong is out messing around* theory at all. It was like she just knew.

And so did I.

She watched me as I struggled to poke my Nikes into the toe clips and took off at a wobble. But it's true what they say about riding a bicycle. Even though I hadn't been on one since I was fourteen, I only had one near miss with a grocery cart driven by somebody's honorable grandmother before it came back to me. It's a good thing, because my mind was churning too hard to concentrate on gearing and pedaling.

Glancing furtively around for Big Foot, I wove through town. The dude had to have given up on me by now. All they wanted was to be sure I was going to stay out of the way and quiet. So I'd seen a plastic bag full of white something. Was that worth chasing me all over Oakland for?

I swallowed hard on the fear and focused on Phong. They didn't have him. So where was he?

I'd told Tram I knew Phong's hideouts, which was only half true. On our cross-country hikes from the pool to the apartment, we'd never lit anywhere. I'd just gathered from the greetings he got from people along the way that once in a while he did stop in someplace to do something besides hotwire their produce. Gripping the handlebars, I plowed on through the dark. I hit pizza dives, pet stores, the fire department. The Tribune Tower was long since darkened, but I scanned the steps from the sidewalk. The pain in my chest tightened. Not long ago the three of us had sat there slurping frozen yogurt. Now I didn't even know where the heck he was.

He's not lost. He's just being an eleven-year-old kid.

My head came up. City Square. The big "art gallery." I was halfway there before my backside hit the seat.

It was starting to drizzle by the time I flung Tram's bike into some bushes and tore up the steps of the Center into the Square.

Somebody'll probably steal it or strip it or both. Congratulations, man. You're getting in deeper with this family by the minute.

But I fought to keep those thoughts from smothering me. I had to keep going until I found him.

Okay, okay, he's up here. He's got to be. Come on—you'll get to to the top of the steps and there'll he be, staring up at that monstrosity sculpture thing and committing it to memory—

He wasn't there. The Square was bare and glistening with new rain. If he'd been there, I would have seen him, sliding across the tile, whipping down the banisters, mashing his nose against every plate-glass window, seeing me and yelling, "Josh Dingbat—where you been, man?"

I couldn't stand it. He had to be there. I could feel the panic rising as I darted to the candy store, and then the toy shop, and back to the yogurt place. All of them stared blankly back at me with cold, glassy eyes. "You've seen him—I know you have!" I wanted to scream at their yuppiness. "This is his home—come on, where is he?"

Okay—don't lose it, man. Check the waterfall down the steps. Go back to the sculpture. How about the entrance to the BART station? He likes to stand there. The candy store again. Maybe he came in behind you. The toy store. The yogurt—

"Phong!"

I froze and grabbed at my chest, which was heaving painfully. Man—I'd screamed—out loud.

A door opened on the mall, and a middle-aged man poked his head out. I ran for him, careening crazily on the wet concrete.

"I'm looking—for a—little Vietnamese—little Vietnamese kid!" I groped to get some control. "Have you—have you seen him?"

The guy shook his head and hastily pulled his door shut. A shade came down, and his store went dark.

Everything in me collapsed as I turned toward the steps. I caught a glimpse of myself in the window of a men's store. Hair still up in spikes and soaking wet. Face dotted with miserable rain. Eyes wild. *No wonder the guy dodged me. He's probably calling the cops.*

That has to be my next step too, I thought as I descended the stairs. But before I did that and called the hospital and wherever else—I had to get back to Tram. She was either pacing a trail in the apartment floor—or she was this minute reaming Phong out for turning us into borderline lunatics.

But somehow I knew that wasn't the case. Every step I made toward the bike was heavier and harder to take.

It was raining for real as I got on the bike, and it went down my back in cold rivulets. But I didn't feel it, and I didn't see the grey buildings skulking around me as I wove back through town. I didn't feel or see or hear anything.

If I had, maybe things would've been different.

◆　　　◆　　　◆

I knew Phong hadn't come home when Tram answered my buzz. When she came down to let me in, we both just shook our heads at each other.

As I followed her up the stairs she didn't say a word. I'd never seen her look that way. Everything about her was unnaturally still, as if she knew she'd crumble like plaster if she let anything within her move. If anybody was going to move, it was going to have to be me.

"Okay, I didn't find him," I said when we got inside. "But I didn't try everyplace yet. I just wanted to check in with you so you wouldn't—you know—"

She held her face still and handed me a towel. "You look like a wet cat," she said in a voice like thin china.

"Feel like one too."

She stood stone-still and watched me while I shimmied the towel through my hair and dabbed off my face. It was so weird to see her control oozing away under the surface. She was turning into a brittle shell right there in front of me.

Lord, okay, I'm out of ideas. Please don't let her lose it. Please, help us!

"Tea!" I said suddenly. "Why don't you make some? Man, I'm freezing—and he's going to be too when he gets his tail home."

My voice was coming out slow and calm, almost like somebody else's. *Come on, Tram, just trust me. I'm trying to hold us together. Please, trust me.*

Mechanically, she went to the stove.

Next step.

"Where's your—where's Ba My?"

"Working late—at the beauty shop."

I tried to laugh. "Manicures at this hour? I guess Friday night—gotta have your talons for the weekend, huh?"

Laugh. Please, let her laugh.

"When's she coming home?" I said.

A little relief dawned over her features. "Late. Maybe 11."

"Good deal. I mean, no sense her being a basket case too, right?"

"She'd die."

All right. Now what? Cover your own tail.

"Speaking of late, I've got to call home," I said. "Do you have a phone?"

"In the bedroom," she said. She moved to take me there, but the tea kettle started sputtering on the burner. She stared from it to me.

"You get that," I said. "I can find the phone."

I crossed the tiny living room and took the only door I'd never been through. The bedroom with its two rollaway beds was even smaller. Both of them had bright yellow blankets on them that were tucked in so tight I could've practiced flips on them. The end of my search for a trampoline.

I sat gingerly on one and reached for the phone on the orange crate which acted as a bedside table. While it rang emptily on the other end, I looked around. So this was where Tram slept.

It was bare, like the rest of the place, with only a few watercolors in plastics frames—Phong again.

I looked away and stared into the receiver. *Come on, Mom—answer—answer!*

"Daniels residence. This is Denise Stahl speaking."

Wonderful.

"This is Josh," I said.

"Hi."

No shriek. No launch into a barrage of useless information. That was a start.

"My mom home?" I said.

"No. She's coming in late."

Good. No explanation. No long list of questions to answer—

"You going to be there when she gets back?"

"I'm spending the night."

Of course.

But for once I was glad. "Okay, tell her that I'm staying at Phong's for a while and not to, y' know—"

"Have a heart attack or something."

"Something like that."

"Staying—at—Phong's—" She was writing it down.

"Okay, well, thanks," I said.

"Josh?"

Here come the questions. Oh boy.

"What?"

"Are you okay? I mean, you sound, like, weird."

"I'm cool. Just—give her the message, okay?"

Reluctantly she said, "Okay," and hung up.

I sat there for a minute. I almost wanted to stay in that quiet, sparse little room, like, forever. Tram was in the kitchen, ready to crack open like an egg. I had a pressure in my chest that was threatening to suffocate me. Phong was who knows where—in the dark—in the rain—hating me— Man, if that were all that was wrong, he'd be home by now. He wasn't lost. He knew this town like the paints in his paint box.

No, man, you can't lose it. You're surrounded by people who are losing it. Lord, please—whatever You want me to do, I'll do it. I will—I mean it.

I closed my eyes and tried to breathe through the deadbolt in my chest. Slowly the rest of the world came to life again. I could hear Tram rattling cups in the kitchen. I got up and went out there.

"I know why you asked me to make tea," she said.

She pushed a cup at me, and I sat down. "Because it's gonna taste great after the soaking I just took," I said. "I'm gonna get that brother of yours when he shows up—"

"You hate this stuff!"

I looked up quickly. Sometime while I'd been in the bedroom, she'd gotten a grip. She sat down and looked me in the eye.

"Okay—I do," I said. "It tastes like baby lotion."

"You've tasted baby lotion?"

"No, but it tastes like that stuff smells."

"You just wanted me to do something to be busy."

I met her eyes. "Yeah," I said.

"Thank you."

Her face still looked as fragile as one of those porcelain dolls Meg used to collect, but Tram was back behind it. *You don't have to do it alone now, man. You two can do this.*

"Phong's okay, Tram, I know he is," I said.

She cocked her head subtly to one side. "I don't like my own imagination."

"We can't go with imagination. We have to go with what we know."

She leaned forward. "And what *do* you know?"

Okay, MacGyver, what are you going to tell her?

"Look, Tram—"

But she held up her hand, and her head came to attention.

"What—" I said.

She put her hand right on my mouth and listened.

And then I heard it too. Footsteps on the cement steps. Not Phong's. Heavy ones.

They moved haltingly, like two people who didn't know where they were going.

She relaxed. "It isn't Phong—" she said.

But this time I put *my* hand on *her* mouth. There were voices too. Low. Thick. Voices too tough to whisper.

"Which one?" one of them said.

"I don' know," the other one answered.

"What we s'posed to do, go poundin' on every one?"

"Yeah—we gon' find that honkie and shut him up."

Everything in me went on automatic pilot. Later I couldn't figure out why I did what I did—how I knew what to do. They were just instincts. One of them was to get us out of there before they broke down the door. The other was to get back out on the street before Phong came innocently up those stairs.

"I've got big bucks," I'd told them stupidly. "I'll pay you for the kid."

I got up slowly and pushed the chair silently out of the way. Tram watched me. I grabbed her arm and scanned the room. She tried to jerk away, but I held on.

"Window," I mouthed more than said.

I didn't let go of her as I moved in that direction. She planted her feet firmly into the floor.

I jabbed a finger toward the door.

"They want *me*," I said hotly into her ear.

She scowled and tried to jerk away again.

"They have knives," I said. "Now come on."

She took one more look at the door and then let me drag

her to the window. I pushed it open and fumbled with the screen.

Impatiently she popped it out and handed it to me. Of course. These were people who washed windows, screens, everything.

I leaned out and looked down into three stories of wet blackness. *All right, Spiderman, now what?*

Out in the hall Big Black Foot and No Teeth banged on a door. It sounded like it was about two apartments down. The thuds resounded in my cranium.

"We have to get out of here," I said close to Tram's ear.

She pulled her face away and looked at me. At least there was anger again now, and not fear. She operated better when she was teed off. "Just answer one question," she hissed. I nodded.

"Are you the 'honkie'?"

"Yeah."

"Do they know my brother?"

I couldn't answer. I couldn't. "That's two questions," I said. "You ever climb out of here before?"

"No. *I* don't get *myself* into these kinds of situations." She leaned out, her forehead pulled into two lines. "Phong has though."

"Figures."

The pounding thudded closer, and so did my heart. They were next door.

"Come on," Tram said.

Before I could even forecast what she was going to do, she did it—squatted on the windowsill and grabbed for the clothesline. It was wet and heavy, and it bowed sickeningly as she swung on it and got herself to the empty trellis on the side of the building. Nobody had planted roses for years. Nobody had done anything here for years. She skittered down it until she was lost from me in the misty dark. I followed her.

If you can climb to a platform, you can get down a stupid rose thingie.

I didn't think about the fact that I was headed for a mass

of concrete—not a "nice, cool pool." If I had, I probably wouldn't have done it.

When I got to the ground I couldn't see Tram. I stood gawking in a pool of streetlight. She grabbed my hand from a thin wall of shrubbery and yanked me in with her.

"What if Phong comes home while they're out there pounding on doors?" she said.

"You're quick," I said. "We have to find him before he comes back here."

"He might already be back here," she said.

"*What?*"

She shook her rain-dotted hair back from her face. It was no longer china-fragile. She was in control. "I remembered something. When he's mad at somebody he goes down in the basement where we store things and hides for hours."

"Let's go!"

New hope, thin as it was, was enough to pump me up.

"Crawl," Tram said.

I nodded and on all fours crept out of the bushes. Once on the sidewalk, with her, puppy-like, beside me, I snorted and got up. "Any cop comes by, he's going to drag us off to the slammer for sure," I said. "Come on. They're still up there pounding and cussing. We'll just walk in the gate and go down—"

"We can't."

"Why not?"

I looked down at her. She looked back sheepishly. "My keys," she said, and pointed up.

"Terrific."

"Well, you didn't exactly give me time to pack!"

But I was already rounding the corner to the front of the building. "We'll climb the gate. How do you think they got in?"

I didn't wait but shinnied over it. If I didn't make it as a diver, I might consider the obstacle course as a second choice. I was getting enough experience.

Once inside we both stood still and listened. I heard the black dudes, fists hammering. Tram heard something else.

"Come on," she said.

She led me down a half-flight of stairs and pushed open a door. Washing machines were churning inside, and an Asian kid with glasses was folding T-shirts at a long table.

Tram rushed over to him, chattering so fast it took me a full ten seconds to realize she was speaking Vietnamese. Her voice singsonged up and down, and his answered in soft staccato. If I hadn't been going nuts, I'd have stopped to think how it sounded like a duet.

Tram nodded and held out her hand. The guy looked at me as if I were an encyclopedia salesman just come to the door. Then he looked back at Tram, dug into his pocket, and pressed a key into her outstretched palm. She nodded some more as he apparently gave her instructions. With key tucked into her fist she steered me out, the guy still attacking me with his eyes. We stopped just outside to listen. There was still pounding, but only a floor above now.

"Hurry!" she said.

Her hand closed around my arm, clammy with sweat. I thundered down the steps with her and stopped in front of a door that read BASEMENT in English. Below it someone had painstakingly painted the word in three other languages—all of them Oriental. It was dark in the hall, and Tram fumbled with the key.

Feet clambered down the steps.

"Hurry!" I said.

She got the key in. The laundry room door was slapped open above us.

"You seen a honkie?"

No Teeth.

"Let me try it!" I said.

But the key crunched in the lock, and Tram pushed the door open. We stepped onto a landing, and she closed it soundlessly behind us. Simultaneously we held our breath. The voices above were muffled, but I strained to make out the words.

"Ain't nobody can speak English around here?"

Slam.

Footsteps disappearing. Up.

I exhaled.

"Yes," Tram said.

I looked down into the inky blackness below us. "There's no way Phong's in here."

"Why not?"

"He's gonna sit here—in the dark?"

"When he gets mad enough and stubborn enough he will. Either that, or he just turned out the light when he heard us coming."

I felt her reach above our heads and heard a chain pull—in vain.

"Oh—"

"What?"

"It's burned out. Everything in this building is burned out or clogged up or something."

She pushed the door open a crack and let a weak shaft of light in from the hall. "We need something to prop it open," she said.

I went step by step down the stairs and looked around on the floor. A rounded hunk of wood that had obviously dropped out of a box looked like a good prospect. I picked it up. It was a piece of a wooden bowl.

I tossed it up to Tram. As she stuck it in the door I looked around the basement. There were sections of neatly stacked boxes and bags, arranged as if fifteen Vietnamese families had just been down there last Saturday to organize their meager treasures. But I knew by now it always looked like that. Maybe all they had were broken pieces of wooden bowls, but they took pride in that. I almost told Tram to forget the door prop. That chunk of wood was important to somebody.

But she'd already come down the steps and was standing in the middle of the basement in a bare spot.

"Truong Phong Ly!" she said in her high-pitched, singsong style. The following string of Vietnamese was half coaxing, half *get out here before I rip out your nose hairs one by one with red-hot tweezers.* If he'd emerged from behind one of the stacks just then, I'd have had a hard time deciding whether to protect him or laugh my tail off.

But he didn't.

"Game's over, So-Long Phong," I said. "I didn't forget you today. If you'll come out, I'll explain—"

Tram's hand closed over my arm.

"Sh-h-h-h-h," she said.

I shut up and waited. She listened like a crouched lioness for a split second. Just as she leapt for the steps I heard wood bounce on wood.

And then the door slammed. Hard.

Both of us tore for the stairs. My open sweat jacket caught on the railing and catapulted me back with a jolt. By the time I ripped it loose and clawed my way up in the dark, I'd already heard it all.

The siren whining up the street.

The series of cuss words.

The chain wrapping around the doorknob, the way I'd seen it whip around the fence pole.

Big Foot saying, "We be back for you, rich honkie."

The feet receding up the steps.

The siren whining closer. And then farther.

I lunged for the door and smashed against Tram who was already there.

"It's stuck!" she said.

I gave it a shove anyway. But I could almost see the chain, tightening around the doorknob and whatever else it was attached to like a fist.

The door wouldn't open.

It wasn't going to open for a long time.

THERE was a shocked silence between us. When Tram exploded into it, I jumped.

"This is your fault!"

"I—"

"You're the 'honkie' they want!"

"I told you that!"

"Now we're trapped in here, and my brother is out there—and it's *your* fault!"

"Hey, look—"

"NO!"

"Tram, come on, get a grip—"

"No. I will not 'get a grip.' I want to find my brother—and because of *you* I can't even leave this—stupid—basement!"

Her voice was reaching hysterical proportions. She slid past me and down the stairs. I followed and groped to a corner I felt was far away from where she'd gone. It was so black it was hard to tell. I sank onto a box and put my head in my hands.

The real pits of this whole thing is, she's right. Man, you can't even be mad at her because she speaks the truth.

I clutched my hair. Why couldn't I just turn off my own brain?

But it *was* my fault. If I had taken Phong away from those punks sooner . . . If I hadn't antagonized the Mexican in the first place . . . If I'd insisted that I ride with Brain . . . Or if I'd made my dad stop for Phong . . . Or if I hadn't thought he'd be cool about it and I'd asked Brian to get him for me. If—if—if—

"Hey!"

Something a whole lot bigger than a cockroach had just skittered across my foot. I was up and hollering before I knew I was doing it.

"What's wrong?" said Tram from the other side of the room.

"An animal just ran across my toe. Man—"

"Probably a rat."

Her voice was so deadly calm, I hated her for a second.

"A *rat*?"

She didn't answer. A shudder racked through me. She wasn't trying to scare me. Although I'd never seen one except in the movies, it had felt big enough to be a power-rodent. Darn. Why couldn't she be scared too?

I pulled my knees up to my chin and stared at the floor. My eyes were getting used to the dark, but I couldn't see into all the corners.

"What kind of a girl are you?" I said.

In the dark I could feel her seething.

"Why aren't you even scared of a rat?" I said.

She sniffed. "I saw too many of them in Indonesia. And they were the friendliest things we saw."

I swallowed. I could feel the pride going down.

"I've never seen one before, and it scares me, and I hate it. Can I sit down?"

She was quiet a minute. Then I heard her pat whatever she was sitting on.

"Thanks," I said, and sank onto it. "Hey, this is a mattress!"

"Brilliant," she said.

"Were you going to keep it to yourself?"

"Excuse me?"

"Aw, man—I didn't mean it that way!"

I really didn't, and I stood up to prove it.

"Oh, sit down," she said in disgust. "I think I have worse

problems than worrying about whether you're going to come
on to me."

You sure do, sweetheart. Not that I hadn't thought of it—

I sat down slowly, being careful not to touch her, which
was hard because the mattress was small.

"This is a crib mattress," I said.

"I'm sorry I couldn't arrange for a king," she said bitterly.

"I'm not complaining!"

"Nobody in this building would be storing anything but
a baby's bed. Everything else is being used, and if it isn't, it's bad
enough to throw away."

I thought guiltily of the perfectly good bunk beds my parents had stored away when they bought me my water bed.

"I've got bunk beds in storage," I said. "I think I'll give
them to Phong—"

"We don't need your charity," she snapped.

"So you can buy them, all right? I just know it's hard on
you guys—"

"And we don't need your pity either—"

"Then forget it!"

We dropped into sullen silence again. My brain wanted to
think something sarcastic, something that would keep me from
sinking any further. But I was too tired.

Tram stood up with a jerk. "We have to get out of here,"
she said.

"Where are you going?"

"To get us out."

She stomped through the dark without so much as bump-
ing into a crate. I fell over three in her wake.

"What are you going to do?" I called after her.

"What we 'women' do best," she said. I'd have bet money
her almond eyes were slits slanted at me. "I'm going to scream."

That she did—while pounding wildly on the door. I joined
her. We must have yelled for ten minutes, but there wasn't the
wisp of a footfall on the stairs. I stopped to massage my fists.

"Where is everybody?" I said. "Does everybody go out
for *hung pao* on Friday nights?"

"They're here," she said. Her voice was going dead.

"Why can't they hear us?"

"They hear us."

Okay. You answer this one right and you get the prize.

"Then why doesn't somebody come?" I said. I was trying not to sound exasperated, but my chest hurt and my mind was reeling and I knew any minute I was going to either get bitten by a rabid rat or be attacked by dope sellers bearing chains the size of anacondas.

"Everybody is scared," she said from the mattress. "And if you lived in this neighborhood you'd be scared too."

"I don't live in this neighborhood," I said, "and I am scared." I moved back to the mattress and sat down. She was a good two feet from me, but I could feel her defeat.

"Our people aren't like that," she said more to the air than to me. "A community like this in Vietnam would be like a town in itself—people helping each other and sharing. And we do, but not like we want to, because we're so afraid all the time."

"You don't act like you're afraid," I said.

"I refuse to. There's an old Vietnamese saying that my father used to tell us when he'd be giving free food from our store to friends who were hungry because of the Communists. He'd say, 'Faraway relatives are not as important as nearby neighbors.'" I could see her pulling her mouth into a line in the greyness between us. "Pretty ironic now, isn't it?"

"Yeah."

That was eloquent, pal. Why not throw in an uh-huh just to impress her?

What *could* I say? Until tonight the biggest problem I had was making the Olympic diving team. I didn't have to worry about my life, or Phong's life, or for that matter anything that seemed to matter right now.

"I've seen people from my country become so lonely and isolated here," she said. "I'm just not going to do it."

The defeat was gone. There was only defiant strength pumping through the mattress.

"You're not like your mother, are you?" I said.

To my surprise—all right, my absolute amazement—she laughed. It was bittersweet, but it *was* a laugh. "You don't have to be MacGyver to figure that out," she said.

I choked.

"No, I'm not like her. If you're the typical Vietnamese woman in this country, you're going to get swallowed up like Jonah by the whale."

"Typical?" I prompted her.

She ticked the characteristics off on her fingers like she'd named them a thousand times. "Obedient to her father. Then submissive to her husband. Then listens to her grown-up sons when her husband dies." Her mouth went into the line again. "As you can see, my mother loses out entirely. She has none of those men with her, and she doesn't know what to do except make money to support us—and here they won't even let her do what she does best."

"Which is?"

"Manage a store—beside my father, of course, but she could do it on her own. No one is going to believe her, though, because she's so shy and has no self-confidence and is anything but aggressive. That's the Vietnamese woman."

"Doesn't describe you," I said.

"You haven't heard it all. She must also speak gently and carefully—'roll her tongue seven times before she says something.'"

Still no cigar.

"And show good conduct and act in a virtuous way."

I was in dangerous territory, but I figured I had nothing to lose. "Do you?" I said.

"I try. I have to have something to salvage for my father. But it's so hard here—nobody acts that way!"

"Tell me about it! Even the so-called Christian girls I go to school with think virtue is when nobody finds out."

We were quiet for a minute. I don't know what she was thinking, but I was holding her up next to Jill and Kim and Zondra—and she was outshining them all the way.

"With no father and no older brother and a mother who just lives day to day in terror, somebody has to be in charge."

"You don't have to defend yourself to me," I said.

"I'm just afraid my father will be disappointed that I've gotten Americanized. I can imagine him looking at me and saying, 'The tree is now a boat. It can never be a tree again.'"

"Well, maybe at first, but—"

"But I'm not Americanized all the way!"

"Well no, but—"

"I spend half my time trying not to be a Vietnamese wimp so my family won't get run over, and the other half trying not to be a liberated American female so those panting American males will keep their hands off me!"

I stuck my hands in my pockets. "I wasn't even thinking about it!" I said.

She looked at me.

"Honest," I said.

Of course it was dark, but from what I *could* see, Tram was looking down at the hands folded in her lap, the way a Vietnamese girl is "supposed" to. I couldn't decide whether she was embarrassed or just as shocked as I was that we were actually having a conversation.

"I know you weren't," she said finally.

I had to look hard to make sure it was still her. The voice was soft as a piece of silk.

"Thank you," I said. "I really . . . I have a lot of respect for you."

Good grief, man, did you just say that to a woman?

She looked up and laughed, a real laugh. The American was back. "I thought you were a jerk when I first met you."

"I was," I said.

"In fact, I still thought you were a jerk until this afternoon—mostly."

"I was," I said again. "I think I still am."

"Maybe so."

"Thanks. I needed *that*."

"But probably not."

"So make up your mind!"

"Nobody could be a complete jerk and care as much as you do about my brother. I don't know a single boy in any of my classes who would even talk to him in the first place, much less spend a whole night looking for him when he was—missing."

The pressure in my chest was almost unbearable by then. Whatever I was holding back was pushing like a bike pump to get out, and I couldn't even talk.

"So many Americans—and I'm talking teenagers mostly—think we're just refugees—boat people—and they treat us that way."

"Do you feel like you're discriminated against?" I said. "Even *here*—even nowadays?"

"You don't get to Civil Rights until twelfth grade," she said bitterly. "By then it's too late."

Sammy Lee flitted across my brain, and with him the anger. "I thought that was over a long time ago."

"Can you honestly say you never had a prejudiced thought about Phong or my mother or me?"

There was a guilty silence.

"I get so tired of defending myself—defending Phong."

"I'm sure you don't have to do much defending for him."

"You'd be surprised—in school—the teachers. Especially because my mother doesn't speak English that well. I fight all the time to show people that I am somebody, not an ignorant foreigner. That's why I study until my eyes drop out. I know I'll never get anywhere unless I'm at the top. And that's why I've become this American teenager. I've learned to talk like an American. I've learned to be sarcastic like an American. And I've learned how to glare like an American. And do you know what scares me?"

I shook my head.

"I think I'm losing who I really am. I can feel the bitterness and the hate building up in me. I don't want that for Phong."

"I get the point—"

"I can't hate *you*."

I didn't say anything for a long time. Tram got up and paced around and came back with an orange that appeared to be only a day or two out of the market bin.

"Phong must have been here sometime," I said. "This fits his M.O."

We shared it in silence, and I let her eat most of it because I couldn't swallow.

"Thanks," I said finally.

She cocked her head in that way she had. "For what?"

"For not hating me. For giving me a chance to—"

"To what?"

I wasn't sure I knew, but it came out anyway. "To figure out what's really inside me. I don't think I knew until I got sucked in by Phong."

"He does that to people. I thank the Lord for him. He keeps me from being bitter. He keeps me from hating all the time."

Maybe it was the fact that she mentioned the Lord. Or maybe it was the fact there was definitely nothing else to do down there. Or maybe it was just the lack of hating.

Whatever it was, it let us talk—for hours—through the dark with the stacks of boxes shielding us from everything.

"Who are those guys who are after you?" she asked me. So I told her.

"Why do you go to the pool every day?" she asked me.

So I told her—everything, all of it. My dreams and my hopes and my doubts, and the way God fit in.

She shook her head at that one. "I think you're mixed up on that," she said.

I didn't get defensive. I just listened.

"I think some things are important to all of us right now. I mean, I'm determined to go to Stanford, and that's that. I'm not going to be where my mother is—ever. But that's *me* talking. I'm pretty sure God's behind me, but I don't know for certain my ideas are His plan—I mean, I don't think that's the only way I can be a mature, successful woman."

"You don't understand," I said. "I feel like God has told me—"

"Baloney. I think you've told God. And I think He's showing you a different way . . . Right now."

I glanced around ruefully. "He's trying to tell me something, all right. Man, I wish He'd tell me whether we are going to get out of here before Big Foot and No Teeth come back and finish me off—"

We did that several times during the night—panic, I mean. Even Tram did it once. She was talking about the day her brother Huyen died and how she stood on the shore for hours with Phong on her back until they were both baked from the sun.

"I kept going into the water until I was up to my shoulders and then I'd realize I had Phong under and then I'd run back to the shore crying. I never found Huyen. You know, I just stood there and watched and lost my brother." She turned to me in terror. "I can't lose another brother! We have to get out of here. We have to!"

She tore up the steps and banged on the door and screamed until she was limp. I went up to about the fifth step and waited. When she was done I nudged her gently, but I didn't hold on.

"Come on back down," I said. "In the morning somebody will go by, and they won't be so scared because it'll be light, and then we'll get out, and we'll go upstairs, and Phong will be sleeping in his cot. Come on." I looked right into her face. "What happened to 'We will do it'?"

She didn't answer, but my question seemed to calm her down. She sat without saying anything.

Keep talking. Don't let her think too much.

"You're luckier than I am in some ways," I said.

"Name one."

"Well—maybe you don't have them all with you, but you have a real family."

"Don't you?"

If you want to call a father who doesn't even care that his son's trying to make it to the Olympics "family"—a guy who's a slumlord—who—

"It's not the same."

"Family's important in my country," she said. "We're raised to pay off the debt of birth to our parents, but we do it because we want to. If my father weren't going to ever join us, I might have to give up my education and the possibility of a family of my own to take care of Phong and my mother, but that's the way it is."

"That's okay with you?"

"It is. There's a Vietnamese proverb—"

"You're just full of those, aren't you?"

"'Children sit where their parents place them.'"

"I hear that," I said sadly.

We were quiet for a minute. When Tram spoke, I realized she'd been trying to think of the right thing to say—"rolling her tongue seven times."

"I'm sorry. I mean, about your family."

"Nah. It's okay."

"At least you don't have to know the pain of being separated from them."

"Yeah," I said. "I guess."

But she was wrong. Just finding out my father wasn't who I thought he was—that was like having him die. I can't be close to him. That's lonely. That's pain.

Beside me I could feel her curling up on her end of the mattress like a kitten.

"Tired?" I said.

"Exhausted." She sighed. "*Chao*, Phong, wherever you are."

"What does that mean?" I said.

"Everything. Good-bye. Hello. Good night. Whatever you want it to mean."

"Then *chow*, Phong," I said.

She laughed sleepily.

"What?"

"You talk funny."

I tried it again. I could feel her shaking with glee. "I can't help it," I said. "The word doesn't fit my mouth. I can't singsong the way you guys do."

"Singsong!"

"Yeah. That up and down stuff."

"Do you know why we do that?" she said.

"No, but I bet I'm about to find out."

"The words in Vietnamese don't just have a pronunciation. They have a pitch. If you use the wrong pitch, you could say something really embarrassing."

"Okay, well, what—"

"Leave me alone," she said through a yawn. "I'm sleepy."

I felt her curl back up on the mattress.

"Do you mind if I lie down too?" I said. "I mean, I won't if you don't want me to."

"What are you going to do, stay up and stand guard for rats? Of course lie down."

I looked around. It used to be I could only find Christ on my ceiling. Now I laid on my back and propped my feet up on a stack of boxes behind the mattress. Instantly He was there, dusting off His sandals and saying, "So you met the girl, huh?"

"What are you doing?" Tram said.

I opened my eyes. For a minute I considered telling her it was some kind of secret diving technique for preparing for a meet. But she'd have seen through it even in the dark.

"I was praying," I said.

"Oh. I was too."

"To Christ?" I said.

"No, *Jupiter*," she said. "Yes—Christ."

"I didn't know. I mean, when we were talking about God—I wasn't sure—I thought you might be Buddhist."

She sat up and tossed her black, thick hair over her shoulders in that impatient *get a clue* way she had. "Does every black person love watermelon?"

"I don't know."

"No! Does every Jewish person necessarily hoard his millions?"

"I don't—"

"No! I'm a Christian!"

"I knew that."

"Sure, you did. Anyway, I asked Jesus Christ to forgive me and come into my life when I was a small child."

"I remember now—about the cross." I shrugged in the dark. "Must have been hard to give that away."

"It was," she said. "I like symbols. I liked wearing it."

We were quiet for a while, and then she snickered. "I didn't exactly have you pegged as John the Baptist either," she said.

"Did you think *I* was Buddhist?"

"No! It was just your attitude. Self-centered—"

"I memorized that list already," I said. This was reminding me of a conversation I'd had with Meg. Not a pleasant memory.

"Do you know what made me start thinking differently?" she said.

Ah. A reprieve.

"It was that day you and your sister stayed for lunch. You agreed that God took care of Huyen's soul."

"Yeah."

"That's just what you said—'Yeah.'"

"I always was a real poet," I said.

"Can we pray together?" she said suddenly.

Pray? You and me? Together?

I'd never prayed with anybody else before. Half my friends didn't even suspect that I prayed alone. "Okay," I said. "How do we do that?"

"I don't know," she said laughing. "It just seemed like a good idea."

So we went for it. At first it was as awkward as a blind date. Me saying, "Lord—here we are—Tram and me—" And Tram saying, "Yes. Here we are—"

But once we started to pray about Phong, we got it off the ground.

And then we prayed about everything we'd talked about—her father, my family, her hatred, my messed-up path.

Then her breathing started coming in even puffs beside me, and I knew she was falling asleep. Before she went out completely she sat up again. "What does J.D. stand for?" she said.

"Not Josh Dingbat!"

"I kind of didn't think that's what you were baptized."

"It's Joshua Daniels," I said.

"*Chao*, Joshua Daniels," she said. And then she was asleep. I pulled my feet off the boxes, and I slept too.

Sometime during the night I woke up and knew she was crying. I didn't hear her—I just felt it.

"Tram—are you okay?" I said.

"Do you know what is so stupid?" she said. Her voice was faint and wavery, like a little girl's. I guess we're all little kids when we cry.

"What?" I said.

"I used to worry so much about Phong because he insisted on speaking Pidgin English half the time and wouldn't do his homework and just wanted to run the streets and read and paint." There was a soft sob. "I never thought I'd have to worry about whether he was even alive."

The pain came back in my chest, but it was probably nothing compared to what she was feeling. I pushed myself up on one elbow. My other hand landed on hers, but she didn't pull away. Gently and cautiously I curled my fingers around it.

"God's with Phong too," I said. "The little dweeb does too much for too many people—God's not going to take him away yet."

Her fingers squeezed mine until she drifted off again. I stayed there and felt them, relaxed and tiny and soft in my hand. Slowly, gently, I reached over and touched the soft folds of skin over her eyes. She didn't move.

Hey, man, did you know you could ever be—tender?

It *was* different, and I wasn't sure where it came from. It definitely wasn't Oriental submissiveness that brought it on.

Maybe it was because she was so clear and unmuddied. Maybe it was because she believed in things I hoped were still true.

Whatever it was, she touched places in me—places I didn't even know were there.

I guess, I thought as I fell back to sleep, I guess that's where love always begins.

IT couldn't have been past 5 A.M. when they started banging on the door. I uncoiled like a cobra on the crib mattress. Tram was already sitting up, holding her breath.

"Somebody's here," I said stupidly. Five A.M. isn't my most alert hour even if I *haven't* been sleeping in a three-foot square.

But the banging sounded like gorillas tearing apart a cage. It got my heart slamming immediately.

"They came back for you, honkie," Tram whispered. Her voice was steady, but it was scared.

"Josh! You down there, man?"

I came up off the mattress like I was leaving a springboard.

"Brian!"

I shoved a pile of boxes over and groped for the stairway with Tram on my heels.

"Who . . . ?" she was saying. "Who is it?"

It hadn't occurred to either one of us in our stupor that Big Foot and friends wouldn't have banged on the door—they'd have ripped off the chain and brought it down with them to use on me.

"Brian—I'm here! Undo that chain—get us out of here!"

But he was way ahead of me. He had the door open by the time I got to the top landing. Grim as it still was at that hour, the

Oakland morning flooded in. Brian was in the doorway—with Nathan and Young Jon Ricco behind him.

Brian grabbed me with both hands. "Man, are you okay?"

"Yeah, yeah, I'm fine. How did you guys know we were here?"

"What the—" Nathan said.

He was looking at Tram. In fact, all three of them were looking at her, and at me, and back at her. She tossed her hair and looked right back at them.

The reason we were all crammed onto the landing of a Chinatown apartment-building basement snapped me back into gear.

"Tram," I said, nudging her gently on the elbow, "why don't you go upstairs and see if he's shown up yet. We'll meet you at—we can't hang out here—"

"Blue Chevy out front," Brian said.

Jon Ricco and Nathan stepped aside to let Tram through, but Nathan had to grab Jon's arm to keep him from following her. Later I snickered to myself about that. She'd have knocked him right over the banister before he'd known what hit him.

I strode beside Brian on the way to the car, with Nathan and Jon behind us. "What's going on?" Brian said. "We've been cruising around all night looking for you—"

"I haven't got time to explain now."

"No need to," Nathan said, wiggling his eyebrows in Tram's wake.

"Shut up," I said. I leaned on the top of the car, facing the three of them on the other side. "Look, unless he came home sometime after 10 last night, Phong's missing."

"Who's Phong?" Jon Ricco said.

Brian's shoulders expanded. "You think those punks . . . ?"

"What punks?" Nathan said.

"I don't think so—although they're the ones who locked us in there. I ran into them when I was looking for him—saw some stuff I wasn't supposed to see. Anyway, I guess they followed me here, and then they heard sirens and got spooked and took off. But the point is, if Phong hasn't shown up—"

I looked over their shoulders. Tram was coming out the gate. I didn't even have to wait for her to shake her head. I knew from the look on her face.

"We have to find him," I said.

"Who's Phong?" Jon Ricco said again.

"Hey, look, don't you have to dive today?" Brian said to me.

"Not if we don't find him."

"Yes, you do, Joshua."

Tram's eyes were leveled on me, and her voice was firm. Even Jon and Nathan exchanged glances.

"What time is it?" I said.

Nathan looked at his watch. "Five fifteen."

"Okay—the meet doesn't start until 10. That's almost five hours. If we split up we can cover a lot of territory."

Tram was still looking hard at me.

"We'll find him, and I'll dive, and everything'll be cool," I said to her. She didn't say anything. "Has your mother called the police?"

"No. She was too afraid. And she knew she couldn't make them understand."

"Okay—we look for, say, three hours. If we don't find him—and we will—then you can call the cops." *But if we don't find him, I'm not diving. I'm not leaving here until he's back.*

I didn't have to tell her I was thinking that. She knew. "You and me in the car," Brian said to me.

That was a good idea. Phong would know the Chevy and flag us down if he saw us first—if he didn't hate my guts thoroughly by this time. But I looked doubtfully at Tram. "Do you want to go with Nathan and Jon?"

She looked like she'd rather accompany the Boston Strangler. But she nodded. Nothing was more important right now than her brother. She wasn't going to stand helplessly on another shore.

"We'll take good care of her," Nathan said to me. He gave me a wink which I ignored. I had a feeling it was Tram who was going to take care of them. I gave them both a warning look anyway.

"Who the—are we looking for?" I heard Jon say as she led them off. "Who's Phong?"

"Let's go," I said to Brian as I slid into the front seat. He pulled the Chevy out onto the still-wet pavement and to the end of the street. At the corner he looked at me.

"I don't have a clue," I said. Without Tram there to put up a front for, the pain in my chest was worse than ever, and whatever was holding it back was threatening to explode momentarily. "I already looked every place I could think of last night."

"You don't think those punks have him?"

"They didn't last night. That was one of the first places I went—I even offered them money."

"Did you have any on you?"

"Couple bucks in my bag."

"They took it."

"How do you know?"

Brian reached into the backseat and produced my L.A. Gear bag.

"Where'd you get this?"

"Fence was the first place I went too. Then I cruised past the pool—"

"The *pool*!"

"Yeah—"

"I never went back to the pool!"

"You think he did?"

"It was closed, but he might have."

"Want to try there?"

"There's nobody there at this hour—but yeah, go there." It was stupid, but going somewhere, anywhere—just having an idea—kept my chest from ripping open. Brian got me there on two wheels, squealing through alleys I'm sure even Phong didn't know about. I'd have to show him—if I found him—*when* I found him.

I had the door open before the '57 even stopped, and I was pounding on the locked glass doors when Brian joined me. I'd have killed to have seen Overbite at the counter inside, but it was semi-dark and still, and the potted plants weren't talking. I kept banging.

Brian took off down the sidewalk.

"Where you going?" I said.

"To have a look around."

Alone, standing in front of that lifeless building that had held every hope I'd ever had inside it such a short time ago, I could feel myself giving up. Slowly my hands slid down the glass. He wasn't here. He wasn't home. He wasn't anywhere. He'd led me down almost every scuzzy alley in this town, and somewhere along the way he'd gotten me off that straight shot home I thought I'd been taking. And I'd wanted it that way. Man, I'd wanted it that way. Now I'd give up the Olympic dream. I'd give up ever stepping foot on a diving board again if I could just find him. If I could just take him home to Tram—

"Josh!"

Brian was yelling from several yards down. "What?" I said wearily.

"It probably doesn't mean nothin'—anything—but there's a window open down here."

I followed him to the spot in the shrubs where he was leaning down, peering into a basement window.

"Looks like it goes into some kind of boiler room or something," he said.

I leaned in and immediately pulled out. It was inky black and a long way down. I'd had my share of dark basements for the duration of my life.

"I think you're right," I said. "I don't think it means anything."

I stood up, but Brian shrugged and poked his giant shoulders in through the window as far as they'd go. "Anybody home?" he yelled.

"Would you knock it off? You'll probably set off some kind of burglar alarm or something. Come on—he's not here."

I started to move, but Brian grabbed my ankle.

"*What?*"

He held up his hand, and I listened. "Anybody home?" he called again.

And then I heard it too, quavering up to us from the coal-black darkness below.

"Me," the voice said. "I'm home. Can you help me?"

"Phong! *Phong!*" I guess I shoved Brian completely out of the way. I must have, because I had the entire top half of my body through the window before Phong could answer back.

"Are you down there, man? *Phong!*"

"Josh Dingbat," he said. "Watch that first step, man. It's awesome."

I could feel my eyeballs practically popping from my head as I strained to see him. "Wave your arm," I said, my heart slamming. Blackness.

"Did you do it?" I said.

"Here." Brian poked a flashlight into my ribs. I stuck it through the opening—and caught a slice of Vietnamese smile in a shaft of light. It was a face puffy with recent tears, but it was Phong's, and it was grinning now.

"I'm not even going to ask you what you're doing down there, dingbat," I said. "Just get out here."

"If I could do that, you think I woulda have spent the whole night here?" he said.

"Can't you get out the same way you got in?"

"Like I told you, that first step's awesome."

I turned to Brian, who was grinning like Bozo. I was having trouble not smiling my lips out of joint myself. Phong was right here. And the little dweeb was alive!

"You got any rope in the car?" I said.

Brian shook his head. "Already looked."

"Okay." *Come on, MacGyver, you eluded three dope dealers, climbed out a three-story window, survived a night in a rat-infested basement. Surely you can get an eleven-year-old out of a— God, are You there? I could use a hand—no orders, no demands—*

"I'll just have to climb in there after him," I said.

"How are *you* gonna get out then?"

"I can probably—"

"Wait here," he said.

"Why?"

"Talk to the kid," he said. And he was gone.

It was starting to get fairly light by then. If I'd had any sense, I'd have thought how weird it must have looked to anyone going past at that hour to see me, butt to the sidewalk, talking into the basement window of the municipal pool. But I had no sense. I just knew I'd found Phong, and I wasn't letting him out of my sight again.

"Man, you don't know how glad I am to see you," I said.

"Yes, I do," he said matter-of-factly.

"Nice place you got here." I whipped the flashlight around the basement. "Looks a lot like the hotel I stayed in last night. Hey." My light hit on a door.

"Did you try that? Is it locked from the outside?"

"I can't get to the door," he said.

I snapped the light back on him. "Why not?"

"'Cause I think I have a broken leg."

I shined the flashlight on his legs. One was propped over the other, and he'd rolled his jeans up to his knee. The once-olive skin on his ankle was dark and swollen and ugly.

That was it. I groaned and felt my stomach churning toward my esophagus. If the boiler room door hadn't opened just then, I'd have lost it. Definitely.

"I guess it wasn't locked," Phong said cheerfully. Brian stepped into the shaft of light and looked up at me, his beige face as calm as Phong's golden one. I didn't even bother to ask him how he'd gotten in.

"Hi, kid," he said.

"Hi, Brian," Phong said. "Where you guys been?"

"Come on. I'll get you out of here."

"You're gonna have to carry me," Phong said. "I got a bum ankle."

"Old football injury?" Brian said as he scooped him gently up against his big chest.

"Yeah—but I made the touchdown."

They chattered off into the darkness, closing the basement door behind them. I sank against the wall and ran my hand over my chest. It was starting to shake just like the rest of me.

"Let's do it," Brian called from the sidewalk about two minutes later. "We got places to go."

I crawled out of the bushes. He was depositing Phong into the backseat of the Chevy. I scrambled up, and for the second time that day I think I shoved Brian out of the way.

In the backseat I put my hands on both sides of Phong's head. "I'm sorry, man," I said. "I should've met you like always—"

"Don't you gotta dive today?" he said.

He spends the night in a boiler room blacker than his hair—cries his eyes into smaller slits than ever—breaks his ankle somewhere in the middle of it—and he asks, "Don't you gotta dive today?"

That's when what my chest had been holding back burst loose. I put his face against my sweat jacket and sobbed.

And the little dweeb cried with me.

◆　　◆　　◆

All mothers must go to the same school to learn to be mothers. When Ba My got ahold of Phong, she alternated between kissing him all over the face and spattering out reprimands in sobbing Vietnamese. I didn't have to understand the language to know she was telling him he'd had her "worried sick."

With her in the backseat slobbering over him—after I'd gone up to the apartment and did everything short of leave my right arm as collateral to get her to come downstairs—I looked around for Tram. She must have smelled us in the neighborhood because she came around the corner minutes later, and when she spotted the Chevy she broke into a run. Nathan and Jon jogged after her, red-faced but still trying to look cool.

I held out my arms to her. "We found him. He's okay!"

She slapped my hands out of the way and dove into the backseat on Phong's other side.

Okay. So much for romance.

"So—is that 'Phong'?" Jon Ricco said at my elbow. He was breathing like a locomotive. I wished I'd seen the chase Tram must've led them on.

"Yeah—that's him," I said.

I looked in the backseat. Tram wasn't alternating between drooling and blessing the kid out. She'd skipped the drooling completely. But even as she yammered on, her fingers were raking through his hair, depositing the night full of love he'd missed right back into his scalp.

"Hey." Jon Ricco poked me in the rib cage. "The Wicked Witch of the West oughta take lessons from your chick."

She's not "my chick," I thought. I looked back at her. *But she's happy—so what does it matter?*

But there were things that did matter.

"What time is it?" I said to Nathan.

He was staring at my head. "Nice do, Daniels," he said.

I moved my hand across my hair, which was still standing up in spikes from my last dive and a night spent curled up like a snail on some baby's bed. "What time is it?" I said testily.

"Don't go on red alert, man. It's 6:15." He nudged Jon. "This has been a real blast, but we gotta split."

"No, you don't," I said. "You gotta go up to apartment 304 and get on the phone to my mother—"

"No way, man!"

"We can't get you out of this one!"

"I don't want you to 'get me out of' anything. Just tell her to tell Mouse when he gets there—"

"Who the—who is 'Mouse'?"

"—to pick me up at the hospital emergency room. And then she can pick you guys up here."

"What—"

"She won't have time to take you home first—so unless you want to take the bus—"

"Bus?"

"Then tell her she can just bring you to San Jose."

"San Jo—"

"Jam, man," I said, herding Nathan toward the building. "You gotta get her before 7 o'clock."

I didn't give them a chance to argue. I slammed the back car door and jumped into the front seat. Brian, of course, already had the motor running.

"Hospital?" he said.

"Yep," I said.

The emergency room of an Oakland hospital at 6:30 A.M. on a Saturday looks like a rerun of "Trapper John, M.D." If Phong hadn't been Phong, we'd have watched the '92 Olympics on TV in the waiting room. But one "Hey, man, nice dress!" to a male nurse in an O.R. gown and all of us—except Brian, who waited outside to flag down Mouse—were in a curtained cubicle and Phong had a balloon and a date for the year 2000 with an X-ray technician.

"He's a cutie," she said to me as she wheeled him out for X-rays.

I was the one they all talked to. They treated Ba My and Tram like they were invisible.

Ba My's voice rose to a panic as Phong's bed disappeared through the curtain.

"They're going to take pictures of his leg," I said. I was trying not to shout.

Tram stroked her hand lightly down her mother's arm and said something soothing. Ba My sat back and closed her eyes. Within thirty seconds her head was against Tram's shoulder and she was breathing evenly.

"She was up almost all night," Tram said.

"Who wasn't?"

"Where was Phong, Joshua?"

Why didn't I tell you my name a long time ago? I like the way you say "Joshua." It's like honey rolling off the dipper.

Did you also like the way she smacked your hand out of the way when you reached out to her? Forget it. She's not interested.

I sighed. Whispering around Ba My's husky snores, I filled her in.

"That big guy," she said when I was through. "That's Brian."

"Yeah."

"How did he get into the pool building?"

"You got me," I said.

"He's awesome, that's how!" Phong said from the curtain.

The tech wheeled him back into the cubicle and shook her head at me. "Lucky for you all he didn't break his ankle. You'd never keep him down."

"It isn't broken?" Tram said.

The tech looked at her like she'd just squirted out of a hypodermic needle.

Yeah, lady, she speaks English. She also wears shoes and knows how to use a restroom.

But the tech still talked to me. "It's just a sprain, but a nice one. The doctor will be in to tell you how to treat it at home."

"Thank you," Tram said pointedly.

I stifled my dimples.

By the time the doctor got there, Phong had guzzled down a whole Seven-Up and was drawing sketches for everybody, from orderlies on up, on the backs of prescription forms. Ba My barked something at him, and he finally sat still while she watched the doctor wrap his ankle in an Ace bandage.

"Joshua, do you see what time it is?"

I looked down at Tram and then up at the clock. "Yeah."

"7:45. You dive at 10:00."

"*If* Phong's okay."

"He's fine. My mother and I have been through worse than this. You dive at 10:00."

"Okay!"

The doctor punched Phong gently under the chin. "This guy's ready to go home. Keep him quiet today—and good luck."

"They'll wait on me hand and feet!" Phong said as the doctor slipped out.

Tram shot him a look. "Dream on."

"Before you leave, ladies and gentleman," someone said from the opening in the curtain, "there is the matter of how you intend to pay for this."

Her nametag said, "ADMISSIONS." Her attitude said, "RESIDENT BIGOT."

Ba My grew two inches smaller and swept her eyes to the floor. Tram's chin came up, but the two lines reappeared in her forehead.

"It's taken care of," I said.

I felt Tram twitch.

"Oh?" said R.B. She tapped her clipboard like a gym coach.

Oh, is right. How you gonna pull this off, big guy? You've been ripped off for everything you had.

"You will need to make arrangements before you leave," she said to me.

"No problem."

Yeah, dig yourself in deeper.

"Will you be paying with check or cash?"

"Check," someone said behind her.

We all looked at my mother, standing at the curtain, wearing her *I mean business* dimples.

"To whom should I make it out?" she said.

R.B. muttered something and slipped out of the cubicle.

Phong scattered the bashful Oriental silence like pieces of a puzzle.

"Hi!" he said.

"Hi!" Mom said back.

"You look like Meg. And him." Phong tipped his chin toward me.

I grabbed my mother before a discussion of genetics could ensue. Tram went to Phong and fussed with his pillow.

"Mom, I'll pay you back," I said.

"Don't be silly."

"I'll get a job or something—"

"You don't have time for a job," somebody else said from the curtain.

It got pretty crowded in the cubicle, I thought later. Phong, Ba My, Tram, me, Mom—and Mouse. At the time, though, I didn't think anything except that I was dogmeat.

"Coach," I said, "it couldn't be helped."

"I know it. Get your suit. Let's go."

"I have to make sure about Phong. See, it's my fault—"

"Joshua."

We all stopped and looked at Tram. She had a way of making people do that. Then she cocked her head at me. If she hadn't, I wouldn't have just dropped my hands and headed for the curtain. But as it was, I stopped and turned around.

"Phong," I started to say.

He grinned from his bed and wiggled his bandaged foot at me. "You will do it, Josh Dingbat," he said.

He'd forgiven me. He'd probably never been mad at me in the first place. I couldn't tell him I'd intended for him to be going with me—and that now I'd messed that up for him too.

"So long, Phong," I said. I followed Mouse outside.

I started explaining the minute I hit the seat in Mouse's Volkswagen. He cut me off in mid-syllable.

"Josh, I don't know what you were doing last night, and I don't really want to know. I just want to ask you one thing."

There was no threat in his face as he looked at me.

"Okay," I said.

He pulled his hand back over his hair. "Do you still want to compete in this meet today? Do you still want the Olympics?"

My mouth opened automatically, but he stopped me. "No—you're not ready to answer yet. You're exhausted, and you've obviously been through one doozie of a night." He glanced at his watch. "If you're going to do this, you dive in two hours. Once we're there, you'll only have forty-five minutes to check in, change, and get warm. You won't have time to think it through then—and I want you to *know* before you get up on that board."

There was still no reprimand in his voice. He was just being straight with me.

"Okay," I said.

"I want you to use this ride to rest and get your head in the right place. If you decide you still want to go for it, we can. You're wiped out. You're going to have to operate on adrenaline. But if you want it, I'll help you and we'll do it. You just have to decide first."

We're not talking about a game here, man. He means it. You've messed around with your chances. Without him you won't make it to the locker room. And without a clear head, you won't have him.

Mouse started the engine and headed for the freeway. I leaned back on the headrest and closed my eyes. For the first time I realized how tired I was.

But although every muscle in my body was screaming, "For Pete's sake, man, find a bed and die in it," I wasn't sleepy. With my eyes closed, all I could do was chase the two thousand things that were climbing over each other in my head to get my attention.

Those three punks. They *had* been dealing drugs. They had been using Phong. And if they ever saw me or Phong again, they'd probably try to erase our memories.

My father. He owned that rotten little store that cheated the people in the neighborhood. People who didn't deserve it.

Phong. He'd gone so far as to climb through a window to get into the pool to find me. He'd messed up his ankle in the process—and it could have been worse. He'd spent the whole night in there in the dark, and in spite of his bravado he'd probably been scared out of his chop suey.

Tram. She'd slept in a cellar full of rats too, and she'd never shown that she was afraid. But she had shown a lot of other things—

And then there were the unanswered questions. How did Brian know where I was? How did he get my bag without being turned into refried beans by Acapulco Al? How did he get into the pool building? And how about my mother? Why did she pay Phong's hospital bill, no questions asked? Why didn't Mouse chew me out for being out all night before the meet? He didn't know where I'd been or why. Why wasn't he throwing in the Speedo on me?

Four months ago the only thing I'd cared about was going to the Olympics as a diver. Now it was obvious my life was different. I cared about a lot more. Did that mean diving wasn't for me? Did that mean all that time and effort and drive should go down the tubes now because I wasn't completely centered on that one thing?

Maybe. Maybe diving wasn't what I'd thought—the one thing that was going to make me *me*. But what if I didn't go for it? Who was I? Who would I be in my father's eyes? In God's? In Phong's?

In Tram's?

I opened my eyes, and the inside of the car swam. "Help me, Coach," I said.

"What do you need, son?" he said quietly.

"Help me get my head straight," I said. "I have to do this."

So the rest of the way to San Jose, I leaned back in the seat of the Volkswagen, eyes closed, every sinew relaxed, while Mouse kept up a steady, low rhythm of *you can do it* flowing softly into my ear.

"Your body's your diving equipment. It's fine-tuned. You've honed it and shaped it just the way you want it.

"You'll stand on the end of that board or platform, and just the way you stand will command notice.

"You'll see every dive in your head. Perfect. Pristine. Clean. Right through to the bottom of the pool.

"Work of art, every dive. A performance that will steal their breath and not give it back until your numbers come up on the board.

"You'll perform. And you'll feel it. You won't think. You'll do your thinking on the board. When you're in the air it'll be instinct—a reaction to the beauty inside you.

"You'll do it, Josh. Maybe your kid won't be there making you feel like Daddy Warbucks, but you'll still do it for him. And you'll do it for you.

"And no matter how it turns out—you'll be a different man when you leave that pool today."

He was quiet for a few miles while I let all of that sink into my cells.

"You pray?" he said into the silence.

"Yeah," I said.

"I suggest you do it now."

He was quiet again.

"Coach?" I said.

"What?"

"You mind if I prop my feet up on your dashboard?"

◆   ◆   ◆

The parking lot was already teeming with cars and people when we got there. I immediately got that pit-of-your-stomach feeling you have when you get to school late and you want to leap out of the station wagon before your mother puts on the brake.

Mouse pulled me back by the shoulder. "We've got plenty of time. And from here on, I do all the work. You just keep your head together and dive. That means you let me be the boss."

"Yes, sir," I said. And there wasn't a trace of sarcasm in my voice.

"All right now—focus."

I closed my eyes and breathed in.

"Good. Lose that concentration and I'll rip your lips off."

I grinned at him. He squeezed my shoulder.

Josh, old boy, who'd have thought you'd ever be depending on this short little—Godsend?

The tile-and-glass lobby was more hectic than the parking lot. For the second time that day I'd have killed to have seen Overbite Betty at the counter. Mouse told me to stand in a corner while he checked out my locker room assignment, which I obediently did. At least ten guys with bodies like Greg Louganis went by. I closed my eyes.

"Doesn't matter what they look like," Mouse said at my elbow. "It's what they do on the board that counts."

What? Are you reading my mind? Well, listen, Bucko— thank you.

He took me straight to the locker room, which by this

time was virtually empty, and handed me my L.A. Gear bag. I looked at him blankly. I'd been so out of it, I'd forgotten all about the frills—like a pair of swim trunks.

"You almost didn't get this," he said. "That big kid that met me at the hospital just handed it to me at the check-in."

"Just now?" I said.

"Yeah."

"He's here?"

"Yeah—now get changed. I'm going to do the rest of the paperwork. Meet me at the warming pool. There are arrows on the walls to get you there."

He also told me not to talk to anybody or think about anything but staying loose. I listened, and I tried—except for noticing that my Speedo was grimy and smelled like an Oakland sidewalk. It was a little sad in a way. This wasn't the way I'd pictured it at all. *Maybe in this life, man, the silver Speedos only happen in your dreams.*

"You're one of the first up," Mouse said when he ushered me into the warming pool. "New kid on the block—but that's okay. You'll fix an image everybody else will have to match."

I sank gratefully into the water and nodded. What he wasn't saying was that I wouldn't have to watch the experienced divers and freak out. He wasn't even letting me talk to them. I'd barely even seen any of them.

"Now lean back and think that image through," he said.

I did, and I did fine, until I got to the part where I swam to the edge of the pool and Phong wasn't there saying, "All right, Josh Dingbat. You did it, man."

But Brian was there.

"Ready?" Mouse said.

I nodded. "I'll just pretend he's an oversized Phong," I said.

"Lack of sleep's knocked the icing off your cupcakes," he said drily. "Come on."

Until then I hadn't looked around much. Mouse hadn't let me. But as we moved outside to the waiting area, I kept my arms swinging and gazed around, trying to look nonchalant. My eyes locked on the stands which surrounded the pool on three sides. There must have been fifteen hundred people out there in a blur of fluorescent visors and sunglasses. I couldn't even have picked big Brian out.

Fifteen hundred people there to see the Olympic potential—the dreamers who were willing to do more than dream to have it all. These people were there to see hope and talent and drive—the things that made up the Olympic ideal.

And I was part of that. I was here. This was it. I'd jogged in place at the starting line for months. Now I could take a step.

The crowd kept fanning and squealing and waiting. Mouse kept talking softly at my side. But it all became a backdrop for what was suddenly nudging my senses awake.

The bite of the chlorine in my nose. The glistening of pool water on my thighs. The rough concrete on the soles of my feet. The snapping of my trunks against my skin as I adjusted them over and over. Those things were as familiar as if I'd been back at the Municipal Pool. They were home no matter where I was. They were part of me. This was where I belonged.

"Ready?" Mouse said.

I squared my shoulders and nodded. *We will do it, Phong.* The first dive—the required dive—was a reverse. Mouse and I had already decided I'd do my reverse with a full twist to up the degree of difficulty. I didn't even have to think that. "Reverse dive" clicked off a series of pictures in my head, and after a second or two of watching them flip by, I was reenacting them. Nice smooth approach, an easy spring up, and I was looking back at the board. Arch. Twist. Roll. And an entry so clean I could feel myself squeak as I went in the water.

Mouse was there with a hand when I got to the edge of the pool. All I saw was his palm, and then his smile. All I felt was a hug neither one of us expected. All I heard was a singsong voice out of the crowd.

"All right, Josh!" it said. "You did it, man."

Call me crazy. There were over a thousand other voices crowding the air. But I heard him.

Mouse pulled me back to the waiting area and went after me with a towel.

"Looked good, fella. Real good. How do you feel? Not tired?"

I pushed the towel away. "I think I heard Phong," I said. "Is he here?"

"There are hundreds of kids in that crowd."

"Not yelling 'All right, Josh'!"

"Okay, okay, maybe you did. I don't know."

"I gotta look—"

I started for the fence, but he grabbed me. "You stay focused, loose, and warm. Keep that adrenaline pumping. I'll look."

"Do you swear?"

"For Pete—"

There was a mild roar, and Mouse tipped his sunglasses on to look at the scores. I didn't look.

He let out a long, slow whistle. "Dive total award—72," he said.

His face was a wreath of smiles. I'd never seen it like that. "All right, now let's keep it up. You got your next dive in your head?"

I nodded. I hadn't been shaking before the first dive, but I was now.

"Cold?" Mouse said.

"No."

"Scared?"

I shook my head.

"Excited?"

I nodded sheepishly and grinned.

"You're a competitor, guy. Okay—do it again."

I got ready to head for the springboard, and then I turned to him.

"I'll look for him," Mouse said. "I will."

Whether he believed me or not, I knew he would look.

And whether Phong was at the pool or not, the little

dweeb was in my heart. *We won't even give them three drops out of a splash this time, man. You watch.*

My next up was a back two and a half with a full twist. I poised on the board and saw it flip by, but the adrenaline was quivering under my skin, and I couldn't stand still. Approach. Up—

It felt good. Too good. I could feel myself overrotating just a little, arching just a hair too much.

Save. You can pull out a bad dive with a good save.

I corrected when I came out of the pike. I knew when I made my entry I hadn't gone over.

At pool's edge Mouse pulled me out and led me, arm around my shoulder, back through the gate.

"You know what you did wrong," he said.

"Yeah. Do you think the judges do?"

"Of course—but it was a beautiful save. Nice picture. Tired?"

"No way." There was so much cheering and flying and dreaming sizzling through my veins, I didn't think I'd ever be tired again.

There was another roar, louder this time.

"The crowd's with you," Mouse said. "They like the new kid."

I turned my head away. "Read it to me."

"Total dive award—70."

"Yes!"

"Oh, and Phong's on the third row, right side, center section. Between your mother—"

"He's here! I knew it! I knew he was here!"

I also knew my voice was wobbling on the verge of tears, but I didn't care.

"Lose that focus and I'll rip your entire face off," Mouse said.

But I saw the wet in *his* eyes too.

My last eight dives sailed like sea gulls. I'd never had a high like that off a board before.

And each time I came out of the pool I grinned. I knew Phong knew it was for him.

◆　　　◆　　　◆

There was a long wait while the second group of divers took the springboard before it was time for the platform dives. Mouse took me back to the warming pool. Even though I knew exactly what my scores meant, he ran through it in the same slow, even, soft voice he'd been using all day.

"You have a composite score of 750. That puts you within range, depending, of course, on how this group does. You already know the top guys are going to be in the eight, nine hundred range. You can't slack off on the platform. In fact, you have to be just as sharp if not sharper than you were on the board. You're still going to have to hustle to qualify for the Nationals."

"I'm ready to do it *now*," I said. "I hate this waiting around."

"Just stay loose," he said. "How's your fatigue?"

"I don't have any!"

"Like I said, stay loose. You're running on nervous energy."

There was a "but" in his voice. Something like, "but it isn't going to last forever."

Trouble was, he was right. As pumped as I was—with Brian *and* Phong out there in the stands and Mouse at my elbow encouraging me—my arms were starting to feel heavy. If I could just lie back in the warming pool and sleep for ten minutes—

"Let's go, Josh," Mouse said quietly.

The platform loomed as much like a hulking mass as it ever had as we moved into its waiting area. I could feel my stomach tightening into a bunch. I hadn't expected it to do that.

"You're going to go off that," Phong had said to me the first time I'd tried the platform. "You scared?"

I hadn't answered him. "You gonna be great, J.D." he'd gone on to say. "But you really not scared?"

He'd known all along I was terrified. He probably knew right now—that's how much he loved me.

I pulled in a long breath and looked up the ladder. Thirty-six feet. A full twelve feet higher than I'd ever dove from before.

But—every platform is the same. You can always count on it. Don't be afraid of it and you can use it as your strong suit.

At Mouse's nod I started up the ladder. On the way I used every handhold that was in my life.

Mouse's support.

God's presence. Oh yeah.

Phong's love.

Tram's—existence.

I wasn't even finished listing them when I got to the top. "You really not scared?" Phong was probably thinking.

None of your business, I thought back.

And then I dove. It was a forward three and a half, an easy one to get lost in. You have to have the feeling you've come around each time. The first somersault should be above the platform. Open soon enough to make the entry. Don't open too soon, or your heels will start to come back over on you. If you open too late, your upper legs will splash—

I was hurling through the air before I knew I'd left the platform. Over once. *Okay.* Over twice. *Man, am I over? Am I?* Over again. *Now? Now?* A splash. Like a tidal wave in my ears.

I grinned when I got out of the pool, but only for Phong. Once in the waiting area again, I grabbed for the towel and plastered it around me.

"You know what you're dealing with now," Mouse said.

"Yeah."

"You're not scared to do it again."

"No." That was true. But there was a but in *my* voice.

"That one took a lot out of you."

I nodded.

"All right. Let's get it back. Come on now—"

He talked slowly and calmly in my ear, pushing the psych

and pushing it hard. But he and I both knew, if you're tired, you're tired.

Up on the platform, I took double the time to prepare my approach. The moves weren't flipping by in my head; they were being dealt off the deck in slow motion.

Relax. See the dive. Then get it crisp. Make it tight.

I saw myself unwinding in the air like a bad dream. Opening my eyes, I shook my head.

Get on with it, man. You're putting yourself to sleep.

My arms were still heavy, and I could almost sense the crowd getting restless. I shook both arms and then pulled them back tight.

That looked tacky. Come on, dive, man.

Inward two and a half with a full twist. Jump. Backward. Come around—

But the platform was like a magnet. I could feel it pulling me back as soon as I started to spin. The concrete was there. Right there. Right there by my head—

And then I was in the water. I hadn't hit. I don't know how I missed it. But I hadn't saved. I hadn't performed. My legs had come apart, and I'd felt myself slop into the water. I didn't even want to come up.

I couldn't smile as Mouse reached down with both arms and pulled me out of the pool.

"You okay?" he said.

I nodded numbly, but he gave me a going-over anyway as we walked back to the waiting area.

"You didn't hit."

I shook my head. I was starting to come back to reality, and I was afraid if I talked I'd cry.

"I've never seen someone come that close. Buddy, you're lucky."

"I'm stupid," I said. I tossed the towel angrily into a corner. "I blew it before I ever started."

"And you'll blow it again thinking like that."

I looked at him quickly. He had his hands on his snakehips, and his eyes were narrowed shrewdly at me. "If you're going to quit, do it now. Don't waste time climbing that ladder."

I looked at the concrete. "I'm not giving up," I said. There was a spattering of applause. Probably my mother and Phong clapping.

"What are my scores?" I said.

"You don't need to know," Mouse said. "If you aren't quitting, get back up there."

He waited. I looked over his shoulder, down at the concrete, up at the sun—and finally back into his eyes. "Thanks," I said.

So I dove twice more. I didn't hit my head. I didn't even come close. But the flow was gone. The sea gull had obviously taken off for the Bahamas, leaving me with an overused robot. I made the right moves—and scored a 670. When I was through, I fell exhausted into the warming pool.

Mouse left me there to watch the rest of the divers. Normally I'd have done the same thing. But this wasn't normally.

I didn't have to see the rest of the divers to know that I didn't measure up to them. I knew my own diving well enough to know I hadn't even measured up to myself. It had been there at first, all the pieces fitting together and set in place by a high like nothing I'd ever known.

And then that first dive off the platform had finished me off. I was too tired to do anything but go through the motions. Right out there in front of God and Brian—and Phong. I'd let them down. I'd let Mouse down too—just when I'd started to care what he thought, just when I'd started to think he cared about me as a diver.

I'd had my chance, and I'd blown it. I didn't have to hear any more scores to know that. I leaned my head against the side of the pool and tried not to cry.

◆   ◆   ◆

When it was over, I went to the locker room and mechanically took a shower and put on the clothes I'd spent the night in. I was surrounded by divers reliving their somersaults to each other, but I didn't need Mouse to tell me not to talk to any of them. There was no way.

I had my head down, tying my shoes, when I sensed somebody standing over me.

"Very decent showing for a first-timer," he said.

I looked up into a tanned face. His nametag said "JUDGE."

I stood up politely on the two logs my legs had turned into.

"Thanks," I said. The locker room got quiet.

"Work some more on the platform. See if you can build up some stamina."

"Yes, sir," I said.

He moved on, and the chatter started again.

"Who *are* you?" a guy in navy-blue sweats said to me.

Nobody.

"Josh Daniels," I said.

"Does he know you?" he said.

"Who—the judge?"

"Yeah."

"No," I said. "I never saw him before."

The guy screwed up his lips and turned away.

"You set?"

I started to shove my Speedo into my bag and looked up at Mouse. "Yeah, I guess."

Since the cutoff had been announced, he hadn't said much to me beyond, "Why don't you get showered and changed?" But there wasn't disappointment in his face. There wasn't anything in his face.

"Then let's do it."

I began to zip the bag and then stopped. I reached in and pulled out the Speedo. It looked as limp and small and crummy as I felt. I balled it up and hooked it into a trash can. Mouse ran his hand over his hair.

"Let's go, guy. You got people out there waiting for you."

That's what I'd been afraid of. People with disappointed faces who didn't know what to say to a loser. My mother would be wearing her concerned dimples and telling me she understood. Brian would be looking beige and vague. Phong would be wishing he'd found himself another hero.

"Josh?" Mouse said.

I looked at him.

"They love you."

Gee, thanks, Coach. Do you think the judges will tack on a few extra points for love and let me go to the Nationals anyway?

I slung my bag over my shoulder and went for the door. When I pushed it open, something warm and sure wrapped itself around my leg. A six-person cheer went up that stopped everybody in the hall.

"Josh Dingbat—you looked *good*, man!"

Phong.

"Honey, I was so proud of you!"

Mom.

"Awesome."

Brian.

"Shoot, I didn't know you could dive like that."

Nathan.

"I didn't know you could do anything—period."

Young Jon Ricco.

"Joshua."

Tram, standing in that knot of cheering people who didn't know a back flip from a pepperoni pizza, but who loved me. They were yelling and hugging and slapping at my head. Phong was clasped to my leg like a ball and chain. And Tram just stood there and tossed her hair.

"Tram!" I said. Charming—but it was all I could get out.

"Joshua," she said again.

And then she cocked her head at me.

I'd have cried then, I know it, if I hadn't squatted down and grabbed Phong by the ears.

"What are you doing here, dweeb?" I said. "You're supposed to be home resting your ankle."

"I rested it here," he said.

"Right." Nathan flicked the top of Phong's head. "He rests like a pogo stick."

"He had everybody in Section C yelling 'All right, Josh Dingbat!'" Jon Ricco said.

"You're a winner, man," Phong said.

I shook my head at him. "I didn't make it."

He shrugged—not as if it didn't matter—just as if it didn't matter to him. "Not this time," he said. "Next time. You're a winner."

He wasn't lying to me to make me feel better. He didn't know how to do that yet. I looked up at all of them, all those people Mouse said were waiting there to love me. None of those smiles were lying either.

"We were all proud of you, Josh Dingbat," Mom said. "You were terrific."

"You had that crowd right in the palm of your hand."

"They wanted you to make it."

"You will."

I looked at Mouse. He had that pleasant ripple across his face.

They don't know what they're talking about. You know it. But you know what else? Right now, that's okay with me.

I went to bed at 4:00 Saturday afternoon and woke up at 5:00 Sunday afternoon. I might not even have joined the living then if my mother hadn't come through my bedroom door with a tray of turkey sandwiches and a pitcher of protein shakes and wafted them under my nose.

"I know you probably still need more sleep, but I also know how long it's been since you've eaten anything, and I thought you could wolf this down and then snuggle in again."

"Thanks," I said. As Lou jumped up beside me, I took a gargantuan bite out of one of the sandwiches, made with whole-grain bread, spread with low fat mayo, and piled high with alfalfa sprouts. "Could you bring in something that isn't good for me for dessert?" I said with my mouth full. "I'm not in training anymore."

Her dimples dipped. "Honey, I know you're disappointed—"

"Mom, if you tell me you understand, I'm warning you, you may wear this sandwich."

We both froze. I guess each of us was trying to decide how to take that and what to do with it.

It suddenly occurred to me that I still hadn't told her where I'd been Friday night or anything else that would explain my sudden loss of sanity. And she hadn't asked me a single question. Not even after she'd paid Phong's hospital bill.

"Joshua, if you want to go on with diving," she said finally, "I'm behind you. You know that. And so is your father. But I think you should know—"

She stopped. *Good grief, she doesn't know what to say next. Can this be?*

But I turned off my wise-guy switch. She looked drained, the way she had the night I'd come home and found her in the hot tub. In a way it was scary *not* to have her understand.

"What?" I said. I laid the half-eaten sandwich on the side of the plate.

"He's going to tell you this, but I know how seldom you have a chance to see him. And I know you don't want Coach Tulley to have to tell you."

"Mom—come on—"

"Your father has fired him. He's arranging for another coach."

"What?" I came up off the water bed, sending both Lou and the sandwich off the side. "Why—man—no! No way!"

Mom winced with every shout. "I told your father you'd probably react this way, but he's determined. He thinks you'd have made the cut yesterday if you'd had better coaching."

"There is no better coaching!" I said savagely. "I didn't dive my best because I'd been up all night the night before. That wasn't Mouse's fault. That was *my* choice! And Dad would know that if he'd even bothered to show up."

We froze again. After a second she leaned over to pick up the sandwich, but I knew it was because she didn't want me to see the tears in her eyes.

"You know what?" I ripped the covers aside and stood up, ignoring the fact that the room reeled. "Is he home?"

"He was about an hour ago."

"I'm calling him. I'm telling him—"

But I stomped out of the room without telling her what I was going to tell him, because I didn't know myself.

In a way it didn't really make any difference. I didn't know if I'd ever dive again anyway. But Mouse wasn't going to be fired by *my* father.

My father, the dad who didn't know beans about something that meant everything to his son. Who forked over the cash for the expensive coach but never once bothered to come by and check out the progress. Or ask intelligent questions. Or stick around for the meet. Or take care of his property. Or give a rip about the people who worked for him or shopped in his store.

I had my hand on the receiver, and I squeezed it tight. *Maybe he hasn't come through on this one thing you cared about because you didn't make enough noise. But there is one other thing you care about, Josh, man, and he's going to know about this one.*

"Hello?" said a honey thick voice on the other end of the line. The cologne saleslady.

"I want to speak to T.R.," I said.

"Honey, he's in the shower. We just got back from a trip and he's exhausted—"

"My *name* is Josh," I said. "I need to talk to him—now. Would you get him, please?"

She didn't answer. She just put the phone down hard.

We just got back from a trip? We?

I pressed the receiver against my ear to stop my hand from shaking and paced the hall. *You're coming to the phone, Bucko. You may not know it yet, but—*

"Josh!"

What a team they make. Her selling perfume. Him selling used cars.

"Dad," I said evenly, "we need to talk."

"Okay, my man."

I didn't have to see his face to know he was patronizing me. The kid's feeling his Wheaties, he was thinking, talking like a big man with things on his mind.

"I heard you fired Mouse Tulley," I said.

"It's obvious he didn't know what he was doing. I'm going to do some calling around this week—"

"No."

"What?"

255

"I don't want you to fire him. He's the best there is, and he doesn't deserve that."

I was surprised at how calmly my words were coming out, but that chunk of maturity didn't impress my father.

"He's got you brainwashed! I saw you dive. You'd have cleaned up at that meet if you'd had decent coaching—"

"I didn't 'clean up' because I wasn't prepared. I was out all night the night before."

"You're a sixteen-year-old kid! Any coach worth the kind of money I was paying him would've made sure you weren't out partying—"

"I wasn't partying."

There was a sudden silence.

"Then what *were* you doing?"

"You really want to know?"

"Don't be a wise guy with me," he said. "Yes, I want to know—and you're going to tell me."

So I did—everything. I didn't leave out a single detail, not even the part about the store that reeked of rotten meat and didn't carry *nuoc man*.

"Those people deserve better," I said. "You—"

"I put out all this money for you to have a private coach and you blow it all on some little Veet-namese kid?"

I squeezed the receiver. *Veet-namese. It sounded so demeaning.*

"And you say there's a girl involved," he went on. "I don't know, Josh. You're a good-looking, with-it kid with everything going for you. I *thought* you were intelligent. What the—you gonna let this little foreigner mess up your life? You're not thinking with your brain, my man!"

"It's not like that!" I knew I was yelling, but I didn't care.

"You can forget about me paying for another coach—"

"I don't want another coach."

"I'm not paying Tulley another dime either. Did he know about all this?"

"Yeah."

There was a jeering stream of expletives. I held the earpiece away from my head and shouted "Dad!" into the receiver.

"Don't you raise your voice to me—"

"I'll tell you what I do want—"

"*You're* going to tell *me* what you want?"

"I want $10,000 out of my college fund."

Silence. I was talking money now. I knew that would get him.

When he did speak, his voice was thin and nasty. "For *what*?"

I didn't even hesitate. "I want to give it to Tram and Phong to get an exit permit to get their father out of Vietnam."

I can't repeat what came out of his mouth then—mostly because I blocked it out. I didn't need to remember it. It meant nothing to me.

When he'd spluttered out, he waited for me to say something. I didn't.

"What has gotten into you, Joshua?" he said. "I mean— what *is* this?"

I'd wondered what I'd say if anybody ever asked me that question. I hadn't come up with anything original. I could only repeat what Mouse had said to me. "I guess it's the power of love." I laughed a little. "—or something mystical like that."

He laughed too, and hung up.

When I got back to my bedroom, Mom was putsying with the tray, but she didn't pretend not to have heard the whole conversation.

"It didn't go well," she said. It was a statement she could have made before I even dialed the phone.

I flopped on the bed. Lou joined me warily. "No, it didn't."

She sat down beside me and stroked Lou's hair. I knew she really wanted to stroke mine. "I can only imagine what was coming from his end—" She put up a hand to stop me. "So you don't have to tell me, and I don't want you to. But I do know what you said. I'm proud of you."

I shrugged. "Thanks."

"It isn't easy, is it?"

"It's okay." I looked at her. She was waiting. "No," I said, "it isn't. He makes it real hard."

She concentrated on Lou's ears. "I think you probably pray—at least you were introduced to God as a little guy. I'd say now would be a good time to go to your other Father and talk this out, because I'm really at a loss for what to tell you." The tears came back to her eyes. "I still love your dad, but I don't think I know him anymore."

Say something, dingbat. Don't let her drown.

"If it's any consolation, I don't either," I said.

"I know God can help you. He specializes in parent-teen relationships because nobody else understands them!"

The dimples returned, and in spite of myself I flashed mine back at her.

"You're exhausted, honey," she said. "Come on, snuggle in again. Lou, you get in there with him. Make him sleep."

As I got back under the covers, the weird thoughts of almost-asleep curled their confused way through my brain.

Mom cares about kids. She really believes in what Christianity can do for them. She makes a living at it. Too bad you never hit her up for advice before. You probably ought to tell her about the parties and the hypocrites at CCA and all that stuff. She oughta know. She could do something about that—

"Mom, can we talk?" I mumbled.

"Later," she said. But she did pull her hand across my hair. I wanted to purr like Lou.

"Will you call Phong's and make sure his ankle's okay?"

"You bet."

"I want to buy Tram a cross. I want to give it to her."

"Okay. What else?"

But I couldn't get anything else out. I could only sleep.

◆　　◆　　◆

I woke up early Monday morning and wandered down to

the kitchen to find Mom and Denise putting an icing American flag on a sheet cake.

Denise couldn't stifle a shriek when she saw me.

"Do you have to do that?" I said.

"I don't blame her," Mom said. "Are you trying for a new hairstyle or what, Joshua?"

I looked at my reflection in the oven door and had to snort myself. Spikes again. It really was the new me.

"You're hungry, of course," Mom said. "But, honey, you're going to have to help yourself. We've got an awful lot to do."

"For what? What's with the flag?"

"It's Memorial Day," Denise said. "You're having a party."

I stopped stripping a banana in mid-peel. "*I'm* having a party? Why am I having a party?"

"Because you're special," Mom said. "Oh, would you taste this potato salad? I'm not sure if it needs more salt."

Normally I'd have wanted to barf at being called "special" by my mother. But like a lot of other things recently, this wasn't "normally."

"Who did I invite to this party?" I said.

Mom shoved a spoonful of potato salad at me. "Well, if you don't know we're certainly not going to tell you. Right, Denny-Penny?"

Denny-Penny shook her poodle head and smiled mysteriously.

"The way this is going to work," she said, "is you're going to, like, enthrone yourself in the hot tub, and as the guests arrive they're just going to, you know, like, strip down into bathing suits and join you."

"So hurry up and, like, grab a snack so you can shower and—" Mom giggled, "—do something with your hair."

I slapped my hand down over my head, but I laughed. I couldn't help myself.

◆　　　◆　　　◆

Okay, so it was a little weird, but Mom and Denise weren't going to let me get away with playing host to who knows who any other way. I had to get into my bathing suit and park in the hot tub with a limeade and wait. I'd had about as much lying around doing nothing as I could take, so I lost my head and yelled to Denise, "You got a bathing suit?"

"Yeah," she yelled back from the dining room where she was folding red, white, and blue napkins into the shape of a star.

"Do you have it on?"

Semi-shriek. "Yeah."

"Then come talk to me."

She appeared in the doorway, eyes big as checkers. "*You* want to talk to *me*?"

"Don't be a wise guy," I said. "Yeah, I want to talk to you."

She pulled her oversized T-shirt off self-consciously and slipped into the tub like she was afraid I'd never noticed before that she, too, had pipe-cleaner legs.

At first I wimped out. "I'm sorry about your parents' divorce," I said.

"Thanks," she said. But we both knew that wasn't why I'd invited her in.

"I think I need to thank you for something, but I'm not sure," I said.

She looked down at the bubbles and shrugged.

"Friday night when I called here—did you—do something?"

She opened her mouth and shut it again.

"If you did what I think you did," I said, "you did good." Her mouth was trembly, she was so nervous. I felt like a jerk. *Man, Josh, why haven't you ever cut this chick any slack?*

"When you called," she said, "I could tell something was really wrong. You just sounded, like, so—anxious. But I wasn't sure what was going on, and I didn't want to freak your mom out, y' know, so I called Brain."

She looked like she expected me to blow a gasket or something. *You really have been a jerk to this girl, Josh. Nice. Real nice.*

"Go ahead," I said.

"I called him and told him you were at Phong's and that maybe I was crazy, but you sounded like you were in trouble. He didn't even sound like he thought I was crazy. It was like he got kind of scared himself. He, like, you know, muttered to himself that he wished he knew where the—where Phong's was." She wouldn't look at me. She concentrated on gathering bubbles up to her bathing suit.

"So—then?"

"So then I just looked around and there was the address right there on the counter."

"Because Mom was going to pick Phong up the next morning."

"Yeah. So I gave it to him."

"If you hadn't I might not be here," I said. It didn't sound as dramatic and corny as I'd expected it to. It obviously didn't sound that way to Denise. She just stared at me, checker-eyed, and nodded. "Thanks," I said to her.

She shrugged and started to get up. "Well," she said, "I have to go finish, you know, helping your mother."

"Hold on," I said.

She stopped on the edge of the tub and hugged herself nervously. I was a scosch nervous myself. I was new at this apologizing stuff.

"Nobody else would have had the smarts to do what you did," I said. "I guess I never really treated you like you had any brains at all."

"Most people don't. Sara—your mom—says it's because I don't let them see my brains."

I could feel myself grinning. "Well, yeah, she's got a point there, but—"

"But, see, Josh—" She hugged herself harder. "I don't think 'brains' had anything to do with it. It's more that, well, like, you know, I hang out here a lot. This is, like, another home."

"That did catch my eye."

"And so I sort of, like, you know, watch you, and I guess I just know you."

"Oh." *Okay, Josh, man, how are you going to break it to the chick that you don't want to be "known" by her. She's not as much of a dip as you thought, but she still isn't—*

"It's just—I kind of think of you as a big brother," she said. "I wanted us to be Christian brother and sister."

She stopped and looked down into the water. Thank heaven she wasn't looking at me, because I know the words "conceited, egotistical fool" were written all over my face.

"The thing is, though," she said, "for a while I wasn't sure you really were a Christian. I mean, you know, like the way you talked to your mother—or didn't talk to her. And you were so wrapped up in yourself. But then that night you came home and you and Meggie were talking about the Vietnamese family, it was like the Christian Joshua came back. And that's how I knew to call Brain," she finished simply.

I at least had the guts to look up at her. She looked at me for a second too and smiled metallically. My mother was right. She was really going to be beautiful someday. On the inside she already was.

I punched stupidly at her leg. "Could you, like, you know, forgive me?" I said.

She shrieked. "For what?"

"Being a dweeb to you."

She got really still—a feat for Denise—and didn't say anything.

"I want to be your brother," I said. "And I really will— I'll try to be a decent one."

"Assorted Buddies One and Two," my mother called from the doorway just then.

Nathan and Young Jon Ricco were behind her, doing a double take at Denise and me chatting cozily in the hot tub.

I sat up straighter. "Where's Brian?"

"Real nice, Daniels," Nathan said. "Your two best friends show up and you're looking around for somebody else."

"The Brain drove his own car," Jon said. "Too good for us, I guess."

There was a grunt behind them, and Brian filled the doorway. It was a fact, really. He was too good for most people, and he didn't even know it.

Somewhere in the scramble of the A.B.'s pulling off their shorts and getting what they wanted to drink from the complete line of beverages my mother was offering, Denise left the hot tub and I was left with the three of them.

"So," Nathan said, lounging across from me with one scrawny leg slung out over the side, "is anybody ever going to tell us why we spent all Friday night cruising around downtown Oakland?"

"No," Brian said simply.

But I gave them the *Reader's Digest* version, leaving out just how much Phong meant to me. I knew they wouldn't really get that part.

"The thing I haven't figured out," I said when I was through and Jon and Nathan still had their mouths hanging too far open to respond yet, "is how you knew where to find us. I mean, I know Denise called you and gave you directions."

"Yeah," Brian said.

"You're going to have to give me a few more details, Bri," I said. "I'm a slow learner."

Nathan picked it up. "First of all, there's nobody home at the apartment. Brain thinks that's weird, so he hauls us back in the car and takes us to this really heavy vacant lot—the whole time not telling us what the—what we're doing or what we're looking for. Ricco and I are freaking out."

"It really gets weird when he—" Jon Ricco jerked his thumb toward Brian, "gets out of the car, climbs the fence, and picks up your bag off the ground."

"When he finds your trunks out on the sidewalk," Nathan said, "I figure the next time we're going to see you is at your funeral."

"Thanks," I said.

"So the rest of the night we cruise all over Oakland looking for—what was it?"

Jon Ricco started ticking them off on his finger. "You—a Vietnamese kid—two black apes—and a Mexican with an attitude." He laughed. "The only thing I was looking for was you. I mean, in downtown Oakland, who *isn't* black, Vietnamese, or Mexican?"

"We stopped asking questions about 2 A.M. because he wasn't going to tell us anything. Five A.M. we go back to the apartment building, and then the thing is, how are we going to get in? Those Chinks have the place locked down tighter than Folsom Prison."

"Vietnamese," I said, teeth gritted.

He ignored that. "So we pull up, and there's one of them with glasses digging around in a potted plant by the gate." Nathan grinned. "So get this—Brain goes up and starts a conversation with the guy—half English, half sign language."

Jon Ricco demonstrated, and I had to laugh. Brian just leaned back against the side of the tub, eyes closed.

"Finally the guy says, yeah, he's seen you and the girl and if he sees you again he's going to turn you into an egg roll because you didn't leave his keys in the plant the way you said you were going to."

"That must have been what Tram told him," I said. "But go on."

"He says the last thing he knew you two were headed for the basement." Nathan wiggled his eyebrows. "I was all for leaving you alone. I mean, who are we to cramp your style if you've got something going? But Brain practically knocks the guy down going over the gate and making for the basement."

"Me and Nathan, we waited for him to open the gate," Jon Ricco put in.

"Real class," I said.

"We get down there and Brain's banging on the door and yelling for you."

"When we saw the chain," Jon Ricco said, "we figured you weren't in there by choice."

"You're quick," I said.

Nathan turned to Brian. "I got some questions, though. I mean, how did you know all the places to look? You drove around downtown like you lived there or something—and we're not talking about knowing where the high-class restaurants are. We went to some *dives*."

"There's food in the dining room," Mom announced from the doorway.

If she hadn't saved Brian, I would have. It was a question I'd wanted to ask a hundred times myself, but I was pretty sure he didn't want them to know the answer.

All three of them left me in a tidal wave as they followed their stomachs to the dining room.

"Coach Tulley is here," Mom said when they were gone. "I'll keep the Buddies in burgers so you two can talk."

You understand—again. And, man, I'm glad.

"Thanks, Mom," I said.

I stood up when Mouse came out. He shook my hand warmly. "Don't get out," he said. "I'm told you're supposed to play host from here all day."

"Yeah, but—"

"Stay," he said. "I'll join you."

I must have been getting pretty used to taking orders from Mouse because I sat down. He eased himself in.

"So how's your head?" he said.

"Clearing up. I guess I have some explaining to do to you."

"Not if you don't want to."

But I did want to, and I told him everything. His face flinched when I got into the stuff about the street gang, but he didn't launch into an *I warned you* lecture. As a matter of fact, I suddenly realized, Mouse never launched into a lecture. Like I said, I'm a slow learner.

"You love that little boy," he said.

I nodded. "I guess I do."

"Then it was worth it." Mouse ran a hand slowly back over his hair. I thought I was going to cry. I was going to miss seeing him do that. "Let me tell you something, Josh," he said. "Diving has been just about my whole life, ever since I took my first Red Cross swimming course and they couldn't keep me off the diving board long enough to teach me what to do once I got in the water."

I laughed.

"Anyway, I was lucky. I had the body to be a diver, and like you I just worked my way up through the ranks, and I didn't think about anything else but going to the Olympics."

I sat up in surprise.

"Yeah, me," he said. "When I made it to the '76 games I thought, okay, this is it."

I sat up even straighter.

"Dream come true. Even if I didn't even win anything, I could say I competed with the best in the world."

"I hear you," I said.

"But as it turns out, I didn't. I wasn't there a day when I came down with the chicken pox. Embarrassing. I've never been so sick in my life."

"Aw, man!"

"That's pretty much what I said. But then I figured, okay, four years to get even better. In four years I'd have a real chance. I worked my tail off in those four years. Made a pretty good showing in the National and International competitions. Then 1980 came along."

He stopped.

"1980," I said slowly. "The U.S. wouldn't compete in the 1980 Olympics."

"Exactly," he said.

"Man—you must have been so ticked."

"Oh, I was. I had never felt disappointment like that. I'll never know if I had what it took. But the reason that disappointment came so harsh to me was because I'd pinned all the hopes of my life on that one dream. When I lost that, I didn't even know who I was. And I don't know if a person who doesn't really know who he is is gold-medal material."

"I don't get you."

"It takes more than being an athlete to be a medalist. You have to have heart. You have to be a whole person. It's a hard balance to strike. You've got to be willing to put so much into honing your skills—so much that you practically isolate yourself from everything else. And yet in your heart there have to be other powers operating."

"You have to be Sammy Lee."

"You could say that."

"Why didn't you ever tell me any of this stuff?" I said.

That pleasant ripple passed over his face. "Would you have listened to me if I had?"

I looked down. "I guess not."

"Don't worry about it, Josh. The most important thing isn't just the win. It's what you learn on the way. It's the trying that counts."

I let the air out through my nose. "I didn't go through all that just to try."

"You're sixteen years old! We expected so much, but, let's face it, you were just a kid."

"I'm still just a kid."

He cocked his head sharply. "I disagree. A kid becomes a man when there's a need for a man. You made some tough choices Friday night. A kid doesn't make those kinds of choices."

We were quiet for a while. But there were still things I had to say.

"I want to apologize for my father," I said.

"Why?"

"Because he fired you. Treated you like scum."

"You're twice the man your father is. Don't apologize for him."

I looked closely at Mouse, maybe for the first time ever. "You don't like my father, do you?"

"Not particularly. He didn't take an interest in your talent, and that held you back. He put you in a position where you were trying to win him by winning at diving. I think that's criminal."

"Did you just work for him for the money?" I said.

He shot me a look. "I didn't need the money, Josh. I agreed to coach you because I'd seen you work and I thought you had potential."

"You already knew that before he hired you?"

"I make it a point to take in the meets. I like to see who's coming up. I knew I'd be seeing you somewhere if you had the drive. First time I met you, I knew you did." He rippled. "I also knew you had an attitude. If anything was going to stop you, it was that. I didn't know if we'd ever get past that—until Phong came along."

I was really confused by then. I guess he picked that up from the way my upper lip was curling into my nose.

"He was your balance. He loved you—I've never seen a kid worship an older boy like he did you, and I've worked with a lot of kids. And when I saw that you cared about him—then I knew there was something in there." He pointed at me. "You had the heart to make your diving more than just a sport. That's when I knew you could do it."

"And then I blew it," I said ruefully.

"You blew one meet—and for the right reasons. And you could even have pulled that off if you'd had more experience. That Regional meet wasn't the end, Josh."

"I don't know. You're my coach. Without you—"

He waited, but I couldn't finish.

"When you decide, come see me," he said. "Bayside Health Club."

"You work there?" I said.

"My wife and I own it. Every Tuesday is kids' night. We open the club at a cut rate and mess around with the little guys. Start getting them in shape young." He watched me as he spoke. "Bring Phong. He can lift weights while we talk."

"I can't afford you," I said.

"We'll talk," he said.

I knew Mouse well enough by then to stop. But there was one more thing I wanted to know.

"How come they call you Mouse?" I said.

He glanced over his shoulder. "I don't tell too many people this."

"I'm a clam," I said.

"My name's Ralph Aaron Tulley. Initials for that are—"

"R.A.T."

"Kids started calling me Rat in kindergarten. How many parents do you know who are going to sit still for that for very long?"

"Not mine!"

"Mine either. They substituted Mouse, and it stuck."

"It doesn't fit you," I said.

"Thanks," he said.

If my mother hadn't made another well-timed entrance, I think we'd both have cried.

"Are you ready for the next entourage?" she said.

Whether I was ready or not, Meg burst in, with Phong draped across her back.

"You couldn't keep this kid quiet if he was in a body cast!" she said. "Get down. You've completely rearranged my vertebrae."

Mouse got out of the tub to meet Meg. Phong hopped toward me on one foot and then stopped.

My eyes followed his to the water. "I'll get out," I said quickly. "You can't get in with your ankle."

"We can take the Ace bandage off," Meg said.

She couldn't have known about Phong's fear, but I growled at her anyway. But Phong plopped himself down and stuck out his foot to her. "Take it off," he said. "Josh Dingbat won't let me go under."

So Mouse watched—misty-eyed, though he'd never have admitted it—while Phong wrapped his arms around my neck and let me circle around the hot tub with him.

"Feels great, doesn't it?" I said.

He nodded stiffly.

"You're a brave man," I said.

He shook his head.

"Are you scared?" I said.

269

He nodded.

"But you trust me," I said.

"Yeah."

"Then you're a brave man," I said.

"Yes, he is," said someone else.

I looked up sharply. Tram was standing on the edge of the tub, cocking her head at me.

"Can I interest you in some potato salad and a hamburger, Coach?" Mom said.

Phong scrambled right out of my arms. "You can interest me!"

Mouse pulled him out of the hot tub and carried him piggyback into the house with Meg bringing up the rear with the Ace bandage. She looked over her shoulder, first at me, then at Tram. "I'm going to go get a spoon," she said. "You have some words to eat, Josh Dingbat."

But my eyes were on Tram, wearing a shiny blue bathing suit that she did wonderful things for.

"He does get in the water with you," she said.

"I threaten him," I said.

I looked at her some more. I knew before that that I loved her. But it had been something else that made me feel that way. It wasn't the way she looked. But now, the way she looked—natural—like Meg—

Yeah, I'm interested.

"May I get in?" she said.

"Oh—man—I'm sorry—"

I stood up to help her into the tub, slipping on the step, splashing her, and generally acting like a dingbat in the process.

"Klutz," she said mildly as she stepped gracefully in, sat down and knotted her hair up on top of her head.

"Where's Ba—your mother?"

"She was too shy to come. But she sent spring rolls."

"Naturally. No meatballs, though?"

She shook her head. A smile twitched around her lips.

"Well, heck, I didn't even know *you* were coming," I said.

"What would you have done if you had?" she said.

I didn't get to answer that. My mother's powers of persuasion only went so far. The tub was suddenly full of Nathan and Jon Ricco, who had hung around with Tram long enough to know to keep their hands off and their mouths shut, but who weren't above gawking at her. Denise and Meg must have talked my mother into letting them out of the house too, since everybody else was horning in. And of course Phong wasn't going to miss out on any of the action.

And it was okay. In fact, it was one of those days I knew even then was going to fall into the *Remember that Memorial Day* category when I was forty years old.

Tram was near enough for me to watch her all afternoon.

Meg and Mom and Denise never stopped serving sodas and trays piled with cookies and plates heaped up with burgers and spring rolls.

Except for the five minutes when Mom took me aside.

"I got this for you to give Tram, like you asked," she said. She put a small white box in my hand. "I don't know if it's what you wanted," she said as I opened it. "You were too sleepy to give me any details."

Inside the box, nestled in cotton, was a silver cross. My mother obviously hadn't needed details. The cross was Tram— simple and fragile and strong. Unmuddied.

I looked up at Mom.

"She's a lovely girl, Joshua," she said. "And you're a fine person to think of this."

I could feel myself getting choked up, so I just said, "Thanks."

Of course she understood.

Back in the hot tub, Nathan and Jon Ricco had everybody laughing. It looked like they weren't ticked off at me any more. Maybe they hadn't been for a while or they wouldn't have cruised around a whole night looking for me and come to my diving meet or come here today. It was a wonder they weren't grounded for life. There was hope in there somewhere. There probably was in all of them—Jill, Kim, everybody. They were going the wrong direction, but maybe Mom could help. Not that I had it all together, but at least I knew who to follow, and maybe I could help them find the way too.

And then there was Brian. I watched him a lot that day. He had Phong in his lap most of the time, or he was wrestling on the floor with him, or they were planning sneak attacks on Nathan and Jon Ricco. When I got the chance—when everybody was inside cutting the cake and they left Brian with me to make sure I wouldn't get too far from the hot tub—I asked him some things I'd wanted to know for a long time now.

"It's none of my business," I said. "Your life, I mean. So I'm gonna ask you some stuff, and if you want to answer it fine, and if you don't—"

"Go for it," he said.

"Okay. How come you used to live in downtown Oakland?"

"That's where I was born—where my dad raised me. We lived in an apartment. A block from the vacant lot."

I tried not to look shocked.

"You want to know how I ended up here."

"Yeah, but—"

"My dad got on drugs when he was in Nam. He came back with only one arm. My mother couldn't take it, so she left, and he couldn't take that, so he stayed on drugs. Then when I was eleven, I got on drugs."

I stared.

"So they took me away and I got rehabilitated."

"At eleven?"

"And at thirteen. And at fourteen. Every time I went back to my father I got in more trouble. Stealing. Vandalism." He sounded like he was going through a shopping list. "But something in me said, I hate this. I asked them to find me a foster home. They did. Here I am."

He'd skipped a few steps, but I got the gist. "So the 'they' you usually talk about—those are your foster parents."

"Yeah. It worked too, because they had a kid who was a photographer in Nam. He got killed."

"So you're kind of taking his place."

"No. They told me when I moved in that would never happen. But now it's, like, they like me for *me*—so I'm not like that son—I'm like another son."

"That's why they send you to California Christian."

"They'd do that anyway. It's more that they gave me his car."

That would definitely do it.

"Hey," he said.

"Hey, what?"

"Are we gonna keep watching out for the kid?"

"I want to," I said. "But I won't be going to the pool anymore."

"Doesn't matter. We'll take the Chevy."

"You don't have to."

"Yes, I do. I know what happens to kids down there. He's too cool for us to let that happen to him."

I nodded.

"I'll meet you after school tomorrow. We'll go down."

Mouse had to leave then. Before he went, Phong presented him with a painting.

"It's you, Josh," Mouse said. Everybody, of course, had to crowd around.

"It is," Nathan said. "I can tell by the do."

He was right. It was definitely me, sailing off the diving board in perfect form—with my hair sticking up in spikes.

Eventually Nathan and Jon got tired of looking at Tram and never having her look back, so they took off. Denise hadn't shrieked all day, so they offered her a ride home.

"Don't bully my sister," I called after them.

They looked at me, looked at her, and looked at each other. Denise mouthed a tinselly "thank you" to me. Brian trailed out behind them.

Meg and Mom went somewhere in the house with Phong. I could vaguely hear him discovering Lou and leading him into some adventure in Phong-dom. But it was all background for being alone with Tram. She'd pulled on a sweatshirt and was brushing her hair on the deck beside the tub.

"Is it safe to get out now?" I said. "I'm a prune."

She tossed me a towel. *She looks so cool and together, and I'm falling apart like I never talked to a girl before.*

But I had to say something. They'd be leaving soon, and I wanted to know where that really left me.

"Thanks for coming over," I said. "I know with Meg you probably didn't have much of a choice—"

"Yes, I did. I like your sister. She isn't pushy. Besides, if I hadn't wanted to come, I wouldn't have."

"Yeah." I laughed wryly. "I guess I knew that."

She put her brush down and tossed her hair. It was shiny. Her eyes were shiny. Her face even shined. Man—

I took a breath. "Denise told me—you know, the chick with the braces—"

"Nice girl."

"Yeah. She was doing a report on Vietnamese teenagers—"

"I know. She interviewed me."

Man, am I ever going to get this out?

"Great. Well, she told me you guys, in your country, don't really—date."

"That's true."

"You don't, like, go out with that kid with the glasses, from the laundry room?"

She looked like she was smothering a laugh. "No."

"Oh," I said, ever the poet.

She cocked her head at me. I wished she wouldn't do that. I loved it when she did—but when she did, I turned into one big speech impediment.

I swallowed. "So—how Americanized are you—about dating?"

She shrugged. "Once in a while an American guy who doesn't have a clue will ask me out. I tell him no way."

My heart sank. "Because of your culture."

"No. Because he's a jerk."

I pulled at the sleeves of my sweatshirt. "Most of us are."

"You aren't."

"You thought I was."

"Until the other night."

I couldn't stand it. I got up and wandered around. Once when I'd been sick I'd watched an afternoon of soap operas out of sheer boredom. The characters had done a lot of that—wandering around when they were talking. I'd thought it was dumb. Now I knew why they did it.

"The other night. Yeah," I said. "The other night kind of like—" *Man, you sound like Denise.* "Well, it meant something to me and what I'm getting at—not exactly in twenty-five words or less—is whether—"

"Would you please sit?" she said.

I did. She snuck her hand over on top of mine.

"I got to know you some the other night," she said, "and I figured out that you aren't a jerk. I never let myself get to that point with any guy yet, especially an American."

"Okay." *And?*

"See—" She searched for words. "I've had to be the one everyone leans on for so long. The other night *I* leaned. It made me feel—it just made me feel like there are things I want to know."

The things she wanted to know smoldered in her eyes.

"So that wasn't just—it? The end of it?" I said. *Gee, Josh, man, you're really smooth at this.*

She started to pull her hand away, but I grabbed it. "Stay right here. I have something for you."

I left her on a lounge chair while I went to the table for the cross. *Okay, don't blow this. Don't try to be a wise guy.*

I stopped with my hand on the box. What was I thinking? There was nothing to blow. It was time to get real.

I sat on the end of the lounge chair, box in hand.

"You know what?" I said.

"No, but I bet I'm about to find out." Her eyes were shiny.

"I thought you were a jerk too at first—I mean, if girls can be jerks."

"At my school they call them something else," she said drily.

"But then I started figuring out you were acting like a 'she-jerk' to me because I was a wise guy *and* because you've had to give up just about everything that's important to you."

She didn't say anything. She just slowly pulled her hair back.

"I can't give you back hardly any of what you've lost," I said, "even though I want to. But I can at least give you this."

The tiny lines puckered as she looked from me to the box.

"Open it," I said.

She sat up and took the box from me. Hesitatingly, almost as if she didn't know how, she opened it. When she did, her eyes came up to me. It was only the second time I'd ever seen her look like a china doll.

I shrugged. "It's just to replace the one you had to give up," I said.

She picked it up and started to put it on, but she stopped and squeezed it in her hand.

"Here, let me," I said. I took it from her and slipped behind her to put it on her. It was a good excuse not to see what was going on in her face. Just in case—

Fastening a chain isn't easy when your fingers have turned into stumps, but somehow I got it on her. Then there was a minute when she just ran her finger over it.

"My mom did this with me," I said.

"She's a good lady," she said softly.

"If you don't like it, I can take it back and get another one."

Her whole hand closed over it. "Na-na-na-na-na!"

Relief bubbled out of me. I could feel her relaxing too. I got brave and pulled her shoulders back so she was leaning against me.

"Joshua?" she said.

I started massaging the arms of the lounge chair. "Yeah."

"Okay—" Her voice got stronger. "See, the thing is, there isn't even a word in Vietnamese for girlfriend or boyfriend."

I looked down into that black hair. "Do you want there to be? We could make one up, y' know."

She cocked her head to one side. "When nothing else works, you can always use sign language."

"Sign language?"

She twisted to look up at me. Her eyes danced just the way Phong's did.

She wants you to kiss her, dingbat.

"Will this work?" I said.

She never answered. I didn't give her a chance.

Tuesday I saw Mouse for the last time—at least for a while.

We talked at his health club while Phong learned how to play racquetball with a bunch of other kids.

"You have a lot of things to get straight in your head," he said, "before you can decide whether you want to compete as a world-class diver or do it in some other capacity."

"Like what?"

"Like teaching. Watching you with Phong, the thought does come to mind that you'd be good at it."

I toyed with my shoelaces. "I don't know—"

"Exactly—you don't know. And for Pete's sake, you're sixteen years old. How many people make up their minds at that age about what they're going to do the rest of their lives?"

"You have to compete these days," I said.

He reached up and squeezed my shoulder. "You can afford a few months. It could make the difference between a wise decision and a big mistake."

I could feel my eyes starting to swim again. Since Friday they'd been doing that a lot. "How do I know?" I said. "That's the problem."

"Pay attention," Mouse said. "You have indicators all around you. You know, when I said it's the trying that builds you, I didn't mean to mislead you. That judge didn't come into the locker room and compliment everybody. He singled you out because you have talent. That's an indicator." He glanced over at Phong who was emerging from the racquetball court with a grin like a slice of honeydew melon. "There's another one."

When it was time to go and Brian had the Chevy waiting out front, Mouse wouldn't say good-bye.

"One way or the other, you're still going to need some coaching," he said.

"I told you—I can't afford you, now that my father's pulled out on me."

"Arrangements can be made. We can trade coaching for some hours put in working here—it can always be worked out." That pleasant ripple moved across his face. "So, no good-bye. Just so long for now."

"So-Long Phong!" Phong singsonged.

When I looked back on our way out to the car, Mouse was in the doorway, running his hand back across his hair. I looked away.

That was Tuesday. Now it was Wednesday, after school, and for the first time in months I didn't have anyplace to go.

So there I was, lying on my back on my queen-sized water bed with my feet up on the dirty spot on the wallpaper, arms behind my head like usual, with Lou curled up in one of my armpits.

But there were no dreams to plug in. I wasn't sure what to even pray about. I just thought. And then I thought about what I was thinking.

Who are you now, Josh Daniels? What is it you want? I mean, for real? That plan you thought you had all worked out with God. Something was missing, wasn't it?

The phone rang out in the hall. Mom wasn't home yet, so I got up and answered it.

"Hi, Baby B.," Meg said.

"Hi," I said. "What's wrong?"

Funny. A month, maybe even a few weeks before I might

not have even noticed that Meg's voice didn't have its usual sizzle—much less asked her about it.

"Is Mom there?" she said.

"She isn't home from work yet. What am I, pastrami on rye?"

"I really need to talk to her. Josh!"

"Yeah?" I said carefully. She was just barely holding back the tears. I was afraid if I said much of anything she'd flood the receiver.

"I am *really* sorry about what happened with you and Dad."

I picked up the phone and carried it into my room. I was going to need the bed, the wallpaper, *and* Lou for this conversation.

"I thought you wanted me to find out about him," I said.

"Not like that." She was crying for real by then.

"You knew he wasn't coming to the meet, didn't you?"

"You know I couldn't tell you."

"Don't worry about it," I said. "I handled it."

"I'm proud of you. And I want to thank you."

"Thank me? For what?"

"For saying what you did to Dad."

"Okay." I groped for something I could have said that Meg would be grateful for.

She took a second—probably to wipe off everything that was streaming out of her eyes and nose. "When I got home after the party yesterday, that was the first I really knew about any of this because you didn't tell me, and Mom didn't either."

"*Mom* didn't?"

"No—or haven't you noticed that she never bad-mouths Dad to us?"

No, I guess I haven't noticed a lot of stuff about Mom.

"So how'd you know?" I said.

"Dad."

I snorted. "I'd like to hear *his* version."

"Oh, I took it with about a *pound* of salt, believe me. He was just oozing sarcasm—even when he told me what you said—about why you spent all night looking for Phong instead of resting for the diving meet. He says, 'You know what the wise guy told me? He said it was the power of *love*—or something mystical. I'm gonna vomit.' That's what he said—that he was going to throw up."

I thought I might just then too.

Meg gave a huge sigh. "I couldn't get that out of my mind, Josh—and that's what clinched it for me."

I was lost. "Clinched *what*?"

"I'm going to marry Carl."

"Well—awesome," I said. I meant it, but in terms of logic she'd left me.

"If you can sacrifice everything you dreamed of because of the power of love, I can take a chance on it too. Maybe my life will change some, and I won't be quite as independent as I am now—but Carl and I can work that out."

Okay. I was getting closer.

"It's like that Bible reference I gave you," she said.

I nodded guiltily, even though she couldn't see me. *Yeah, the one I read once and threw back in the closet.*

"It's just another way to the same place—a better way."

I grinned like Phong, canteloupe-style. "So you put that ring on, huh?"

"You bet!"

"Then why are you crying?"

By then she was laughing *and* crying, but that cranked out the tears again.

"Aw, man, I'm sorry," I said.

"No, it's okay, it's just—I can't stay here with Dad, even just until I marry Carl. He's living a bad life, Josh."

I squeezed Lou up close to me. "Yeah, I'm starting to figure that out."

"I just can't live under this roof and still live with myself." She sniffed up what had probably been a whole afternoon of bawling. "I'm going to ask Mom if I can come live with you two until the wedding."

"All right! That'd be cool."

"Let's hope Mom thinks so. I mean, I'll pay rent—"

"She'll probably be over tonight to help you pack."

She laughed through the tears.

"So—the crying," I said. "I still don't get it."

"I'm just so torn up about this split with Dad. We had a major fight—I mean a *major* fight. I always knew he was a little out of it about some stuff, but it hurts to know he's this messed up. Josh, there's this woman he goes out with—"

"I know," I said.

"His business dealings aren't just a little shady—they're downright inhumane. Did you know he also owns that so-called apartment building Tram and her family live in?"

I closed my eyes. The rats and the shattered steps and the broken windows danced in my mind. "No," I said. "I didn't."

"I'm disgusted. But I'm also so sad. He knows better than that, Josh."

I'd been so busy being angry, I hadn't thought much about the sad part. And this latest piece of information drove me closer to homicide than tears. But, yeah, my dream about my hero-father—that was gone too. It *was* sad.

I left Meg blowing her nose but not sobbing anymore. I was only off the phone a minute or two when I heard Mom come in the door, the inevitable grocery bags rustling in her arms.

"Did you get any Top Ramen?" I said, strolling into the kitchen and poking my head into the nearest bag.

"Oh!" Her hand went to her chest. "You scared me to kingdom come! I'm not used to you being here when I get home."

"I'll leave," I said mildly. "Soon as I scarf up some of this stuff." I pulled out a package of mushrooms. "You gonna sauté 'shrooms?"

She didn't answer. She was flipping through the mail, and she'd come across something she wasn't crazy about.

"What's wrong?" I said.

She held the envelope out to me. "It's for you," she said. "It's from your father."

She put both bags on the farthest counter from me and started quietly putting stuff away. I sat down at the table and stared at the envelope.

"Daniels Properties," the return address read. A business letter from my father. Was I being written out of the will? Dropped off the insurance policy? Served for insubordination?

Slowly I tore it open and unfolded it on the table. It stared up at me in stark, formal black and white.

Dear Joshua,

I have considered your request for the early release of $10,000 from the college fund I have set aside for you, and I have decided to deny it. It is still my feeling that you need an education, and you will find it difficult to obtain one without the necessary financial backing.

I looked at the salutation again. It did say, "Dear Joshua." He *was* writing to his son, not a client. You could have fooled me.

However, whereas it is obvious that you are determined to spend money on some idealistic "mission of mercy" and whereas I obviously have not done my duty as a father and taught you the value of a hard-earned dollar, and whereas you, in your infinite wisdom and experience in these matters, feel that you can criticize my management of certain of my properties, I make you the following business offer.

As of June 1, Daniels Market in Oakland will be signed over to you, and all legal matters pertaining to it will be handled through my attorney, Lawrence Dwyer, until you reach twenty-one years of age. The market can be run in any way you and legal counsel see fit, and all proceeds will be yours solely to do with as you wish. By the same token, any financial losses incurred by you in the operation of the market will be your total responsibility and will be drawn from your college fund as necessary. Please contact Mr. Dwyer for further details. I will have no dealings with this piece of property, as it will no longer be in the name of Daniels Properties.

I wish you good luck in this venture. Quite frankly, you're going to need it.

I didn't even have to look to know it was signed "T.R. Daniels" and not "Dad."

"Josh?" Mom said quietly. "Anything you want to talk about?"

I pushed the letter toward her and stared at the table.

A letter from my father, so full of *whereases* and *by the same tokens* it made my blood run like ice water. In the middle of that snarl of legal language it was so plain, he might as well just have typed it in: "Here you are, wise guy. I'll show you. If you're so noble—you handle it."

But how are you going to make money off that store? You don't know the first thing about running a store. And neither does that poor old geezer who's growing out of the stool over there right now.

And once you do get the money—what do you know about getting an exit permit?

What do you know about anything?

I pulled my hands up over my face.

"Oh!" I heard Mom slap the letter on the table. I looked up in surprise. There were no dimples—just tight, livid lines.

"This is unconscionable," she said.

"He just dumped it on me."

She sat down next to me. "I'm still looking into the exit permit situation. And Mrs. Sanderson told me you'd shown an interest. She's looking for materials for you. I know you want to help Mrs. My and there are other ways besides your father—"

"Whoa!"

I was halfway up off the chair.

"What?" she said.

"Mrs. My!"

"Uh-huh—" Mom wasn't following, but she was trying.

I stood up all the way, heart racing. "Tram said they had a store that did great in Vietnam. Her mom knows how to manage a place like that!"

"But, honey, you said she barely speaks English."

I laughed, a little wildly I'll admit. "Neither do most of her customers! But Tram does!"

Mom folded her arms, and the dimples came back. "So you're thinking of hiring them?" she said.

"Then they'd have money to live on."

"And they could make such a go of the store that a percentage of the profits would also be theirs, and that money would pay for the permit. Then they wouldn't think of it as charity."

Why didn't you think of that, dingbat? Because you're sixteen years old.

Suddenly sixteen felt very old. The adrenaline quit pumping, and I sat down again.

"You okay?" Mom said.

I nodded. "I need to go—think or something," I said.

"I understand," she said.

I let that go. I think she really did understand. And I was glad.

◆　　◆　　◆

Upstairs, I put my feet up and closed my eyes. Christ came in, dusted off His sandals, and said, "What do you have for Me tonight, guy?"

I don't have anything for You. I used to tell You, "I'm going to do this" and "I'm going to do that." Didn't I?

But where everything used to seem so sure—I've got so much doubt.

I think it was about then that my voice stopped and His started. It didn't come in real sentences the way mine did. It was just there, like an idea that springs out of nowhere and doesn't have words.

I sat up straight on the bed. Lou wasn't there with me this time. He'd gotten sick of getting knocked off and had retired to the windowsill with a piece of dental floss. He watched disdainfully as I dove for the closet and pulled it out.

King James Version. Now what had Meg said to read? Mark? No—Matthew. Chapter 2.

I flipped to the page, and I read—in spite of my questions about why Meg wanted me to read about the Christmas story, for Pete's sake.

Wise guys hearing about Jesus and thinking they knew what God wanted them to do.

Wise guys going for it—traveling all those miles for it.

Wise guys running into Herod along the way. So much for their original plan.

Wise guys seeing Jesus.

Wise guys being warned in a dream: Find a serious other route.

And they departed into their own country another way.

I let the book slap closed across my chest and leaned back on the bed again. I didn't think. I didn't pray. I didn't dream. I didn't imagine. I just listened and let God talk.

I only wanted to be a man. I thought God said diving was going to make me a man.

It didn't.

But I was still getting to be a man—everybody was telling me that. But it wasn't diving that was making it happen. It was the thing that had been missing before. I was getting there by *loving*.

Loving some of the good things in strange people—like Overbite Betty and Mrs. Sanderson.

Loving my freckle-faced sister who shot from the hip.

Loving the narrow-eyed coach who believed in the real me.

Loving the porridge-faced lug who cared more about me than any other friend I'd ever had.

Loving the poodle-haired chick who just wanted to be my sister in Christ.

Loving the dimpled mother who was a real parent.

Loving the smart-mouthed, slanty-eyed, worldly-wise kid who'd taught me how to love.

Loving the almond-eyed, smartest girl in the world for whom I'd have even traded in Lou to have love me back.

Man, that's like a whole family. It's like a home I didn't even know about. It's—like—everything I need.

You're a wise guy, too, Josh, God seemed to be saying. *You knew I'd take you home. But there are Herods out there. You better let Me send you another way.*

That was it, of course. Where I was going—that was the same. It was just the way I was going that was different.

◆　　◆　　◆

I couldn't go diving that afternoon. I couldn't even dream about diving. Instead I started a new map. Right there on the ceiling, with my feet up on the wallpaper and Lou—well, Lou nearby. I just started a whole new map.

Wait—let me rephrase that. *We* started a new map.

Christ and I started traveling home by another way.